THE GLIMMER BLADE

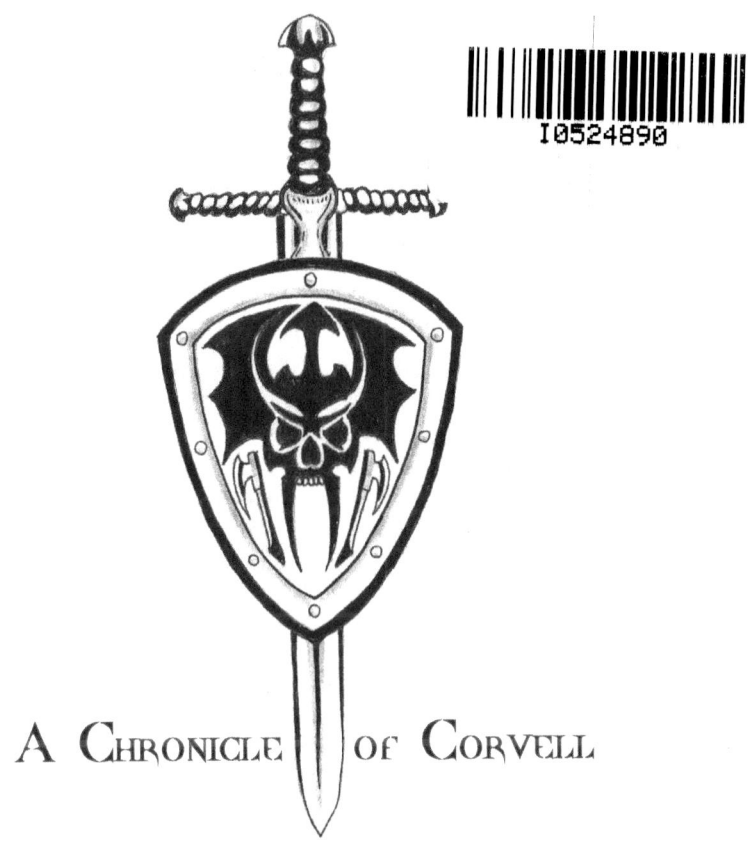

A CHRONICLE OF CORVELL

The Glimmer Blade

A Twiin Entertainment Book
Books by Jason L. McWhirter

The World of Kraawn
Cavalier Trilogy
The Cavalier
The Rise of Malbeck
Glimmer in the Shadow
Shadow Knight Books
The Shadow Knight

The World of Corvell and Belorth
The Steel Lord Series
BannerFall
Banner Lord
The Chronicles of Corvell
The Glimmer Blade

Non-Fantasy
The Life of Ely

Published by Twiin Entertainment
www.twiinentertainment.com
Copyright © Jason L. McWhirter
Library of Congress TX 8-460486
All rights reserved
Cover Art by Mario Teodosio
Map and other art by Jason L. McWhirter

Author's Notes

This is a work of fiction. Names, characters, places, and incidents are the product of my imagination or are used fictitiously, and any resemblance to actual persons, living or dead, business establishments, events, or locales is entirely coincidental.

My plan for the Chronicle's of Corvell novels is for them to be stand-alone stories about Brant, as well as other cast members from the Steel Lord Series, along with possible new characters that spring forth from my imagination. With that in mind, I think it still makes sense to read the Steel Lord series first so you have a strong background of this particular world I created. I hope you enjoy them.

Dedication

I would like to dedicate this book to my readers who love to imbibe a tasty spirit or two, savoring the unique essences as you analyze the nuances of so many tantalizing flavors, from rich and malty ales, bold and peppery wines, to lush caramel and vanilla notes of an aged scotch. If you are like me, enjoying a few glasses of your favorite spirit, while reading a good book, is one of the best ways to pass a cold winter night, or a raining Washington day. Cheers to you! And as always, thanks for your support.

PROLOGUE

Endler Ral stood alone on the sixty-foot wall gazing out through the battlements to the gentle waters of the Bitlis Sea. For once, it was a calm evening, although the stillness did little to relax him. Even the salty clean air of the sea, which he normally loved, did not settle his tense soul. Tanwen, Dy'ain's northern most city, had been destroyed over nine years ago, and just this year the work to rebuild was nearly complete. Captain Ral had been an integral part in managing the city's rise from the ashes, placed there by Jarak Dormath, the King of Dy'ain, to help oversee the proceedings. The first three years he helped direct the military in leading the construction; but now, as the new Chamberlain, a post he reluctantly acquired from the previous ruler, Lord Rathiam, he was feeling the weight of his new role. Nine years ago Jarak Dormath had burned his own city to keep the Saricon Horde from using it to winter their army. Now the rebuilding of the city was mostly finished, but the stresses of the job were weighing heavily on the new administrator. He was a fighter, a leader of men. He wasn't sure he was up to the task of being the Chamberlain of a busy trading port. There were countless administrative decisions to be made every day, each one somehow causing one group or person to be unsatisfied. Despite the honor bestowed upon him in receiving the title, he wasn't sure it was something he wanted.

He sighed and ran his hand through his long dark hair. Tomorrow he had an early meeting with his council. The city's coffers were nearly empty; their allotment from Cythera spent, and up for discussion was raising taxes to help finish the last remnants of construction. It would be a heated discussion, one that Chamberlain Ral was not looking forward too. He did not want to raise taxes on a people who had suffered much over the last ten years. When Jarak Dormath burned his own city, the occupants were forced to leave and find their way on their own. War always conjured up difficult decisions and destroying one's city so your enemy could not use it to winter their army was a prime example of that. Needless to say, the people of Tanwen struggled, and raising taxes when they were nearly done rebuilding was not something he wanted to do to them. They had a few other choices, one being asking for more money from the capital, Cythera. But that city had also been damaged greatly when Jarak had raised a new army and taken it back from the Saricons. That battle was brutal, destroying the rear and main gates in the process. Along with the help of the Varga and the Marastian mercenaries, they had defeated the Saricons, but the cost in life and property was staggering. The capital city of Cythera had been rebuilt as well, but the cost was strenuous on an already struggling economy. Not to mention the city of Kreb that guarded the western border had also been razed to the ground, and the cost of rebuilding all three cities had put an enormous strain on their coffers. On top of this great expense was the fact that the Kul-brite mines had not been operating at capacity, many closed as Jarak worked to rebuild the Dygon Guard, the Mergers trained to protect the precious metal stores. Most of the guard had been killed during the war, including Kulvar Rand, the guard's leader. Jarak's new army had defeated the Saricons, but the costs had been impactful, then, and now. While the costs to rebuild Dy'ain escalated quickly, the income from the Kul-brite mines could not match the expenses. Needless to say, asking for more money would not go over well, especially from a Chamberlain who was young and relatively inexperienced. He needed to find another way.

Chamberlain Ral's mind was so occupied that he failed to hear the light footsteps to his right.

"Greetings Endler Ral."

Startled, Endler turned towards the voice. A man stood before him holding a slim Kul-brite blade in his right hand, the moonlight reflecting off the bright silver steel. He wore a black hooded cape that was gently fluttering in the wind, a black mask of cloth, leather, and what looked to be plates of dark steel, hiding the man's face beneath the shadows of the hood.

Endler felt the threat immediately. Drawing his own blade, he stepped back, increasing the distance between them.

The black masked man tilted his head as he looked at Endler's blade. "Kul-brite," he said, "I did not know."

It was rare for anyone outside the royal family or the Dygon Guard to have a Kul-brite blade, the steel worth ten times that of any precious metal, and much harder to find. The steel was the only material capable of harnessing the aura energy of a Merger, not to mention it was nearly unbreakable and could cut through almost anything. But Endler, who had worked with King

Dormath for years, and in fact helped save his life when he was attacked on the road many years ago by four Saricon Shadow Riders and their torgs, had become fast friends with the new monarch. They had barely survived the beasts and their riders, and in fact some had not, including Kaan, Brant Anwar's friend who had given them shelter when they had escaped from Cythera after Jarak's parents had been assassinated by his own uncle, Daricon Dormath. It was safe to say that Endler had become good friends with Jarak Dormath, and as part of his service had been given a Kul-brite blade, despite the fact that he was not a Merger. Endler Ral was a Channeler, someone gifted in the Way who could pull aura energy from others around him, filter the energy to clean power and give it to an Aura Mage. A skilled Channeler and Mage were a deadly duo. But Endler had no Mage with him now. He was on his own.

Endler ignored him. "Who are you?"

The man paused before answering. "Your past, coming back for revenge."

"I don't understand."

"You will."

Endler was an accomplished swordsman, but there was something about the way this man moved that sent a jolt of nervous energy through his body. The man was so confident, and he moved with a slightly enhanced speed. Was he a Merger?

The assassin glided over the parapet wall, his sword arm attacking in a blur. Their weapons kissed several times before the assassin's blade slipped under Endler's, scoring a shallow gash across his forearm. Endler grunted as the man stepped back from him, his head slightly tilted in a confident, almost arrogant manner.

"Does it hurt?" he asked, his voice soft and controlled.

Endler wasn't wearing armor, and the man's Kul-brite blade had easily sliced through his leather sleeve, a small line of red visible. He could feel the warm blood drip to his hand. "Who are you?" Endler asked again, this time more strained. Looking around, he hoped to see guards nearby.

The assassin's head tilted the other way. "Any guards that were close are now dead. You will not receive any help, just as I did not."

"What do you mean? Who are you?" Endler asked, his voice frantic. He turned on his towd, his aura sight, and was surprised at what he saw. He had never seen an aura like it. Most men or women gifted with the Way, had solid auras of various colors, depending on whether they were Mergers, Mages, or Channelers. This man's aura was pulsing with colors of blue and purple, with intermediate flashes of bright white. He had never seen anything like it before. He took the brief moment to wipe the blood from his sword hand on his pant leg before re-gripping the hilt.

"In time." Then the man resumed his attack.

Again, their blades met as they moved across the stone surface of the parapet. The ring of steel was loud in the calm night, but after a short exchange the clatter of steel stopped as the swordsman flicked Endler's blade away, dropped low and forward, his own blade arcing across Endler's exposed stomach.

Pain lanced through Endler as he stumbled backwards, his free hand going to his deep wound.

The swordsman was so fast. The wound was bad and he could feel his life's blood pour down his leggings. Gritting his teeth, he looked up at his attacker. "Why are you doing this? I have done nothing to you," he stammered.

"Oh, but you have," the warrior said as he stepped closer, his free hand pulling the mask from his face.

Endler's eyes struggled to process the man's face, his expression one of confusion and uncertainty. There was something about his features that looked vaguely familiar. He was a young man, perhaps in his mid-twenties. But little else was noticeable as he could not look past the man's eyes. They were all black, with irises of steel gray lightning strikes. It wasn't the blackness one sees when you snuff out the last candle before bed; it was much darker, a depth that feels like nothing could escape their dark clutches. Finally pulling his own eyes away from assassin's deep pits, he tried once again to analyze his features. Then slowly it came to him, his eyes widening as recognition flashed before him. "Is it...really...," then he dropped to a knee as he became dizzy from loss of blood, the pain from his gruesome wound nearly unbearable. Gritting his teeth, he looked up defiantly at the assassin.

"Yes, it is." Then the assassin's eyes narrowed in anger as his blade flashed through the air.

Endler registered the attack, and even tried to raise his own blade in response. But he was too slow, and the only thing he felt was a release of pressure at his neck, then he fell forward, everything fading black before his body hit the cold stone pavers.

Chapter One

Brant had been holding the position for nearly five minutes, his legs strong and firm, sweat dripping from his brow. His eyes were closed in concentration. The move was called the Swaying Oak, the last position of the Gaton, a training regimen taught to him by Tangar, the Schulg warrior who had captured him and forced him to fight in the pits. Tangar was dead, killed by his friend and mentor, Kulvar Rand when he had escaped from the Schulg. Despite being a slave to Tangar for over two years, he had learned much from the Schulg Warrior. He had turned him into a warrior, a man that was good at killing. The series of poses were designed to work on strength, stamina, and speed. It had taken Brant months to be able to perform all the maneuvers, and nearly a year before he could do it with any fluidity and power.

Nearly ten years later he was still practicing what Tangar had taught him, eager to keep his body strong and powerful. He had added a final step to the Gaton. Long ago his mind had been opened by a man named Angon, a Kynan with great power who showed him the true energy of the world. Kynan were once the keepers of the earth's magic, but long ago had been hunted down and persecuted by the Argonians. The faith's propaganda had been successful at demonizing the Kynan, and now they were thought of as killers and baby eaters. Most were long dead, their names whispered to scare little children before bed. But Brant had learned the truth of things, befriending the Kynan many years ago. Angon had opened the door for him, cracked it slightly so he could see in his mind's eye the energy of all things, and over the years he had further opened that breach, gaining more access to the earth's energy. No longer was he restrained by just his aura's energy, which in fact unconsciously drew from the earth's power. Now he could connect to the river of power consciously, drawing from it when needed. His adaptation to the Gaton was during the last move, when he was the most tired and his muscles were strained. Holding the Swaying Oak, a low squat position, he concentrated on the earth's energy, drawing it up from his feet and into his body. As he did so he strengthened his body and mind, as well as improved his connection to the earth's river of power.

"How long must I wait before you teach me this?"

Brant's eyes fluttered open and he smiled, slowly standing from the difficult position. Shaking his tired legs, he wiped the sweat from his forehead. "Soon," Brant said. "The poses require great strength. You are nearly ready."

Tobias was leaning against the wood fence that penned in their six pigs. He was now twenty one years old and was a spitting image of his father. His brown hair was long and slightly wavy, his young body short, but with strong thighs and forearms. Indeed, Brant had planned on training him in the Gaton very soon. "You have been training me in the blade for most of my life. Why not show me the Gaton?"

Brant picked up his cotton tunic and wiped his face with it. "As I've said before, I'm not hiding it from you. It's just that you must be very strong to even perform the maneuvers one by one, let alone in consecutive order." Brant's body was covered in scars, but even they paled in comparison to the six Schulg sigils branded across his chest, marking him as Ull Therm, a conqueror of the Schulg fighting pits. Each mark represented five men killed in the pit, or they could be earned if you killed a fighter who had already earned the brand, his kills transferring to you. He was not proud of the marks, but at the same time they represented a part of his past that had molded him into the man that he had become. He was not fond of thinking of the men that he had killed, but nor was he ashamed of the sigils. After all, he had had no choice. Reaching for his shirt, he slipped it over his head and stepped closer to the young man.

"But I *am* strong," Tobias reasoned.

He was right. Brant had been training him ever since his father had been killed by the Saricon Shadow Rider. Combine that work with the difficult labor of running their farm, and Brant had turned the young man into a powerful fighter. He was strong and quick and had become a fine swordsman. Brant placed his hand on Tobias's muscled shoulder. "How does tomorrow sound?"

Tobias's face lit up with a genuine smile. "You are not jesting?"

Brant shook his head and smacked his shoulder playfully. "Bright and early."

"I will be ready. And the Kilting Way?" The Kilting Way was a complicated set of sword forms taught only to the Dygon Guard. The maneuvers focused on powerful wrists and forearms, the strength required only acquired through a combination of genetics and specific muscle training. Kulvar Rand had taught Brant, and over the years Brant had continued the training. One so skilled in the Kilting Way became a master killer. Tobias was not quite ready for that.

"All in good time my eager disciple. Now get your sword. Let's get some work in before supper. Besides, these pens need to be cleaned."

"No doubt you are referring to me," Tobias said as his smile disappeared, but it returned slowly, the excitement of learning the Gaton overriding his lack of desire to clean the smelly pig pen. He walked excitedly towards the cabin to get his blade.

Brant watched him, his mind drifting to his friend, to Tobias's father. Kaan had died ten years ago when the Saricons had invaded Dy'ain. When the war was over, Brant had taken on the responsibility of raising his children, Tobias and Jana. Kaan was his first real friend, and he missed him dearly. He blamed himself for his death, and despite trying to rationalize that it was not his fault, he could not overcome the blame. It *was* his fault. He had brought the fugitive king to Kaan's cabin when they had escaped, bringing the Shadow Riders to their door, resulting in his death. No matter how he tried to paint the picture, the visual image of Kaan's body ripped and torn apart in the pig pen would never leave his mind.

After the war he had married Thea, the serving girl he had met at Amorsit, and together they had raised Kaan's children as their own. Jana was already married to the inn keeper's son and living in town, and soon, Tobias would find his own way. He was already talking about joining Jarak's army, and although Brant was against it, it was hard for someone with his martial reputation to convince the young man that war was not glorious. After all, when Brant had killed the Saricon Tongra, he had become famous; the Defender of Dy'ain, the Barbarian Slayer, the Glimmer Blade, all names whispered everywhere he went. Brant had trained Tobias to fight in order to defend himself, but war was a different matter altogether, and his heart ached when he thought of him fighting, and maybe dying in the mud in some far-off land.

Tobias returned carrying his long sword with practiced ease. Brant thought it interesting, that no matter your trade, when you were good at something, whether it was the sword, a blacksmith's hammer, a farmer's scythe, or even a sewing needle, the tool that was mastered looks as if it was a part of your body, an extension of yourself, like you were born with it. Tobias carried the blade with practiced ease. He, although no master yet, had been practicing with tenacity under Brant's tutelage, and Brant would put him against most veteran soldiers.

Tobias was smiling. "You are tired from the Gaton. Should we wait until after dinner for you to rest?"

Brant said nothing, reaching for his Kul-brite blade leaning against the fence railing. Unsheathing it, he turned to face Tobias. At the start of their training years ago, they used blunted steel swords. But now, after many years of swordplay together, they had advanced to use their real blades, the exact weight and feel difficult to duplicate in a training sword. Even after all these years, Tobias still failed to hide his awe every time he saw the famous weapon. The amount of Kul-brite steel that was required to make just that one blade could feed a family for their entire lifetimes.

Before viewing Brant's blade, Tobias had never seen the rare steel before. The metal was extremely strong and never lost its edge. It was the only steel that could withstand the aura energy of a Merger. Amongst the Merger nobles, it was the most sought-after prize. It was the reason for the Saricon invasion to begin with. They wanted to control the Kul-brite steel trade, as well as propagate their faith, their belief in their one warrior god, Heln. After the Saricon Tongra died in their duel, the army, according to their tradition, had to leave, and they could not return for twenty years. Brant held no doubt that they would in fact return, and he wanted Tobias to be ready.

"I'll tell you what," Brant answered. "If you touch me just once, I will clean the pens tonight."

"Fair enough," Tobias responded, raising his blade, knowing full well that in time he would be knee deep in the smelly muck. After all, he had never touched Brant with his blade before.

Brant attacked him quickly, his sword sweeping low and coming up and across his body. Tobias parried and they both moved quickly across the dirt clearing, their swords ringing as they connected again and again.

Brant was a Merger, but he was not accessing his ability as Tobias would never be able to keep up. But there were few as strong and fast as Brant, and within moments his blade spun over Tobias's and smacked his left bicep.

Tobias didn't pause or show his frustration, reversing his blade quickly and coming back around for Brant's thigh. But Brant was faster, snapping his foot out he connected solidly with Tobias's wrist. Tobias grunted and nearly dropped his blade, retreating from Brant and gritting his teeth.

Brant had trained him well and toughened him in the process. It was not uncommon for him to walk away with bruises, and occasionally small cuts. It was the price you paid when training with an Ull Therm, the title Brant earned, although he was not proud of it, by being the best killer in the Schulg pits. There were few who ever made it that far in the pits, and the brands across Brant's chest reminded him every day of what he had been forced to do to survive. Brant's life had forged him into a killer, a man capable of withstanding great pain, and equally capable of dealing it out. Even his youth had contributed to this skill set. He had been raised by an abusive father and trained by him to fight in the mines. Then, when he was eighteen, his father had died, and he left the mines without a second thought. Then things just got worse. He had been arrested for killing a drunken brawler in a bar, sold off to the Schulg fighting pits where he learned to kill for two years before becoming Ull Therm. Then he escaped, and soon found his way into the service of Kulvar Rand, the great Dygon Guard leader and the finest swordsman in all of Corvell. Kulvar had continued his training, elevating him to a warrior that seemed to have no equal. More importantly Kulvar had trained him how to fight as a Merger, something he had known very little about at the time. Then the war came and Kulvar had been killed defending the main gate, the thirty Dygon Guard he led killing hundreds of the enemy before being cut down. They still sang songs of the brave thirty and their famous swordsman. In the end, they had won the war, and now Brant had retreated to a life of solitude, living in peace with Thea and raising Kaan's two children. The last ten years had been the best of his life, free from violence and death. At least that's what Brant told himself. He hid it from all, embarrassed by the thoughts, but there was something about the violence he missed. Brant felt at home with his sword in his hands. It was like telling a sailor that he would never feel the gentle sway of a boat beneath his feet, or smell the salty sea air ever again. He never voiced it, but he missed the violence.

Brant didn't give Tobias time to rest, pressing the attack further. Tobias grunted and flipped his blade to his left hand, meeting Brant's attack in a flourish of parries and attacks of his own. Brant's face was stoic as it always was when he fought, free from emotion. Emotions could get you killed. A practiced killer can read much from his opponent by his facial expressions, and Brant had learned long ago how to mask his emotions. But inside, Brant was smiling. Tobias could use his left hand nearly as well as his right, something they had been working on tirelessly for the last year. And now it was paying off. Brant was proud of him.

Brant had yet to train Tobias in the Kilting Way, and although it was forbidden to teach the technique to any outside the Dygon Guard, Brant planned to eventually train him in the deadly sword forms regardless. He figured Kulvar had taught him, and he would pass it down to Tobias. But the young man was not ready, his forearm and grip strength not yet at the levels required to even start the most basic portions of the technique. But soon, very soon, he would be ready for the next level.

Brant purposely over extended himself to see if Tobias would take advantage of the error. And he did. Tobias moved forward, avoiding the strike with a slight sway of his body, his elbow leading and aimed directly for Brant's nose. It was a well-executed move, but Brant was ready. Brant too swayed around the strike, bringing the flat of his blade around to smack Tobias on the back. But Tobias's attack was a ruse. Brant had thought he was attacking with his elbow, but he was not. He had quickly flipped his blade from his left hand back to his right, and while Brant's blade finished its arc, Tobias's swept down and nocked his blade away. Tobias was now very close to Brant and he followed the parry up with a kick to the back of Brant's knee, hoping to drop him to the dirt.

In complete composure, his surprise at Tobias's ruse not evident the least bit, Brant pivoted his body and planted his legs firmly in the Swaying Oak position of the Gaton. Tobias's kick, instead of striking him on the back of an unprepared knee and collapsing his leg, struck his leg at the wrong angle, and instead of dropping Brant to the ground, it looked as if Tobias had kicked the trunk of a tree. Tobias was so committed to the attack, that he barely noticed Brant's blade slice the air in a blur, stopping a hair's length from his throat. Tobias froze. He knew he had lost.

Finally, a smile broke through Brant's façade as he stepped away from Tobias. "Well done, that was an impressive move."

Tobias shook his head in frustration. "Not impressive enough."

"You are wrong. That maneuver would have worked against nearly any opponent."

"But not you," Tobias responded with a playful smirk.

Brant held his arms out mockingly. "I am Ull Therm, the Glimmer Blade."

Now Tobias was smiling broadly. "What did I do wrong?"

Brant pursed his lips. "Nothing. I just saw it at the last moment, reacting appropriately. That's what training is all about. You want your body to react without thought to every conceivable attack. When you are strong and fast, you have given your body, and mind, the tools it needs to stay alive."

"So my attacks need to be *inconceivable*, so your body does not react fast enough."

Tobias was serious, but Brant was still smiling. "Good luck. Come on, get in there and get those pens clean while I help Thea prepare supper."

Tobias nodded, still thinking as he stepped away.

An hour later they were together eating a meal of tulkick steaks with gravy, roasted potatoes from their garden, and fresh baked bread. Thea had not been much of a cook when they had met at Amorsit, a town a few days walk from them, but now, she could arrange some decent table fare. The small stone cottage was warm and comfortable and it had been a good home.

Thea was still stunning, and every time Brant looked at her he wondered why she was with him. It's not that he wasn't handsome. He guessed he was in a very rugged kind of way. His face was sharp and angular like carved stone, with

ago. Over the years, every time he was out plowing the fields, collecting wood, or hunting, he had searched for big flat stones, collecting each one methodically. Finally he had found enough, and had completed a stone patio just outside their front door, Thea's garden flanking the two chairs and a rough stone fire pit erected in the middle. It was their favorite place and many a night were spent by the fire looking up at the bright stars. The night was clear, with an occasional smudge of cloud floating across the glowing moon. Fire danced in the stone pit, the smell of wood smoke drifting around them as they sipped on expensive wine from Layona, a gift from Jarak Dormath.

They sat close together, Thea huddled under a soft cotton blanket, her hand gently touching Brant's muscled forearm. "Do you ever miss it?' She asked softly, stroking the scars on his arm and looking up at the brilliant stars.

Brant was looking deep into the flames, his own mind lost in thought. He looked at her, his appraising eyes taking in her beauty, as they always did when he looked upon her. "Miss what?"

"Fighting."

They had talked about it before. Many times actually. She seemed to sense something missing in him, something that even he didn't want to admit. He was a fighter, a warrior, and he was good at it. When one is good at something, it is hard to ignore. Brant didn't miss the killing, but deep down inside there *was* something missing, and Thea felt it. She saw it in him when he stared into the fire, or when his eyes lit up when training Tobias. She seemed to know him better than himself. He missed the adrenaline of battle...the feeling of skill and training coming together to defeat an opponent.

"No, I do not," he lied.

Her eyes were gentle, but she did not look away, pressing him further. "You cannot lie to me, my love. You know it's okay, right?"

"Okay to kill?"

"Okay to miss what you are skilled at."

Brant pursed his lips in thought. "Not when one's skill sheds blood and ends lives."

Her grip tightened on his arm. "I do not mean that you should want to fight and kill. I simply mean it's okay to miss the feeling it gave you."

Brant drank from his wine and looked deeply into the fire. The flickering colors of orange and red were mesmerizing. Brant had spent many nights looking deeply into the burning embers, watching the wood slowly burn beneath heated colors of red, orange, and blue. The reality was that he was not looking into the embers; he was looking into his soul. It was when he was the most honest with himself.

"I do miss some of it, but the sword has brought me nothing but pain and violence. Too many people have died as a result of it."

She knew he was talking about Kaan, Kulvar Rand, Ardra and Orin, the twins Gyths, and many more. "But look at what else the sword has brought us. It ended the Saricon invasion, it allowed you and I to meet and be married, it kept Jarak alive so he could rebuild Dy'ain." She sighed. "I'm not saying that violence is okay. I'm just saying that sometimes it's necessary, and if you happen to be one so skilled, then you must embrace it."

"I do not miss the feel of my blade sinking into flesh," Brant said as he looked over at her. "I do not miss the look on a man's face as his life's energy leaves him."

Thea leaned over and kissed his cheek. "And that's why you are the one, and others like you who must carry the burden of violence. You do not seek it. But do not feel bad when you miss it." She smiled at him and sat back in her chair. "I see you thinking about it, and I do not want you to feel ashamed. Okay?"

Brant nodded his head, a slight smile forming. "What did I do to deserve you?"

"Interestingly enough, I ask myself that same question when I look upon you."

This time Brant's broad smile broke through his thoughts. Lifting up his cup, they toasted together under the bright moon. "To deserving each other," he said. And they both drank heartily, the bold wine washing away their deep thoughts, warming their bellies nearly as much as the fire's heat that bathed them, their love somehow shining bright even in the dark night.

***

Eltus, the capital city of Kael, was now Saricon, conquered by the foreigners ten years ago before they invaded Dy'ain. The local people were forced to flee, convert, or die, and most chose the first two over the latter. However, there were always outliers, people that had never sworn allegiance to the Saricon god, Heln, and lived in the shadows. They did not want to leave their home. They survived, and in their own way they continued to resist.

Eltus had been rebuilt, and every remnant of the Argonian faith had been destroyed. Temples to Argon and Felina were converted to worship centers to Heln, statues of the two gods were torn down and replaced with great, impressive figures of Heln's muscular form, his long beard and hair expertly fluttering in the wind, both hands resting on his huge sword.

The population of Eltus was now nearly forty percent Saricon, and despite the small resistance to them, the Kaelians and the Saricons more or less got along. The Saricons were very adept at killing and war, along with administration. Once a land was conquered, they were well versed on how to maintain control of the populace. Besides the forced conversion, the daily life of a Kaelian had changed very little since their defeat.

ReeOnen walked quickly down the narrow alley, both sides flanking her were tall stone walls that blocked out most of the sun. It was almost dusk, the disappearing sun's rays were nearly gone, the alley painted in dark shadows. As a Saricon, she was a full head taller than most Kaelians. Her long blonde hair was pulled back and woven into a tail that hung to her lower back, each side of her head shaved to the scalp. Scars, now painted black, were intricately cut into her skin making graceful designs that covered the skin above her ears. She carried a sword at her hip and a quiver of javelins on her back. Before her was a large steel door that blocked entrance into the newest building in Eltus. At one point it was an Argonian temple, converted six years ago into a facility built for a new military program...a program that she ran.

The door was blocked by two massively built Saricon warriors. They both stepped aside when they saw her. Standing before the huge door she reached her hand into a hole built at waist height. It was a Saricon lock, designed by their engineers. Once your hand was inside, you pressed a series of levers that would unlock the door. If you pressed the wrong combination, a blade would drop, severing your hand. Needless to say, those that entered took their time in entering the sequence.

There was a click, and the door swung open. ReeOnen pushed it further inward and walked in, shutting it silently behind her. There was an audible noise as the lock reengaged. She knew the facility well and made her way through the vast complex of hallways and rooms, before entering the center of the structure, the core reason for the building's creation.

The room was large, like a king's conference room, but mostly empty. In the center were six beds, three of which were unoccupied. The wall opposite the beds was filled by rows of shelving and work benches, the surfaces covered with beakers, tools, and other equipment that ReeOnen knew nothing about. Sitting in a chair, hunched over his tools, was a Saricon Overseer. His name was ThoraDin. The man looked up when she entered.

"Come to see the progress?"

He was tall, like all Saricons, but his old frame kept him in a perpetual bent posture. The man's hair was gray and long, his beard reaching to his belly button and his long hair mingled with it creating an unruly mess. He wore a long gray robe with a leather over-jerkin, the symbol of Heln, a horned helm, etched beautifully into the black leather in red. Despite his unkempt appearance, his intelligent eyes sparkled with vitality.

"I have," ReeOnen replied, flicking her gaze to the three men that occupied the beds. One was asleep and lying under a light white cloth. He was thin but muscular, and clearly Kaelian, as his hair was dark as night and his skin the color of brown leather. The other was naked and uncovered, his arms and legs strapped to the bed with various tubing leading from his wrists to a strange contraption off to the side. This man was more heavily muscled, his body covered with scars. He was a warrior, there was no doubt, and by the looks of him he was Marastian, his skin more red than brown. The third body was a woman, and she was clearly dead, her skin pale white in contrast to her jet black hair. ReeOnen could see various holes in her neck and dried blood caked around them. She had been dead for at least a day and was beginning to smell.

"I am just getting ready to inject subject ten with the blood. Would you like to watch?"

"Of course. Proceed."

ThoraDin went to a steel box built into a near wall and opened the door. Cold air billowed out as he quickly reached in and removed a glass jar filled with blood. Keeping the box cold required ice to be shipped across the strait from Argos, the island nation south of Kael, which was also controlled by the Saricons. There was a tall peak there, the only place within a week's ride cold enough to provide ice all year round. Needless to say it was expensive, but necessary to keep the contents viable. Quickly he shut the door and carried the jar to the table near the man's bed. On the table was a strange machine of sorts. There was a main chamber attached to a billow, and coming from it was a tube made from the gut of some animal, the end capped in a narrow steel needle, the sharp point already buried into the man's forearm.

"What dose is this?" ReeOnen asked.

"First one." The overseer looked up at her as he poured the blood into the mechanism's chamber. "Have you seen a first dose yet? My old mind cannot remember."

"I have not. Will he survive?"

ThoraDin shrugged his shoulders. "Hard to say. Most do not. He is physically strong, but, as you know, it requires more than that. He must be able to withstand the pain and harness the power. His will must be strong. If not, it will consume him."

ReeOnen knew that most of the subjects never survived the blood transfer. In fact, only five men over the last five years have, and two of those men had already been killed in the field. As of now, they only had three men in play.

This building, what they were doing, was called the DarPool Program. It was a program created to transform men and women, those who were not Saricon, who could blend into the foreign surroundings, into assassins loyal only to Heln. It was started by ThoraDin, the most skilled Overseer in Corvell. Most Saricon's were warriors to some degree, but not all. Some, the Overseers, were born to serve Heln another way. They did not wield steel, but intellect and ingenuity. They were the most intelligent of the Saricons. They dabbled in science, engineering, alchemy, anything to advance the conquering agenda of Heln. They brought with them a great deal of technological expertise, more than most peoples that they conquered. What made them so skilled was that they borrowed from all the cultures that fell under their axe, making them the most learned men in all the lands.

Once the blood had filled the chamber, ThoraDin looked up at ReeOnen. "Ready?" ReeOnen nodded.

ThoraDin slowly pumped the billow and ReeOnen could see the blood move through the tubing and into the man's wrist. ThoraDin slowed the pumping, moving the bellow steadily up and down.

It didn't take long for the man to react. His body went rigid, like a board, and as the Overseer continued to pump the blood into him, the warrior began to shake. The shaking was so violent that the bed began to move.

"Hold the bed if you will," ThoraDin asked.

ReeOnen went to the bed side and held it still, watching the man's face as he shook. His eyes bolted open and he screamed. It was piercing and filled with pain. The man convulsed further, his body shaking so fiercely that the bed bounced up and down, forcing ReeOnen to put her weight onto the frame to keep it still. "Is this normal?!" she said loudly over the man's horrible screeching.

ThoraDin nodded and continued to pump the blood into him. The screaming and convulsing went on for a minute until finally blood begin to drip from his ears and nose and the man fell silent, his body still. ThoraDin finally stopped pumping, his head shaking.

"Is he dead?" ReeOnen asked.

"Yes. We need more men."

"I will work on it. Whose blood was that?"

ThoraDin looked up. "The Tongras"

Tongra Orgul had been ruling Kael for nearly ten years, taking the place of ReeOnen's father, Tongra Taruk, after he was slain in the *Gratatuit*, or War Duel, by the Dy'ainian swordsman known as Brant Anwar. ReeOnen's family had lost honor and respect in the eyes of the Saricons. But she had a plan. She would avenge her father.

"His blood is powerful."

ThoraDin nodded.

They had used his blood before, and all but one man had died. "What of her?" She added as she flicked her gaze to the dead woman.

"We have drained her of blood. As you know, finding anyone gifted with the Way outside the royal families is no easy feat. We need as much blood as we can find."

ReeOnen nodded. "I will bring you more men within the week." The second part of the program involved using blood of those strong in the Way. If a DarPool candidate survived the influx of blood from a Saricon lord strong in the Fury, then the second stage was enacted, adding blood enhanced in the Way. The mixture of enhanced blood either killed them outright or created something totally unique. Generally, in all his research, ThoraDin found that if they initially survived the blood of the Saricon lord, then they would not succumb to the blood of those gifted in the Way.

ThoraDin nodded again as he began unstrapping the man's wrists. ReeOnen turned and left. She had another quick inspection to make.

She was eager to check in on the training of the only man they had currently who had survived the blood transfusions. She walked through several quiet halls heading towards the indoor training grounds. She knew the man had spent the last four weeks enduring arguably the most grueling portion of the training. Nearing the door she heard the man's screams before her hand even found the handle.

Entering the room she found the subject strapped to a statue of Heln, his arms lashed tight to the expertly carved wooden arms of their god, while his legs were bound to Heln's carved feet. The statue was in the shape of a cross, thus so was the man's body. The room had several similar statues, various tables filled with weapons of all sorts, whips, books, clay pots filled with various liquids, and plenty of space for weapons training. There were several large glass windows built into the ceiling that let plenty of natural light in during the day. At night, torches and lanterns lit up the large room. A broad shouldered female Saricon turned when ReeOnen entered, her eyes burning with frenetic zealotry, a long bloody whip held at her side.

The man lashed to the wood statue was naked, his body covered in crimson valleys, blood pooling at the statue's base. He was panting heavily but his eyes were tense, his face a mask of concentration. ReeOnen nodded for her to continue.

Snapping her arm forward, the whip carved a hand span cut across his shoulder. He screamed again, but it was not one of pain. It was born of rage, almost like he was welcoming it. "Heln's forty fourth code?" the Saricon yelled.

"Benevolence is a weakness attained through mercy!" the man answered, taking several rapid breaths, preparing himself for more pain he knew was coming.

She struck him again, this time across his muscled chest. "Heln honors your courage!" she stormed, worked up nearly as much as him. "Strength begets strength. Now, what is Heln's fifth law found in the Crenelation?"

There was a brief pause before the man answered. "Any child born weak must be left at the highest peak to die. Any woman to birth such child will never birth again, on pain of execution!" The Crenelation was the second book in the Torgot, the Helnian sacred text.

The man before her was a Kaelian named Sanik. He was taken as a slave and eventually forced into the DarPool program. Few made it as far, and ReeOnen was happy with his progress. She knew he would be healed and then the pain would commence again. He would be cut, bones would be broken, all the while learning the Torgot and becoming Heln's weapon. The idea was to mold a warrior who did not fear pain, or even death, as he had already experienced it. If he survived, he would be given his new Saricon name, and the training would continue. It was a long process, but the end result was the deadliest warriors she had ever seen.

She nodded in satisfaction to the trainer and turned and left the room. She had another meeting to attend.

It didn't take her long to reach the rendezvous site. The sun had set and her path down the alley was lit by no more than the stars and bright moon. She didn't worry about thieves or cutthroats, as few would be stupid enough to attack a Saricon officer, her armor painted with Heln's red symbol marking her as such. She was nearly at the apothecary shop, their meeting point, when she felt a slight whoosh of air behind her followed by a soft voice, its tone eerily deadly, like the slither of a viper in the grass.

"Kulgarrion, I am here."

ReeOnen turned at the mention of her title. It was a Saricon word that meant leader, and the only ones that called her such were the three DarPool assassins that had thus far survived the training. Standing before her was a man dressed in shadow, his dark clothes and black mask making him nearly invisible.

"What is your update?"

"The merchant is dead, as you requested."

ReeOnen was the head of the DarPool program, but she was just a puppet to the Tongra. She was given orders, and those orders were passed down to the three assassins that had survived the blood transfers and training. If the subjects survived the transfers, then they spent years training in stealth and combat, the best teachers brought in from all around Corvell and even Belorth. There was no expense too great and with coffers overflowing with wealth taken from conquered lands they could afford the very best military trainers. They taught them how to use every conceivable weapon, how to track, hunt, how to hide in the shadows, and how to speak handfuls of languages. They not only shaped their body like a swordsmith hammers out a blade, but they brainwashed their minds, creating devout assassins loyal to Heln and the Saricons.

The man standing before her was their finest assassin. They called him TorGynin, or *first killer*. He was captured and taken as a slave ten years ago when he was just fourteen, soon learning that his aptitude made him an ideal candidate for the new program. He was not as strong physically as other candidates, but there was something deep inside him, a will to survive, a will fueled by revenge. He too was given the blood of the Tongra, the most powerful in the Fury. Tongra Orgul's blood had already killed eight men, but TorGynin had survived, the Tongra's blood giving him abilities that none without the Way possessed. After that, he had survived more blood from a Sapper and a Merger, developing abilities that none thus far had reached. ThoraDin had learned through trial and error that when powerful Saricon blood, blood drawn from men who were strong in the Fury, was added to the normal blood of a subject, that incredible changes could happen. That is if they survived. Few had thus far, so they were still learning what capabilities the survivors might develop. Not all changes were good, however. Several men survived the transfer of blood only to die later of mental and physical abnormalities. But for whatever reason, TorGynin had survived the

transfers of blood, giving him powers similar to the
Saricon Fury as well as the Way, making him the
deadliest of the DarPool assassins. His entire
training had taken six years.

"And what of *your* task?"

"Endler Ral is dead."

"And how does that make you feel?"

"Unsatisfied. There is more to do."

"Yes there is. But remember, the game we
are playing is dangerous. No one can know what
we are doing."

"I understand."

"Have you completed our next play?"

"I have."

"Good," ReeOnen said. "Now remember, you
have other missions ordered by the Tongra, which
you must complete so he is not wise to our plans."

TorGynin had been stark still, not moving in
the slightest bit. But now he shifted subtly from
one foot to another. "As always, your will is my
command. I will do as you ask. But you promised
me revenge. And I shall have it." His voice was
eerily gentle, but somehow it carried the weight of
a broadsword before the killing stroke.

ReeOnen unconsciously stepped back from
him. Even she, with all her military prowess, was
afraid of the assassin. So far the training had held
him in check, his loyalty to Heln and the Saricon
cause not wavering. They had spent years molding
him into a killer, a killer who obeyed, but
nonetheless ReeOnen was wary of him. After all,
she knew what he was capable of. "You will have
your revenge. But the façade must be kept.
Besides, I too want to make them pay, and our

paths converge on this point. I will not deny you that which I also crave."

The assassin said nothing, but after a few heartbeats he nodded his head in acquiescence. "What would you have me do?"

CHAPTER TWO

Brant leaped from one boulder to another, barreling up the river bank in powerful strides, Tobias only four arm lengths behind him. The sun had barely crested the tallest peak of the Devlin Mountains, waking for its daily rise and decent. They ran like this nearly every morning, before the real work began on the farm. Years ago, Tobias could not come close to matching Brant's speed, strength, and endurance, falling far behind in every run. But now, as he aged, he could keep up well enough, and if Brant did not push himself, then he might even outdistance him.

Clearing the dry river bed, Brant wove between a grove of trees, the path before him as well known as the sword maneuvers that he practiced daily. They had run their current path so many times that they had created an obvious trail from which to follow even in the dim light of the early morning.

Brant looked back and smiled at Tobias, taunting him to push himself. Tobias narrowed his eyes, grunted, and dove deep for more energy, pulling up closer just a few paces behind. They both broke through the glade and their tiny cabin was just before them, the pen fence fifty paces away marking the finish line.

"Come on!" Brant yelled encouragement. "Dig deeper!"

Brant's lungs were heaving like a horse pushed to exhaustion and his muscular legs were on fire. If he was tired, he knew that Tobias was nearly at his limit. They had been running like this for over an hour. He heard Tobias growl and felt him move nearer. This was the closest he had come to catching him, and Brant was extremely proud of the boy.

Twenty paces to go and the young man yelled into the morning air, pushing his legs and lungs even harder. Then moments later Brant raced by the corner of the fence, his hand touching the old wood that marked the corner of the pen as he ran by. Three blinks later and Tobias was at the railing, nearly crashing into Brant as he slowed.

They both stood up tall, arms raised behind their necks as they sucked in much needed oxygen. It was several moments before they spoke. "So close," Tobias muttered as he paced slowly, breathing deeply and cooling his tired muscles.

"That was the fastest you've run yet," Brant agreed. "It won't be long before you will be able to beat me."

"You'll just blame it on age," Tobias responded with a playful smile.

Brant chuckled. "Maybe so."

There was a water bucket nearby and they both took turns drinking from the ladle. "I'm going to wash up and then head into town. I should be back before dark."

Tobias nodded. "You still want me to bring in that lumber we felled last year?"

They had dropped several trees a few hours up stream and now that it was dry it was time to cut it into sections and haul it home.

"Yes. Don't forget to check the wheel on the cart before you go. It should need some grease."

"I'll do that now while I'm out here," Tobias said, heading towards the barn.

"See you inside for breakfast," Brant added, turning toward the cabin.

Brant made it into town just before mid-day. It wouldn't take him long to get his supplies and get back on the road, so he wanted to check on Jana first as well as pay a visit to Anders, his friend and owner of the local tavern, the Axe Room. There were only two places to rent a room in the small town, the Axe Room, and the local inn called Randers, named after the inn keeper, Gorrin Rander. It was his son, Taryn, who married Jana two years ago. It was there he went first.

The inn was small but cozy. The main room had vaulted ceilings made of thick timbers, each one put in place by Gorrin and his father over thirty years ago. There was a river rock fireplace on one side and several tables and chairs placed before it. The opposite end was the desk where Gorrin, Taryn, or Jana, welcomed guests. Gorrin's wife had died ten years before and he now lived alone in a nearby cottage, allowing Jana and Taryn to occupy the comfortable home attached to the inn's main building. They more or less ran the inn, while Gorrin spent his days hunting the lands around them. The house attached to the inn was where Taryn was born and raised. There was one door that led to six rooms, each small but well taken care of. They served breakfast and dinner and offered a small selection of wine and ale, but nothing like the Axe Room. Most visitors stayed at Randers, but they drank at the Axe Room, his ale famous throughout Dy'ain, especially after the king himself was known to order kegs for his personal

consumption. King Jarak Dormath had met
Anders many years before when he had wintered
his army in town and the surrounding lands. It
was this army that he had used to take back
Cythera from the Saricons. There was even an ale
named after him called Dormath's Dream. It was a
thick dark ale brewed with roasted oats and
accentuated by a dark nutty coffee. It was an
extremely popular beverage, especially in the cold
winter months.

Brant stepped into the room and warmth
from the fire welcomed him. It was deep into fall
and the days were getting colder. The room smelt
of wood smoke and something savory cooking in
the adjacent kitchen. The fire had been recently lit
and already the room was warming comfortably.
Brant looked up, like he always did, and gazed
upon the massive mountain elk rack secured to
the opposite wall. It was the largest rack he had
ever seen, and according to hunters who knew
more about it than he, it was probably the largest
he would ever see. Gorrin's grandfather had killed
it when he was young, hunting the edges of the
Devlin Mountains before the town of Bygon had
even been built. It was a beautiful trophy. Gorrin's
family had a long tradition of hunting, and there
were few who knew the lands and wild game better
than he.

"Brant," a voice came to his left. Turning, he
saw Taryn approach from around the counter, a
warm smile greeting him. "It's good to see you," he
said, shaking his hand. Taryn was a rugged
looking young man, with wavy dark brown hair
and steel gray eyes. He was soft spoken, but tough
like his father. Hard work and manual labor was a

daily occurrence, molding him into a reliable husband for Jana. Brant liked him immensely.

"And you as well," Brant replied, looking around the room. "I was hoping to see Jana, is she around?"

"She is in the kitchen. What are you in town for?"

"Need some axle grease and a few other supplies."

"Will you be staying with us?"

Brant shook his head. "No, just here for a quick visit before I get back on the road."

Wherever Brant went he always carried his sword and wore his armor. It was the same armor that Kulvar Rand had given him so long ago. Something about the weapons comforted him. His sword was typically strapped to his back, as it was now.

Brant noticed Taryn's gaze flick to his sword, his furtive glance returning quickly. Brant had never been one for lofty words of praise, and despite the fact that Taryn had known him for two years now, he still seemed nervous around him. Perhaps it was Brant's martial reputation, or maybe his quiet brusque demeanor; combine both with the fact that Taryn had married his adopted daughter and that was a recipe for nervous tension at times. Brant tried his best to comfort the young man, but soft emotional words were just not his forte.

"You have time for an ale while I get Jana from the kitchen?"

Brant pursed his lips. "I think I can manage one."

"Good. I'll bring some smoked sausage and ale for us. Feel free to warm yourself by the fire while I fetch Jana and some food."

Brant nodded and moved to the table nearest the fire. He took off his travel cloak and draped it over a chair. Unbuckling the strap securing his sword to his back, he leaned the weapon against the edge of the table.

Just then the door opened and five people herded in, talking softly as they moved to the counter. Brant's inspecting gaze flitted from person to person, taking them in and appraising them quickly. They too were looking around the room, all sets of eyes settling on him before looking away indifferently. Immediately he felt something wrong. It was in their eyes...a reflection one got when looking at a soldier, or a fighter, someone who had seen violence. But in this case, it wasn't just someone who has experienced bloodshed; it was the look of someone who enjoyed it. Brant knew the look.

Four of them were men, while the other was a woman, although she mirrored no womanly attributes. In fact, at first he had assumed she was a man. Next to a female Saricon, she was the largest woman Brant had ever seen. Her black hair was short and her shoulders broad, with narrow hips typically seen in a male. Intense green eyes glanced his way and paused, a slight smirk flashing across her pock marked face before she turned back to the men who were now standing around the counter.

Brant kept his eye on them as he moved his chair further away from the table, giving himself room if needed. It was probably nothing, his overstimulated imagination forged from years of violence always suspecting the worst. But he couldn't shake the feeling. They all wore traveling clothes dirty and worn form the road. Glinting steel could be seen under their cloaks and jerkins, probably chainmail or pieces of plate. They each carried swords at their hips and they moved with the practiced ease of one who had a lot of experience doing so.

Taryn opened the door behind the counter that led into the kitchen and was surprised to see them. "Oh, hello," he offered, setting the tray of ale and sausage on the counter. "What can I do for you?"

It was the women who spoke, the other men casually leaning against the counter, several facing Brant, their eyes like that of a predator. "We be lookin fur rooms for the night." Her voice was deep and brusque and laced with an accent Brant could not place.

"Sure. How many?"

"What you see here," she added.

"We only have four available. Two would have to share."

The women nodded. "See to it."

"Give me a moment," he replied. "I'll be back shortly."

Taryn lifted up the tray and made his way to Brant, just as the door opened again, revealing Jana with a wide smile on her face. Instantly it vanished as she saw the group before her. Looking past them, she saw Brant by the fire, her smile returning as she followed Taryn.

One man stepped in front of her, his colossal body blocking her from moving around the counter. "Pardon me, sir," she said politely.

"I'm Ardren," the man said. "Who might you be? Such a ripe thing you are."

Jana flushed and her eyes narrowed. "Excuse me," she said again a bit harder, pushing past the big man as he let her by with a laugh. A few others nearby joined in, their hushed snickers not going unnoticed.

Brant was already standing, his hand reaching for his sword. Jana rushed to him, her eyes saying *no, leave it.* She hugged him fiercely. "Brant, I'm so glad you are here."

"Me too," he replied, his green eyes looking past her to the man at the bar.

"It's fine," she whispered. "It's not the first time."

Taryn's face was a mask of anger as well, having just witnessed the end of the brief confrontation. "What did he say to you?" Taryn asked, his jaw set.

"Oh, nothing. I told you, I'm fine. Just men being men," Jana added as she casually brushed it off.

Taryn didn't look so sure. "Jana, stay and talk with Brant. I'll take care of these customers."

Taryn went to leave when Brant grabbed his wrist. "Be careful," he said. "There is something about them I don't like," he added, his voice just a whisper.

Taryn nodded and left them together. Jana sat down opposite Brant and they both picked up a mug of ale. "To family," she said, clicking her mug to his. They drank deeply before Jana smiled warmly again, obviously trying to alleviate Brant's concerns. "So, how are you?"

"Doing fine. Just coming into town for a few supplies. How's the business?"

Jana pursed her lips and nodded from side to side. "Comes and goes. But we are surviving. Did Tobias come with you?"

"No, you know my rule."

"That one man must always protect the home," she said mockingly, smiling through the jest.

Brant held his arms to the side, placating. "I'd rather be cautious when it comes to those I love."

She reached across the table and held his callused hand. "I know. I'm just kidding."

Brant placed his hand over hers. "But, Tobias is coming into town tomorrow. He wants to see you."

"Oh good," she said with excitement. Then her look turned coy. "I'm hoping he wants to visit a certain someone as well."

Brant smiled. "Oh, I'm sure that's on his list."

Brant looked up as the large women approached the table. Immediately he sat back, his right hand closing on his sword. Quickly he drew energy from his aura and flushed it into his limbs, readying his body to use the energy if it was needed. Jana caught his movement, her body going rigid and her smile disappearing. Taryn was leading the other men through the side door to their rooms. Brant had turned on his towd, or aura sight, and was relieved to see that she was not gifted in the Way.

"I'm sorry to be interruptin youze folks," she said as she stood next to Jana, her huge size dwarfing her. "But do you happin to be Brant Anwar?"

Again, Brant noticed her strange accent, one he had never heard. His eyes narrowed and his hand tightened on his sword. "Does it matter?" he responded, his voice harder than he had hoped.

She didn't like his tone, but she stepped back, aware that she was putting him on guard. "I just wanted to meet ya, that be all."

Brant relaxed some, releasing the handle of his blade. But his aura energy was ready nonetheless. "I am called by that name," Brant said. "How did you know?"

She nodded to the sword. "Your blade is quite famous you know." She smiled. But something about it seemed insincere. "You are the Glimmer Blade," she added in excitement. But again, it seemed forced.

Brant nodded. "Who are you?"

"My names Orna. We are traders, moving through Dy'ain."

Brant looked her over again. She did not look like any merchant he had ever seen. "Where you from?"

"Vyalia, in Belorth." He couldn't place her accent, nor did he know what someone from Vyalia would sound like. He guessed her origins explained her unusual accent, but he could not be sure.

"You are a long way from home."

She shrugged her huge shoulders casually. "Just hopin' to get some Kul-brite. Like everyone else. Is it true you killed that Saricon war leader in five heartbeats?"

"It's not something I like to talk about. Besides, I'm visiting family," he said, indicating Jana. He added nothing more, hoping she would take the hint.

The large trader looked at Jana and smiled, stepping back a few paces. "My apologies." She nodded curtly to them. "Good evening to ya both." Then she turned and followed Taryn and her companions through the closed door.

After she had left, Jana turned to Brant. "I know you hate being the hero of the war, but perhaps kindness is the proper response for your admirers." She was smiling, but Brant knew she was serious.

"There is something I don't like about that group. Stay away from them. My bet is they are not traders."

"Always seeing the worst in people," Jana said mockingly.

Brant leaned forward, his expression hard. "I'm serious, Jana. Stay away from them."

Jana sighed. "Fine, now, let us talk of pleasant things."

***

Tobias led the ox pulled wood cart through the small glade of trees, smelling the smoke before he saw it. His heart started to beat rapidly as he quickly guided their ox through the maze of timber, reappearing around the river bend. Not much could provide that much smoke and none of them were good. Realization and horror struck him when he pushed through the trees. He froze; his heart sank in his chest when he saw the smoke billowing from the thatched roof of their cabin.

"Thea," he whispered, releasing the reigns and grabbing the loaded crossbow and his sheathed sword from the ox's saddle. Whenever he went out, he carried the loaded crossbow, both for protection and the off chance that he came across some wild game. He raced at full sprint towards their home, not sure what he was going to find. A chill ran up his spine when he heard Thea scream, moments later five men came around the side of the house, Thea shoved before them.

She stumbled and fell to the ground, the men around her carrying bare blades. Her nose was bleeding and her shirt had been ripped off her shoulder, exposing her bare flesh. "Thea!" Tobias yelled in anger as he neared.

She looked up from the ground and her wild eyes matched her scream. "Tobias, run!" But her crestfallen look that followed showed that she knew he would not.

The men turned when they saw him, glinting steel held before them matching the gleam of their villainous smiles. Tobias had never fought a real fight before, but he had no time to ponder his lack of experience. Anger erupted from deep within him, giving way for a massive amount of adrenaline to course through his body. Instinct took over and he simply reacted, skidding to a halt ten paces away and leveling the crossbow at the man nearest Thea. There was an audible click in the tense silence followed by a thud as the man was catapulted to his back, the bolt buried to its fletching in his chest. One man yanked Thea off the ground from her hair while the other three charged.

Tobias's heart was pounding in his chest and he threw down the crossbow, drawing his blade from its scabbard just as the first man was on him. Their swords met, and despite the fact that Tobias had little experience, his training with Brant guided his strokes. He blocked a powerful attack, the man before him much larger. Remembering his training, he pivoted as he blocked, the strength of the man's attack throwing him off balance. Tobias spun the blade up and across his body, slicing the man across his armored chest, his sharp blade deflecting off the steel and cutting through his exposed chin, blood spraying from the gruesome wound.

The man stumbled backwards and Tobias barely had time to parry the next attacker. Immediately, Tobias sensed a better swordsman. The man was a little taller than he, wearing chainmail under a road worn tunic, a gray cape fluttering behind him. His long sword rolled over Tobias's parry and nicked him across his bicep. Grunting, Tobias spun away from the man, only to face the third opponent who came at him in a wild rush. Tobias's blade was up to block it, and faster than his opponent thought, his blade spun back around to cut him in the thigh. The man grunted and stumbled backwards, away from him.

The two men circled him, the third groaning on the ground, his hand covering his broken and cut chin trying to staunch the flow of blood. Tobias's was breathing hard, but he was oddly calm, his sword held still before him.

The better swordsman smiled, accentuating a nasty cut across his lips. "So, the pup can use a blade."

The other killer was holding his sword with one hand, his other hand clamped over his cut thigh, blood dripping freely to pool at the ground. "Should've known he could fight," he growled through the pain.

"Who are you?" Tobias asked. The men had an accent although he could not place it. He had never heard it before.

The swordsman shrugged casually. "It matters not. You will die, and the woman will come with us." His wicked smile clearly reflected their intent.

"Brant will hunt you down and kill you all," Tobias said.

Again the man shrugged. "He will not be able to find us."

Thea was struggling in the fourth man's grasp and he violently kicked her in the back of the knee, dropping her to the ground. The man holding her was large and heavily muscled, a long sword in his right hand, the other wrapped tightly around her neck, his strong grip capable of snapping her neck. "Leave him alone," Thea grunted through the pain. "Don't hurt him...I will go with you."

The man holding her was heavily bearded, but Tobias could see his smile nonetheless. "Sorry missy," he said. "Orders are to grab you, and kill him. Do it!" he ordered.

The swordsman smiled and lunged, simultaneously the man with the injured leg attacked, his sword sweeping low. Tobias brushed his blade aside, holding his attack as he leapt to the side of the man's injured leg, hoping to distance himself from the other man's attack. He felt the whoosh of air behind him as the attacking blade missed him by a hair. The injured man tried to turn towards him, but his leg caused him to stumble. Tobias pivoted quickly, his own blade arcing down and across his assailant's neck, biting deep into the flesh. The man cried out as blood sprayed through the air, crimson splashes coating Tobias's face and chest.

The man fell to the ground as the better swordsman continued his movement, attacking Tobias with several lightning attacks, trying to find an opening. Their blades clashed many times as they danced across the ground, each swordsman looking for an opening. The man was a killer, but Tobias's body was reacting on years of swordplay with one of the finest warriors in Corvell, and that training was now saving his life.

They were both sweating profusely when Tobias snapped his leg out, connecting with the swordsman's knee. The man saw it coming, but could not retract his leg in time, Tobias's foot glancing off his knee. The man stumbled and Tobias took advantage, his blade darting in and penetrating the flesh on his bicep. The man swore and jumped back to regroup.

"I tire of this!" the man holding Thea said. "Gandren, get out of the way!"

The swordsman jumped to the side and Tobias found himself looking directly at the man who had been holding Thea. But he wasn't holding his sword anymore, or Thea, who was unconscious on the ground. In his right hand Tobias caught the glint of steel as his arm retracted and threw. His mind registered the movement, but his body could not react fast enough. There was a sharp pain in his chest as the dagger slammed into him.

Tobias stumbled backwards, his eyes wide with shock as he looked at the cold steel buried in his chest. Pain shot through his body and he nearly dropped his sword. Falling to his knees, his mind flashed through his last thoughts. *I failed them...*he thought. *I could not protect Thea.* He looked up and saw the swordsman approach. Again, his mind saw the threat, but his body could not respond. His arms felt like led, and he could not bring his sword to bear.

Blood gushed from his mouth as he spoke his last words. "Brant...will...kill you." And for some reason that final thought comforted him, the realization of what Brant was going to do them somehow causing him to smile through the agony. He saw the flash of the blade, and felt no more pain.

***

Brant had left with his supplies the tail end of mid-day, soon after his brief visit with Jana as well as his friend, Anders, the proprietor of the Axe Room. The journey went by quickly, his mind preoccupied by the group of men and the mysterious women he had met at Randers. He couldn't put his finger on it, but something about them didn't seem right. He couldn't shake the feeling, and it worried him. *Was he just being over protective and worrisome?* Possibly. But his feeling was like a bee sting, it just kept nagging at him, and despite how furious he scratched it, it just got worse. He was so wrapped up in his thoughts that he failed to notice the smoke rising in the evening breeze just beyond the glade of trees that surrounded their home near the creek.

Brant's heart slammed in his chest as all his worries coalesced violently, surges of adrenaline rocking his body. *Was his home burning? Were Thea and Tobias alright?* His sword was already strapped to his back, and without a second thought he pushed his aura energy his legs and raced along the river bed, his Aurit powers bringing him quickly to their fence. Once there his eyes quickly took in the scene, the smoke from their ruined cabin languidly rising into the evening air, as if it had no worries to ponder, oblivious of the destruction scattered below it.

Ripping up the dirt, Brant skidded to a halt as he saw the bodies littering the ground. His wide eyes flitted from one body to another, discerning their identity in less than a heartbeat. When his gaze landed on the third body, it felt like all his energy was ripped from his body. His legs buckled and his arms hung limply. Sprawled across the ground, lying in his own blood, was Tobias. In the back of his mind he knew he hadn't seen Thea among the dead, but that knowledge did little to mend his shattered heart. Stumbling towards the boy, Brant dropped to his knees, his shaking hands reaching out to touch him.

"No...no...this can't be happening," he mumbled, he hands touching Tobias's cold arm. A dagger was protruding from his chest and his bloody sword was still grasped tightly. His eyes were open, staring, blank, devoid of what made Tobias *himself.* Tears streaked down Brant's face as the pain worked its way through his body. Part of him pushed it away, as if that action could turn back time, could make it all go away. But he knew what he was seeing. Tobias was cold...his blood was everywhere...he was dead. Brant screamed as loud as he could, the pain and loss needing to be released or it would consume him.

He reached for Tobias's head and laid it gently in his lap, sobbing loudly as he closed his eyes against the image of his dead adopted son, wishing for it all to go away. But it didn't. He sat there for a few moments, hoping that denial would somehow erase what he was witnessing. But he knew it wouldn't. Brant took a deep breath, calming his mind and body, and opened his eyes once again. He reached down and gently closed Tobias's eyes.

That action switched something inside him, like a massive stone shifting, unmovable except for the ravages of time. His heart turned to stone, calming at the same time. His eyes narrowed and his steady gaze looked more intently across the scene, all emotion disappearing over a cascade of steady, calm, anger. The killer had been awoken. He felt like a potter's ball of clay on the wheel that had suddenly hardened, one moment he was softened by pain and loss, the next moment hardened by something deep and dark. Taking in the scene, he noticed three men were dead. One was on his back, a crossbow bolt buried to its feathers in his chest. That's when Brant noticed their crossbow four paces to the right. He recognized the worn wood, one edge of the handle chipped from constant use. Brant gently laid Tobias's head down and rose to inspect the other bodies. The other three had died from sword wounds. Two bled out from various cuts, one vicious one had taken a man in the chin, and another had cut deeply into a man's neck.

Brant couldn't smile. He wasn't capable of it at the moment. But he knew that Tobias had killed three men, and that knowledge, although barely perceptible beneath the controlled anger, was somehow reassuring to him. Whoever these men were had underestimated a young man, and had walked away with three less because of it. And Tobias had not died of a sword thrust. He had not been beaten in a duel. Some coward had thrown a knife at him from a safe distance.

The thought of Thea came flooding back to him and he hastily searched the grounds. The cabin's roof was smoking and the wood rafters and thatch had caved in, catching the contents of the cabin on fire, their belongings burnt wood and ash. The main door was open and partially burned. Brant passed through it, feeling the heat from the fire and embers immediately. Quickly, he searched the home where he could, covering his mouth as the smoke made it difficult to breath. He couldn't find her and raced from the cabin, coughing and squinting away the sting of the smoke, his eyes watering profusely. She was nowhere to be found.

What had happened? Who were these men? Were they connected to the *traders* he saw in town? He could not be sure, but finding no body meant that Thea could still be alive. He had to find her, and *now*. But he could not leave Tobias's body sprawled across the ground, lying in his own blood, to be scavenged and picked apart by birds and other carrion feeders. He knew he needed to get on the assailant's trail while it was still warm, but burying Tobias was something he had to do.

It took him two hours to dig a reasonable hole next to Tobias's parents who had been buried in a grove of trees behind the cabin. He would do more when he had more time, but for now it would do. After lifting the body into the hole, he laid Tobias's sword on his chest, placing both hands on the handle. He died as a warrior, and he would be buried as such. He spent the next hour carrying stones that outlined their garden's beds to the grave, placing them neatly into a cairn that would do well to protect the shallow grave from the wild animals. He didn't cry once during the task. He couldn't. His mind was focused on one thing and one thing only...locate Thea, find who did this, and kill them all. His anguish would only be washed away by blood.

The ride back into town was the quickest he had yet accomplished. After grabbing a pack, any rations that were still intact and not destroyed by the fire, his crossbow, armor and weapons, and coins he had buried in the barn, Brant had mounted their fastest horse and rode with all haste. The last two hours of the ride was completed in the dark, but luckily for Brant the sky was clear and the moon bright, its blue glow lighting the worn road well enough. He was forced to slow some, but only some.

A flashing lantern light at the entrance of the town slowed him down, pulling in tight on the reins as he saw two men holding crossbows, one lifting the lantern up high. "Hold traveler!" one man yelled as Brant came to a stop before them. Brant had been traveling to and from the town for ten years, and not once had he seen men guard its entrance. It wasn't a good sign. "Who ye be travelin at such a fast pace?" The same man asked.

Brant narrowed his eyes in the darkness, trying to see who it was before him. The lantern light reflected yellow off of a familiar face. "Tyvus, what be the meaning of this?" Tyvus was the town's cobbler, and he was no warrior.

"Brant, is that you?" He sounded relieved, and worried at the same time.

"It is," he replied as the two men lowered their crossbows and moved closer. "What is happening?" Brant recognized the other man as well. It was Beargan, Tyvus's younger cousin. Both of the men looked concerned, to say the least.

It was Tyvus who spoke. "Brant, I'm sorry to have to tell ya this. But some men killed Taryn last night and took Jana with them. Emy is missing as well. Taken after her shift." Emy was a serving girl at the Axe Room, the same girl that Tobias was hoping to visit the next day. He would never visit her now, or any girl for that matter. He pushed the morose thoughts quickly away, focusing on what the men had just said.

Brant's gaze hardened, his jaw flexing, but he said nothing. He had already prepared himself for the worst. Nudging his horse, he raced past the surprised men.

Moments later Brant's steed skidded to a stop and he leapt off in one smooth motion, shoving open the door to Rander's Inn. It was late into the night, only hours from morning, and yet the room was occupied by three men. Two were sitting by a smoldering fire, and a third paced across the wood floor boards. All three turned when Brant entered.

"Brant!" Ander's said, standing hastily to greet him. "We were just deciding who was going

to ride to get you." Ander's was the owner of the
Axe Room, and Brant's longtime friend. He looked
tired and distraught. "Brant, Jana and Emy were
taken."

Brant looked at Gorrin, father to Taryn. The
man looked tired as well, but something else was
there, something deep and primal. Brant
recognized it immediately as it had always been his
companion. Anger...a boiling almost
uncontrollable anger.

"They killed him." It was all Gorrin could get
out. His voice was a whisper, but Brant knew it
was the gentle sprinkles before a massive
rainstorm.

"Was it the group staying here?" Brant
asked, his voice cold.

The other man that had been sitting with
Ander's by the fire was the town's head
councilman. His name was Orlin, and although
Brant did not know him well, his reputation was
that of a hardworking, honest man. He stepped
closer to Brant. "Why are you here? Has
something else happened?" Orlin could tell
something was wrong with Brant. And besides, no
one had sent word to Brant. He had no reason to
be there at such a late hour.

"Men attacked my home. Tobias is dead.
Thea is...gone." He barely got the last word out
before looking back to Gorrin. "Was it the men
staying here?" This time his voice was strained,
like the low growl of a caged mountain cat.

Gorrin nodded. "It was. They struck near
midnight."

"How do you know?" Brant asked.

"I found Taryn's body in the kitchen," Anders answered. "It's not uncommon for me to have a late drink with him after the night crowd goes home. It was a slow night. I came over early and figured he would be in the kitchen cleaning up with Jana. He had been stabbed in the back." Ander's eyes were rimmed red and puffy. Bygon was a small town and the homestead families had known each other for a long time. The young man's death had clearly hit him hard.

"Did you have any newcomers in your bar tonight?" Brant asked Anders, his voice all business.

Anders nodded. "I did. An unruly lot who claimed to be traders. They didn't look the part, more like mercenaries to me."

"Slavers more like," Gorrin spat.

"Perhaps," Orlin agreed. "But Brant, they clearly had a vendetta against you. Why else would they attack your home and take Thea, as well as Jana."

"But they took Emy as well," Anders added quickly.

Orlin pursed his lips. "Perhaps it was a grab of convenience. When did those men leave the Axe Room?"

Anders thought for a moment, sighing heavily as realization struck home. "Just after Emy left for home."

"Something tells me they were trying to hurt Brant, and Emy just happened to be in the wrong place at the wrong time."

Brant's mind was spinning, but it was hard for him to think past his pounding heart and reeling anger. He was barely keeping it in check. But who would do something like this to him? And why not attack him? Obviously they took the ones he loved. Whoever did this wasn't just looking for slaves. They were trying to hurt him.

Brant looked at Gorrin. "They have four hours on us. We need to get on their trail."

Gorrin nodded. "I would have left already. But I was waiting for you."

Brant was no tracker. Gorrin, however, was the best tracker and hunter west of the Devlin Mountains. He was well into his fifties, but a lifetime of hunting the mountains and forests, as well as manual labor, had chiseled him into a sinewy man built of muscle and grit. Not to mention he had spent four years in the legion. He was as tough as they came. "Good. Fill your pack. We leave now." Brant looked at Orlin. "Are there any of the king's men in town?"

"Unfortunately, no. You want me to send word to Amorsit?"

Brant nodded. "Get the word out." Bygon was too small of a town to hold a garrison, but Amorsit, the nearest village, manned a small garrison of ten men. If slavers were about, the king's men needed to know. Slavery was illegal in Dy'ain.

Brant turned to leave as Ander's stepped before him. "Be careful Brant. Something doesn't smell right."

"Regardless, I'm going to kill them all."

Chapter Three

There was no sense in riding hard at night, so Brant and Gorrin had left just before sunrise. That had given them an hour to pack and organize their supplies. They had no idea where they would be going, or how long, so they wanted to be prepared. It was an excruciating wait for Brant, his mind reeling over the catastrophic events of the previous day. One moment he was content, even happy, and the next, everything had come crashing down. Brant had never felt this lost, this alone, and this angry, and his aura energy was flashing through him, eager to be unleashed in a bloodletting fueled by revenge. Whoever had killed Tobias and Taryn, and taken Thea and Jana, would pay. They would die at his hands. There was nothing else he could think about. The thought of snuffing out the life of the killers was like a comforting blanket, soft and heavy, the only thing warming him against the chill of such a great loss.

While they waited, they had come up with a plan. They hoped that Gorrin could track them, but if not, they would head to Cythera, the capital city of Dy'ain. Brant had remembered that the woman named Orna had mentioned she was from Vyalia, which was south of Argos in the Alsace Sea. It was likely that if they were returning home, if Vyalia was indeed their home, that they would secure transport on a ship departing Cythera. It was a big gamble as they really had no idea who they were, or where they were going. But it's all they had to go on. Finding them soon was paramount. Both knew that if they got too far ahead of them, that their trail would disappear like smoke in the night. If Gorrin could find their tracks, then they might have a chance.

They pushed the horses hard that first day, stopping often as Gorrin inspected the ground. The road was well traveled and pocked with dirt and mud, prints of man and steed peppering the ground. Some were fresh, and some were not. Luckily for them it had not rained, and Gorrin was able to read the road well. There was recent travel from a large group of heavy riders, the depth of the hoof prints indicating such. Wagon ruts pushed through the horse tracks before it. Gorrin thought there may have been two wagons. And they were laden, heavy from goods. Brant ground his teeth in anger as he thought of his Jana and Thea trussed up and tossed in a wagon. Who knows what they had already done to them. That thought had to be pushed deep within his conscience or it would overwhelm him. He needed to think straight, and dwelling on that would do him, or them, no good. He would deal with those emotions when the time came.

Gorrin looked up from the muddy ground, his age lined face scrunched in worry. "It be them," he growled. "They are a half day before us."

Brant looked up at the sky. "Not long before dark."

"What do you want to do?"

Brant hated to admit it, but they needed to rest the horses. Not to mention if they tried to pursue them at night they might miss their tracks. There were plenty of smaller cart paths that branched off the main road, some leading to small villages and settlements. They couldn't risk losing the scent. "We best set up camp and rest the horses. We leave at first light."

Gorrin pursed his lips in frustration, but knew he was right. "They have to camp as well," he said, trying to ease their anxiety at having to stop when they knew their quarry was out there somewhere.

There was a clearing off the side of the road and it wasn't long before they had a fire lit and Gorrin was heating a bowl of beans and dried meat over the flames. Neither man was much for conversation, even at good times, and now their minds were both occupied, the silence a proper bed mate to their turbulent thoughts.

Gorrin sat up to grab the bowls when suddenly he grunted and his hand snapped to his neck. He stumbled and fell to the side, unmoving on the flattened grass.

Brant reacted instinctively, pouring aura energy into his limbs. His body was a blur as he reached for his sword. But he never made it. There was a sharp sting at his neck and his body dropped like a sack of stones. His eyes widened as his body shook, releasing the aura energy harmlessly into the ground. But he couldn't move. There was a numbing sensation at his neck and no matter how hard he tried his arms and legs would not respond.

"Do not fight it, Brant." A soft voice came from the darkness as a dark shadow stepped above him. In the dim light of the fire, Brant could not see the person well, his head covered by a black hood, his features hidden behind a dark mask. "The poison comes from a rare mushroom far to the north." The man squatted lower, so Brant could see him better, the orange firelight flickering across his torso. "Do not worry. It will not kill you. It paralyzes you see, and it will make you sick for days."

Brant growled and dug deeper for the energy to move, but all he managed was a slight turn of his body so he could view his assailant better. He was sweating as the numbness from the poison spread down his neck. It felt like ice cold water was entering his blood stream.

"Very good," the man said, clearly impressed. "Most cannot even blink, and yet you managed to actually move. But you are Brant Anwar, so that is not entirely unexpected. Ironic, isn't it...that the Glimmer Blade was brought down by a simple plant? You can thank the Gyths for that. One in particular taught us many things." TorGynin paused, as if thinking if he wanted to finish that particular tale. He chose not to and continued. "But do not worry. I will not kill you. In fact, it is I who has saved your life. There is another that wants you dead. I persuaded them otherwise. I owed you that much. But they needed their revenge, and so your loved ones have unfortunately filled that void. I cannot have you rescuing them. So, you and your friend here will succumb to the poison. It will be days before you can ride, and by that time the trail will be gone. You will never see them again. Every moment of every day will be occupied with the thought of them. Where will they be? Are they alive? Are they slaves? It will nag at you, eating you from the inside. You see, it's the not knowing that tears you apart. Trust me, I know." The man rose from the ground quickly, the darkness of the night shadowing his face once more. "Perhaps, in time, I will come to you again, and tell you the story that set into motion the events you are now experiencing. But for now, your companion will be the pain you feel from the loss of loved ones, as it was for me." Then he was gone, the dark night swallowing him in a blink.

***

Brant woke slowly; his body feeling like a gang of Saricons had used him for a training dummy. He hurt everywhere, and his body was clammy and cold. Focusing his eyes, he looked around the room. Where was he? What had happened? His thoughts were hazy, and trying to wrestle with them hurt as much as his body.

The room was gloomy and shadowed, the only light coming from a warm fire on the far wall and several oil lamps placed around the cabin. That's what it looked like, a cabin, not so different than his own, although older and more dilapidated. But he had no cabin anymore, and now that single thought forced everything to come rushing back to him. Thea and Jana were gone, likely taken by slavers. They had been poisoned on the road by a stranger, shot by some dart. And now he was here, wherever *here* was. Frantically, he tried to move, but his body barely complied, and everything ached when he did. That's when he noticed Gorrin laying on a wooden cot in the corner, near the roaring fire. He seemed to be sleeping, covered with a thick brown fur.

"You are awake, that is good." A voice came from Brant's right, near the door that was now opening, a bent over old woman entering slowly, shutting the heavy wood door behind her. Her gray hair fell to her mid-back, pulled back in a long tail that was lashed with a black leather cord. Two of her teeth were missing and her skin was so aged that that there was no portion of her face free from lines, like hundreds of valleys, the heaviest concentration around her eyes and lips. She went to a table and poured a glass of water from a clay jar, her hands shaking in the process.

"Where am I? Who are you?" Brant croaked, trying to clear the last of the fogginess. He was so tired that he could barely speak.

She brought the water to his lips and that's when he noticed how thirsty he was. The water poured down his dry throat and he swallowed greedily, quickly emptying the glass. "Me names Morwin. Dis be me cabin. My grandson founds uze on de side of de road, bringing ya back here he did. I don't know what be aflictan yeah, but uze seem to be doing better."

"How long have we been here?"

"Three days. Ya ought to be hungry as a bear."

Panic hit Brant as he realized the implication. If they lost the slave trader's tracks than they might never find them, and that meant that he would never see Jana or Thea again. Three days! Their trail would be cold now. Who was this man who poisoned him and why? Everything the man said had made no sense. All except the reason for poisoning them. That made sense. If the mysterious man really didn't want them tracking Thea and Jana, than keeping them bed bound for a few days was a good way of going about it. But why not just kill them? The assailant acted as if he knew him. He had too many questions that he could not answer, and he was afraid that he might never get the answers.

One thing was for sure, he would never get the answers lying in a bed. "I have to get up," Brant groaned, trying to lift his body off the bed. He got his torso half way up before he came crashing down. He had no strength.

Morwin shook her head. "Nots lookin' like ya goin anywhere soon. Me bet it be a poison of some sort. I'll look afta ya, but was wonderin if ya have any coin to repay de favor."

"Topi, we should help dem regardless." The voice came from the door again as a young man entered, dressed in rain-soaked furs. The young man was in his early twenties, but his face was covered in a week's growth of black stubble making him seem older. He hung his wet coat up on a peg by the door and moved towards Brant. "We'll help ya get on ur feet. No need fur de coin. Me names Caelin."

"Shut ur pious mouth," Morwin said as she slapped his shoulder. "We be needin the coin and we know he can pay."

Brant realized for the first time that he was naked, his eyes worried as he looked around the room for his belongings. They must have gone through his stuff, finding his coin purse in the process. "Where are my things?" His voice was laced with accusation, but he had no strength to back it up.

"Don't fret, ur things are safe over there," Caelin said, indicating the corner of the room. He was smiling as he looked from Morwin to Brant. "Sorry bout ur clothes, but when I brought uze in you were both burning up and sweatin like pigs in de desert."

Morwin smiled and put her hand on Brant's muscled bicep. "Tis was the most exciten thing this old woman done for years now," she said with a flirtatious wink.

Caelin lovingly put his arm around his grandmother. "Don't be minden her. Ur safe here. Now, what be ur name? Me grandmother and I have sort of a bet on who uze might be with all those scars and such."

"My name is Brant. My companion is Gorrin. We were on a very important mission when we were attacked on the road and poisoned. We need to get back on the trail."

Caelin smiled at his grandmother. "I told ya. Topi, he be the Glimmer Blade. No one else has scars like that." Then he looked back at Brant, his expression more serious. "I know who you be, sir, and I want you to know that we be willin to help in any way we can. I never would've known but fur ur sword and scars."

"Thank you for your help, Caelin. Is Gorrin alright?"

It was Morwin who spoke. "His heart is strong...his color better. Should wake soon. We need to get food in ya bellies." She winked at him again. "Uze be needin a sponge bath, and I be available."

Caelin nudged her again. "Stop it, Topi. I'm sure Brant be on important business. What can we do to help?"

"Thank you. We need to get on the road and we could use your help in nursing us back to strength." He looked at Morwin. "I can pay. As soon as I can walk, we will leave. Our mission is very important." Brant's tone was urgent, and they both picked up on it.

"Topi, let's get some food cookin now that he is awake. I'm sure ur friend, Gorrin, will wake soon enough."

Morwin frowned before turning towards the kitchen. She stopped and looked back, a mischievous smile following. "How about the sponge bath?"

Despite the tension flowing through Brant's body, he couldn't help but smile. It seemed rude not to. "Let's just start with the food, which is much appreciated."

They talked well into the evening after they ate a savory vegetable stew, dipping chunks of fresh bread into the salty broth. They were famished. The food was simple, but nourishing, washing it down with mugs of cold water.

Morwin had convinced Brant and Gorrin to drink a brown tonic of her own creation. Brant had learned that she was something of apothecary, and her skill was the main source of their income. The tonic was bitter, but she promised that it would get them on their feet sooner than later. Caelin supplemented their livelihood from coin earned from hunting and farming potatoes, the latter being the reason he had found Brant and Gorrin's immobilized bodies by a smoldering campfire on the side of the road. Caelin had been transporting a recent batch of potatoes to a coastal town called Gashwin. He was returning home when he found them early the next morning. He did not know who they were, but Brant's sword alone was reason enough to help them.

"Thank you again for your help," Brant said, sitting on a wooden chair facing the warm hearth. Gorrin had woken an hour before, and after he had eaten, had enough strength to join them by the fire. "You know who I am, which means you know my sword is made from Kul-brite steel." Caelin was looking into the warm fire, his gaze moving back to Brants. "The steel alone could keep you and your grandmother comfortable for the rest of your life." Brant's tone was serious as he looked to Morwin and Caelin. "It's not often one meets honest folk as you. Again, we thank you."

Morwin nodded and winked at Brant. Caelin's serious expression cracked into a smile. "Well I couldn't very well sell it without being caught."

Gorrin chuckled as Brant leaned back in his chair, adjusting his body to ease out the soreness caused by the poison. "Just the same, we appreciate your help." Then he looked at Gorrin. "We will be leaving at first light."

Caelin's expression grew serious once again. "Uze sure ur fit fur travel?"

Brant shook his head. "Honestly, no. I've never felt such a drain on my body. But we cannot wait any longer." Brant had already told them what had happened and why they were on the road. They both understood. Brant reached into his pocket and set four gold dracks on the side table. "This is for you."

Caelin's eye's widened at the exorbitant sum. It was obvious that he had never seen so much gold, but he tried unsuccessfully to mask his surprise. "We be more than grateful. Thank you. Which direction you heading tomorrow?'

Brant shook his head, clearly worried. "If Gorrin can't find their trail, which is likely now, then we will head towards Cythera. They are way ahead of us and any sign of their passing was likely washed away in the rain. If I were betting on their destination, Cythera would be it."

Caelin frowned and looked into the fire. He sighed and ran his hand through his greasy long hair. "I was thinken bout what uze said, and remembered somethin. On de road back from Gashwin, before Ize found ya, I passed a rather suspicious lot. Ten men, armor and weapons all, leadin two covered wagons. They were headin towards Gashwin."

Gorrin sat up straight in his chair, looking hopefully at Brant. "Can you remember anything else?" He asked.

"Think hard, Caelin," Brant added. "What else do you remember?"

Caelin shrugged apologetically. "Not much I'm afraid. Just remember dem being an unruly lookin lot. Weren't kind either, nasty stares and deep frowns all around. And they were big, warriors clearly. Oh, and they were moving fast."

Brant looked at Gorrin. "What do you think?"

Gorrin let out a deep breath. "Could be them. What choice do we have? We could head to Cythera, with no idea if they went that way. Or we could head west to the coastal town. At least that decision is supported by *some* evidence."

Brant looked at Gorrin. "How far is Gashwin?"

"Two days hard ride. On foot? Best reckon four to five days."

Brant rubbed his eyes, clearly frustrated they had lost their horses. Whoever had poisoned them had made sure of that. They had very little to go on, and what Caelin had said was so far their best information. Gorrin was right, what choice did they have? "At first light we head to Gashwin."

***

As best as Thea could tell, they had been traveling for nearly two days, chained to the bench in the back of a wagon, a leather gag stuffed in their mouths and strapped around their head. They had not had a drink or eaten anything since their capture. Blood caked the side of Thea's mouth where she had been hit and her head still throbbed. Her mouth felt like it had been sucked of moisture, the gag tasting like salty leather and damp earth, the skin around her lips rubbed raw. She had nearly thrown up several times, but luckily was able to hold it back. Her back and neck ached from being chained in her present sitting position, her wrists fastened to the bench, allowing for little movement, her legs similarly manacled and pinioned to the floor.

She blinked, exhaustion nearly overwhelming her as she looked at Jana and Emy. They were chained just as she on the opposite bench, and looked even worse. Emy's eyes were closed and she swayed back and forth, until the chain was pulled tight on her wrists, startling her awake. Jana was awake, barely, her eyes drooping with exhaustion. Dried blood covered the side of her head forming a layer of dark crimson throughout her disheveled hair. The wagon was empty and smelled of sweat.

Thea could barely think, lack of water and food finally taking their toll. But she had done nothing but think for the last two days. Who had taken them and why? What had happened to Brant? Was Tobias dead? Fresh tears streaked the side of her head when she thought of Tobias. She didn't think she had any tears left. He had been so brave. Was it possible he had survived? She didn't think so. What was going to happen to them? Surely they would at least be given food and water soon. If not, they would all three collapse, whether chained or not.

As if her thoughts had been heard, the wagon suddenly came to a halt. They had been traveling hard since her capture, stopping only a few times to water the horses and allow them to relieve themselves. Thea had counted ten men and one woman. At least she thought it was a woman, her tall and massive shoulders masking any feminine attributes she might have had. The flap flipped open and two men entered, one dangling a key chain. They stank of sweat and tobacco smoke. Quickly, they released the locks and pulled them all out, none of them able to offer any resistance, which they had originally. Thea had kicked one man in the groin, earning her a smack across the face that nearly landed her unconscious a second time. They were dropped unceremoniously on the ground while they went about their business setting up camp. It was nearly dark and they had pulled the wagons and horses into a clearing off the side of the road. Tall trees surrounded them, their leafy branches looming above them. Normally the setting would feel comfortable, the drooping branches providing a sense of peace and tranquility. But not now. Thea looked up, feeling trapped as the dangling branches danced in the evening breeze. They looked foreboding, like undulating arms of skeletons eerily scratching at the coming night.

Fires were lit and the horses were fed. It wasn't long before the group was eating and laughing. By this time Emy had lay on her side and fallen asleep, exhaustion finally victorious. Thea looked at Jana, her eyes rimmed in tears. Jana looked scared, and Thea could do nothing to help her. It irked her that they thought so little of them that they left them sitting in the grass unguarded. Thea was sure they were keeping an eye on them, but the reality was that they didn't have the strength to do anything. And they knew it. Their legs were still chained together. Even if they had the strength to run, they would not get very far.

Eventually two bodies rose from the fire, one grabbing a lantern, both heading towards them. They loomed over them and held the lantern high. Thea could barely make out their features. One man was tall and thickly muscled, with an angled jaw and feral eyes. His skin was fair and his wavy shoulder length hair a light shade of brown, like the hide of a tulkick. He was clearly not Dy'ainian, or even Kaelian, perhaps coming from the south, maybe even Belorth. It was the same man who had knocked her unconscious at the cabin. The one holding the lantern was the woman, her dark brown hair cut short down the center of her head, the shaved sides accentuating the stripe. Several scars marked her face and her eyes were black and deep, void of emotion.

It was her that spoke. "We will feed and water you, like our horses. Bronas, remove their gags and wake up the bitch on the ground."

The muscle-bound man moved with a grace that belied his bulk. Smiling, he stepped forward and kicked Emy in the side. She grunted and flipped on her side like a beached fish, crying through the gag as she pulled her body into a fetal position, trying futilely to protect her body. But no other kicks came. Bronas roughly undid her gag and immediately she vomited on the ground. The big man laughed as he removed the gags from Jana and Thea. They both dry heaved and sucked in air, trying to relieve their sore and dry mouths. But nothing they did would help. They needed water.

Thea licked her lips, hoping to wet them. But there was no moisture left. She sat straight and looked up at the woman. "Who...are...you?" She stammered, barely able to get out the words.

The woman squatted down next to her, placing her huge meaty hand on her cheek. She was eerily gentle. "Me names Orna, my pretty one. I were told you were quite a looker, and even covered in sweat and blood, half dead, I'd welcome uze in me bed."

Thea wanted to spit on her, to yell at her, to pull away from her, but she had no spit, and no strength. But she could manage a few words, and uttering them gave her some satisfaction. "Brant's...going...to kill you."

Bronas laughed. "That's funny," he said, "that little shit eater said da same thing. But heez dead now, I killed him myself."

Thea closed her eyes, her nightmare coming true. She had a feeling Tobias had been killed, but the man vocalizing it brought fresh pain to the surface.

Orna's thick fingers wrapped around her neck under her chin and squeezed, causing her to open her eyes. "Don't ya worry my lovely ting. Dying aint in ur cards. We'ze to take you away, never to be back here again." She gave the lantern to Bronas and lifted her by the shoulders. She was so strong that Thea felt like a sleeping child in her father's arms. Oran looked at Bronas. "Get a few others over here and get em food and water. Once fed, chain em to the wagon wheel and give em a blanket.

Bronas nodded and together they walked to the fire, Orna more carrying Thea than guiding her.

***

Five days later...

"There, lift the rod!" Serix yelled, nudging his nephew who was preoccupied with a sliver in his hand. They had been sitting on the dock for quite some time now, with no bite to show for it. But the little wooden ball at the end of his line was being pulled under. Finally a fish had taken his bait.

Tallin bolted upright, jumping to his feet and raising the rod at the same time. The fish was still on and Tallin was giggling with excitement. "Look, Serix, I caught one!"

Serix was smiling and urging his nephew on. "Keep the rod high and the line tight. Now slowly back up and I will get the fish."

They were at his country estate, a half days ride from Cythera. Every year, during the King's Games, his family visited from Kreb. He looked forward to it immensely and it was typically the only time he could see his younger brother and his family. His father had died six years back, and his mother had been making the journey ever since. This was the first year, however, that she had stayed at home. She was getting older, and the long trip across Dy'ain was much more difficult now.

Tallin was his brother's only boy, and Serix loved him immensely. He was nine years old, but seemed much older, taking on his brother's bulk early rather than Serix's sinewy frame. "How big is it?" Tallin yelled excitedly as he moved further from the edge of the dock.

Serix was leaning over the dock with a net made of fibers from the baylin plant, a fibrous stock that grew in swampy areas. The thin fibers were used to make the strongest cord, their diminutive size ideal for small rope that didn't sacrifice strength. "It's a fat one!" Serix yelled as the fish flopped and splashed across the surface of the water. Serix quickly shot the net down and scooped up the fish, standing tall so Tallin could see his prize.

Tallin dropped the rod and ran to take a closer look. It was a nice fish, nearly as big as Tallin's forearm. "Wow, that's the biggest one yet!"

Serix was smiling from ear to ear. It was indeed a great catch, one of the biggest he had seen in this lake. And he told Tallin just that. "It's one of the biggest fish I've seen in this lake. Well done. I told you, good things come to the patient, especially when fishing."

"Can we eat it tonight?"

"Of course. I will have Loreasa prepare it just for you."

"What is all this commotion about?"

Serix looked up and saw his brother, Lanwin Rilonen, step onto the dock. The grounds behind him were stunning, with green grass and lavish gardens decorating the back of the estate, all splendidly sprawled around his small lake. The ten room, two story home built of gray stone rose up behind him.

"Look what I caught, father!" Tallin said as he took the net from Serix to show his father.

Lanwin, unlike Serix, was a Merger, and one of the better swordsmen that Serix had ever seen. He had joined the king's army when he was eighteen, as most young nobles did, but never pursued a career as a warden or even a Dygon Guard, which was an option for him considering his skill with a blade. Instead, he chose to take over their father's business, running plantations and cattle herds all across Dy'ain. It had made him rich, but whenever he had the time he sought out the weight of a blade in his hand, eager to keep his skills sharp. The King's Games happened every year to mark the winter solstice, and Lanwin used it not only as an excuse to visit his brother, but to test his skills against the old and new swordsmen from all around the lands. He had won the swordsmanship event the last two years, and was hoping to claim the title once again in two days' time. He had just finished his evening training and his long dirty blonde hair was soaked with sweat, wisps sticking to his forehead. As it always did, his Kul-brite blade, given to him by his father when he turned twenty-one, dangled from his hip. "That's quite a fish, son. Well done."

"Uncle said we can cook it tonight!"

"Well, it's getting close to dinner and it will be dark soon," Lanwin said, looking up at the disappearing sun. The estate was surrounded by tall trees, but even so you could still make out the sharp peaks of the Devlin Range. It was a beautiful view from the many terraces of the home, the snowcapped mountains peaking behind the tall swaying trees, the calm lake and stunning gardens in the foreground. Lanwin had several incredible estates all around Dy'ain, but even he was jealous of his brother's home. "Shall we get it up to Loreasa so she can prepare it?"

"Take the fish," Serix said. "I'll get the rods and our gear."

Lanwin put his hand on his son's head and ruffled his wavy hair, wrapping his arm protectively around his shoulder's as they walked together off the dock, the net, and the fish, cradled against his chest like his most prized possession.

Suddenly there was a man there, stepping around a thick trunked apple tree, standing in the shadows of its bulk. He wore a black hooded cape and his face was covered with a strange mask. It was TorGynin, his thin silver Kul-brite blade held in his right hand.

Lanwin saw the blade first and reacted by pushing Tallin behind him and drawing his own blade, his movements a blur as aura energy rushed through his limbs. "Who are you!"

Serix had dropped the rods and ran to his brother's side, drawing power from his mage stone at his belt, his hands flaring blue with crackling energy. Serix Rilonan was an Aura Mage, one of the most powerful mages in all of Dy'ain, next to King Jarak Dormath of course. Serix had trained Jarak for many years, but as the young king aged, his power grew, and now it even surpassed his master. But that was bound to happen, as the Way grew strong in the King's bloodline. Serix didn't dare draw any power from the auras around him, as the energy, tainted now by fear, could harm him more than help him. There was no Channeler about to filter the tainted energy for him, so he was going to have to rely on the power in his mage stone. He wished he had his sword.

"I am not here for you, Lanwin Rilonan." TorGynin's voice was unassuming, and lacking emotion. "It is your brother that I want."

"You did not answer his question," Serix said. "Who are you? Why are you at my estate uninvited?"

TorGynin tilted his head slightly at Serix. "I would have thought my purpose is obvious. I am here to kill you." Then he slowly looked at Lanwin. "I am sorry that your son will have to watch you die, as I know you will not step aside."

Lanwin was already readying his body to attack. "Tallin, run!" Then he shot forward as fast as a horse's kick.

Serix had all the confidence in his brother, and when he attacked he moved to the side quickly, turning on his towd at the same time and readying his spell. His confidence faltered quickly when he saw the speed in which the newcomer deflected his brother's attacks. They were both a blur, their aura energy flashing through them. He did not know the man was a Merger, like his brother, and now he felt a stabbing pang of worry. His brother's aura was bright and edged in blue, as it always was, but the newcomers was unlike any aura he had ever seen. It flashed in bright hues of white, blue, and purple, the power undulating with him as he fought. The ringing of Kul-brite steel echoed in the evening air, and after a few heartbeats stopped as Lanwin stumbled backwards with a grunt. His eyes were wide as one hand went to his thigh, dark blood pouring between his fingers.

Serix's eyes widened in fear and immediately he pushed his hand's forward, blue crackling energy shooting from them like lightning on a stormy day. The assassin didn't move. He simply raised his hand and the blue killing energy stuck it, sucking into him like water in a drain. In a blink the power of Serix's spell was gone, and the assassin stood before him unharmed.

"That cannot be," Serix whispered, clearly in shock. "You cannot be a Merger and a Sapper both."

"Oh, but I am. I am something new."

Lanwin growled and came at the assassin again, their blades sparking as they fought. But Serix could see his brother slowing, and knew that soon it would be over. He didn't know what to do. He didn't have his sword, and even if he did he would be greatly outmatched. The mage stone he wore still had enough power for another spell. Maybe the assassin could only sap so much power. There was a chance he could overwhelm him. He had to try. It was the only thing he could do. Thinking quickly, he drew the last of the power from the stone.

Just as he did so, his brother stumbled backwards, his sword falling to the ground as his hands went to his throat. Dropping to his knees, Lanwin's wide eyes shifted to his brother's, his life blood gushing from his throat, pouring between his fingers in pulsing waves. He blinked once, then fell over.

"No!" Serix screamed, launching into his spell. Great ropes of fire shot from his hands, and expertly Serix whipped them around his body and shot them at the assassin. One struck TorGynin's sword arm, the red fire rope wrapping around his wrist. The other whip wrapped around his neck, and still screaming, Serix pushed all the fiery energy through the whips into the assassin's body.

Smoke sizzled from TorGynin's wrist and neck and he dropped to his knees, fighting against the whips and their power. Fiery hot energy shot through the whips and into him, burning his skin, the smoke from his sizzling clothes and flesh rising into the air. TorGynin screamed as the energy was pulled into him. The pain was immense, but he had suffered worse, far worse actually. Growling it away, he pulled the energy into him and guided it into the ground beneath him.

Serix was still screaming when the energy from the mage stone had depleted itself, the sizzling ropes disappearing in a flash. The assassin stood slowly, his sword still held in his burning hand. Serix stopped screaming and stepped further from the man, looking around hopelessly for a way out. Thankfully Tallin was gone. But what of his brother's wife, and his servants, surely they would come running with all the commotion.

The assassin's voice pulled Serix's focus back to him. "That was well done," he said. "Your power nearly consumed me." Then he glanced at the estate, as if he was reading Serix's thoughts. "I'm sorry, but I had to kill one servant. The others I put to sleep, including the boy's mother. You see, I am a killer, but I do not act indiscriminately. It is tragic they will wake to your bodies."

"Who are you?' Serix asked pleadingly. "Why are you doing this to me?"

TorGynin tilted his head again, as if thinking. Then he reached up and pulled his hood off, removing the strange mask from his face. "Someone from your past. Do you recognize me?"

Serix narrowed his eyes, the evening shadows hazing the assassin's features. But there was something familiar there, although he could not place it. "I don't know...what did I do to warrant this?" Serix asked, his voice frantic, gesturing around him.

"You made a choice, and now that choice is coming back to haunt you. Are you ready to share Endler Ral's fate?"

"Endler? Did you kill him?"

The assassin's face was scarred, but strangely devoid of emotion. He was young, perhaps in his mid-twenties, his features becoming clearer as he stepped closer to Serix. "I did."

"Please...I can give you anything," Serix stammered as he stepped onto the dock.

"You cannot," the assassin said, his voice harder than it was previously. "There are things that you cannot give back to me." Then he launched forward, his Kul-brite blade leading the way. He attacked so fast that Serix didn't even move before the tip of the assassin's blade pushed through his stomach, and shot upwards, punching a hole through is upper back.

Blood gushed from Serix's mouth as the assassin held up his body with his blade. He was closer now, and Serix's eyes widened as he finally recognized him. "You...I...", but he could say no more. Blood gushed from his mouth, splattering across TorGynin's face. He convulsed once, then he was dead.

TorGynin shoved the body off his blade and pushed it from the dock where it splashed into the shallow water. He walked to the edge and looked down at Serix's corpse, his blood turning the water red. "One more to go," he whispered.

Chapter Four

Jarak Dormath, King of Dy'ain, stood on the parapet looking down into the training yard below. Next to him was a giant of man named Baccus. Standing guard behind them both were four sentinels, the private guard of the king, and the finest warriors in Dy'ain next to wardens and Dygon Guards. Below were ten men and two instructors, one of the instructors aged, his gray shoulder length hair blending in nicely to his immaculately trimmed beard. He was slowly directing the men through several sword forms.

Jarak looked at Baccus, his large hazel eyes inquiring. "How goes the training?"

Baccus looked like a dwarf had carved him from stone. He was nearly as big as a Saricon, his muscle-bound body cut and full of edges. It took him a moment to answer, thinking of his words carefully, his steel gray eyes looking at Jarak when he was ready. "Considering..." he shrugged his huge shoulders, "not bad." The large warrior paused again before continuing. "The men are skilled, there is no doubt, but the morale, well, it's not a unit yet."

"Spit it out, Baccus. I have no time to mince words. What is the problem?"

Baccus sighed. "Sir, the nobles are not taking well to the commoners."

After most of the Dygon Guard had been killed during the Saricon invasion, including Kulvar Rand, the most dangerous swordsman in all of Corvell, and perhaps Belorth, they had to work hard at restoring their numbers. But it was no easy feat to train the elite swordsman, let alone find enough that were Mergers with the aptitude and skill to become a member of the most dangerous fighting force in all of Corvell. After Brant had killed the Saricon war leader, Jarak made a commitment to change the kingdom's policies regarding commoners born with the Way. He passed new laws, forbidding any persecution of commoners skilled in the Way, taking it further by sending word out that they were recruiting commoners to be Wardens and members of the elite Dygon Guard. Before the Saricon Wars, these positions were filled from within the noble families. Few commoners signed up, and even fewer had the foundation allowing them to be elite swordsman. In fact, in ten years, only four had passed the training, Baccus being one of them. Baccus was a rarity, winning over the commoners and nobles alike. He was the best of them, and Jarak had surprised the noble families by promoting him to commander of the Dygon Guard, Kulvar Rand's old title. It was unprecedented, and several powerful noble families were very outspoken in their anger that their sons were overlooked for the honor. Of the ten new recruits before them, two were commoners.

"That is expected. It is nothing we have not dealt with before. How are our warriors treating the commoners that have passed the tests?"

"They are treating them well," Baccus said quickly. "But they have a bond forged from blood and death. In my experience, that usually supersedes petty grievances of family lineage."

"So the same will occur with this group. They will fight together, and the bond will be forged." Jarak glanced at the men below. "Will the commoner's pass the final tests?"

Baccus pursed his lips in thought. "I believe so. They are more skilled than a few of the nobles, which is part of the problem."

"Of course it is," Jarak commented, looking back down at the training. "It shatters everything they have been taught, that somehow they are better, stronger, smarter, than those without noble blood." Jarak smiled as he watched one of the commoners execute a maneuver perfectly, gaining praise from the gray-haired instructor.

"What is it?" Baccus asked, seeing his smile.

"It was not so long ago that I had believed just that sentiment. Things have changed so much."

Baccus nodded. "I'm glad that you could finally see the truth of things."

Jarak stopped smiling and looked up at the big warrior. The edge of Baccus's lips slowly curved upwards into a tight smile. "Are you making a jest?" Jarak asked, smiling back. It was a rare thing to see Baccus smile, and even rarer for him to make a joke. "You do know I am your king."

"A good king knows humility," Baccus replied.

Jarak nodded. "I see you are reading that book I loaned you." Jarak had given Baccus a rather large book written by a famous scholar named Landorian. In it, the scholar and historian speaks of the role of government, analyzing the history of Belorth and Corvell through a political lens. He thought it a good idea to have his Dygon Guard commander be well read on the politics of their lands. It was heavy reading, and Baccus, prior to entering the Dygon Guard training, could not even read or write. Needless to say, the warrior and learned many things the last ten years. "Remember," Jarak continued. "Not everything you read is true." But he was smiling, and Baccus knew he was not serious.

"I will remember your sage advice."

"Sarcasm now? I've created a monster." Baccus chuckled in response; his deep voice sounding like someone was beating a drum. Jarak turned serious once again. "Keep working on them, Baccus. Help the commoners fit in. Your own background makes you perfect for the job. And talk with the nobles. They must see them as sword brothers, if not, then the Dygon Guard is not the place for them."

Baccus nodded. "It will be done."

Jarak paused a moment, looking out towards the mountains, seemingly in thought. Moments later he looked back at Baccus, his eyes forlorn. "Any news about Chamberlain Ral's death?"

Baccus frowned. "None sir. As you know I have sent four Dygon Guard there to look into it. They should have arrived three days ago. With any luck, we will hear back from them within a week.

Word had come four days ago about the death of Endler Ral, Jarak's friend and Chamberlain of Tanwen. He had been cut down on the city wall, nearly beheaded. The messenger had no other information. Jarak was angry and worried. Captain Ral, which was how Jarak still thought of him, had fought with Jarak many times. They had formed a deep friendship and his death had hit him very hard. Who would do such a thing, and for what purpose? An attack on his officials was a direct attack on him. Who was threatening him? He needed answers. He would find out who killed his friend, even if it meant he had to go to Tanwen himself. He voiced that sentiment to Baccus. "If they return with no information, I will be going there myself."

"I do not think that is a good idea, my King," Baccus warned. "Clearly, there is a real threat, and going to Tanwen could be just what the perpetrator wants."

Jarak ground his jaw, his eyes narrowing. "Good. I will draw the rat out."

"It is too risky. We will find another way."

"Then find out what happened to my friend." His tone was tense and Baccus felt it.

"It will be done."

Jarak nodded and looked back to the training, hoping it would take his mind off of Endler's death. He had been a good friend to Jarak, saving his life several times during the Saricon wars. Shaking the morose thoughts away, he drew his attention to the aging instructor. "How is old Vorn doing?"

"He is old and slow, but the men respect him."

"Is he able to train them...to show them the proper maneuvers?" There were very few men left who had ever been trained in the Kilting Way, the elite style of fighting taught only to the Dygon Guard. Of the few Dygon Guard that survived the Saricon Wars, most were needed to guard and transport the precious Kul-brite steel. They did not have enough men, as of yet, to train the new members. Jarak had long hoped that Brant would eventually come to him and ask to train the men, to perhaps lead them. But that never happened. Brant was content leading a quiet life with his family, and despite his selfish reasons, Jarak was happy for him. In the end, Jarak was forced to bring back a few of the aging veterans.

"He is, although he no longer as the stamina to pass the strength tests. But he knows the steps, and that is enough."

Jarak knew that before any warrior could be trained in the deadly style, that they first had to develop enough wrist and forearm strength to execute the maneuvers. Vorn was well past his prime, and despite the fact that he knew the maneuvers; he would not be strong enough to execute them in an actual fight. "We will need to bring in some Dygon Guard to work with the men once they find the necessary strength. How far off are they?"

"Six months."

Jarak nodded. "See to it." He looked up and gauged the sun's descent. It wouldn't be long before the sun dropped behind the Devlin Range and the chilly fingers of evening embraced them. "I don't want to be late for dinner. Good work, Baccus." Baccus nodded as Jarak turned and walked away, his sentinels following closely.

Jarak didn't have to walk far to get to his palace grounds. The palace was a majestic three story building located in the middle of the inner castle, their home protected by its own set of walls within the colossal capital city, Cythera. The

Dygon Guard training grounds were situated adjacent to the sentinel's barracks, housing the two hundred warriors whose only job was to protect the king and his family. The parapet wall from which he observed the training was the same wall that protected the inner castle. A simple walk through the palace gardens brought him to his home, and by this time it was dark, the evening shadows pushed back by the many flaming sconces expertly placed along the entire expanse of the palace walls.

Ten years ago the sentinels had been infiltrated, as well as some of the palace staff, ending in the death of Jarak's mother and father, paving the way for the Saricon surprise attack on the capital city. Since then, Jarak had taken extra precautions, better vetting the staff and warriors alike, as well as putting in place various steps to ensure that that type of subterfuge would not happen again. No system was perfect, and in reality, Jarak knew that if one was skilled enough, and possessed the proper resources, that there was no castle security that they could not breach. But he certainly didn't want to make it easier for an enemy.

Jarak had married Cat five years ago and they had a little boy named, Hagen, after her father, who had died valiantly defending the city ten years ago. He was one year of age and no matter how long Jarak was away from him, he longed to hear his voice and to see the innocence in his eyes. He had no illusions that that innocence wouldn't last long, crushed slowly by age and experience in a world filled with war and conflict. But Jarak hoped that he would hold onto it for as long as he could, pressing it dearly to his chest as his most prized possession. Little did the young man know that it *was* the dearest thing in the world. So many things were wasted on the youth. To see the world through the eyes of a child was such a gift, and if somehow all the kings and conquerors of the world could just remember what that was like, then perhaps they could live in a world without violence.

Entering the palace doors he was immediately met by Torleen, the palace manager. She was nearly in her sixties but her hair was still dark and lustrous, shining like glistening oil. Jarak was never able to figure out how, but no matter when he arrived, she was always there to meet him, to serve his every need.

"My king, good evening," she said with a deep bow.

"And to you, Torleen. Is the queen in our chambers?"

"She is, along with the young prince. Would you like dinner brought to your chambers?"

"That would be wonderful. Thank you," Jarak said as he stepped by her, eager to see his wife and child.

"A bath is drawn for you in your chambers if you should desire it."

Jarak turned as he walked away, smiling towards her. "I don't know what I'd do without you." Then he spun back around and walked through the massive antechamber, heading to the grand hall and the stairs that led to the third floor and his chambers. Two of the sentinels stayed behind to join the two guards at the entrance. The other two followed Jarak. They would join with other sentinels who were positioned at various locations throughout the castle.

He moved quickly through the halls, talking briefly with various guards as he passed. There was an antechamber before the hall of the palace that acted as his personal chambers. Six guards were stationed here continuously, and each gave Jarak a subtle bow as he passed. He had casually scolded them on numerous times in regard to their pompous greeting every time they saw him, but it was to no avail. They had reduced their deep bow to a shallow breach of the back and dip of the head, but they would not remove it entirely, despite his pleading.

A wide but short hall led to double doors that marked the entry into their private suite. Two guards were there and they quickly opened the door as he neared, nodding as he flew past them, eager to see his family.

He found them both in their bathing chambers. Cat looked up when she saw him and smiled. Her dark hair was pulled back into a plait but wisps clung to her face, water dripping from her nose as Hagen played and splashed in the stone tub. The room smelt of lavender and roses, an aroma Jarak knew well as Cat's favorite soap. "There you are," she said. "We've been so excited to see you."

Jarak dropped to his knees and kissed her cheek, reaching in to tickle their boy. Hagen giggled and kicked his legs and arms, splashing them both in the process. Cat was holding him in the water and she lifted him out, laughing all along.

Picking up a towel from the corner of the stone tub, Jarak wrapped it around Hagen and held him close. "How has he been?" Jarak asked, drying him off.

"Rambunctious," Cat replied. "He continues to be reluctant to give his mother a break."

"Well I am here now," he said, dancing around and lifting his naked body in the air.

"How goes the training?" Cat was in simple leather leggings the color of coffee with cream, with a white cotton blouse draped below her hips tucked into a brown leather belt that was cinched tight to her narrow waist. A knife the length of her forearm was tucked comfortably at her hip. Cat was no simple queen. She was perhaps one of the finest swordsmen around, trained by her father. She had spent the last four years in the legion, and only ended her service due to her marriage with Jarak and the birth of their child. After all, the legion was no place for the queen of Dy'ain, or a mother for that matter. But Jarak knew she missed being a soldier.

"Seems to be going well," Jarak replied as he kissed and played with Hagen. "Baccus suggested that there were problems between the commoners and nobles, but that is nothing new."

Cat nodded, having had discussed the very thing with Jarak on many occasions. When Jarak had decided to formally welcome all Dy'ainians born with the Way, it had created lots of political and social upheaval. Since then they have worked through those issues over the last ten years, but still old ways and ridiculous biases resurfaced occasionally. "Any news on Endler? I still can't believe that someone killed him. It makes no sense."

Jarak frowned, his playful smile disappearing. "It's too early. We are expecting the Dygon Guard we sent to Tanwen to return soon. Hopefully they will have some answers."

"I hope so. I don't like unresolved threats. And clearly, someone has threatened us. But why attack Endler in Tanwen? Who has a grudge against him?"

Jarak shook his head. "More questions I cannot answer."

"I'm sorry," Cat said, jumping towards him and kissing him and Hagen both. "It's just I've been talking to a two-year-old all day. It's nice to speak with someone who can put a coherent sentence together."

"You do know that you are the queen, right? We have nurse maids and servants at our disposal. You can take a break. Sarellen would be happy to watch him more," Jarak added through a smile.

"And have a stranger raise our child? I will not permit it."

Jarak frowned playfully. "Sarellen has spent more time with Hagen than I have. She is no stranger and you know it."

"I have taken a few breaks here and there, and that is enough," Cat answered. She changed the subject quickly. "By the way, if you end up going to Tanwen yourself, we are going with you. I will stay trapped in this palace no longer." Without waiting for a rebuttal, Cat continued quickly. "What shall we do for dinner? We are famished," she added as she tickled Hagen's belly.

"Dinner will be brought to us soon. And don't change the subject," Jarak added. "I will not have my wife and son travel with me to Tanwen."

Cat expression turned serious, but a soft playfulness was still there, shimmering beneath the fake façade. "This wife of yours is a legionnaire, don't you forget that. And there is no safer place than with you and your Dygon Guards. We will travel with you. End of discussion."

Jarak was just about to respond when she leaned in close to steal a kiss, wrapping her arms around his waist. Slowly she nuzzled the side of his neck, softly brushing her lips around the apex of his jaw just under his ear. "Do we have time, for, well..."

"Yes!" Jarak blurted out, a mischievous twinkle in his eye.

"Good," Cat purred as she slowly pulled away from him, walking suggestively towards their sleeping chambers. Without looking back, she seductively said, "Put him in his bed and join me. We do not have much time."

"I do not think that will be an issue," Jarak said laughing as he followed Cat from the washroom, placing Hagen in the crib near their large bed.

Cat stopped and turned around, her eyes playful. "It is not you I'm worried about, my husband." She winked at him.

Jarak smiled and ran after her, lifting her up and nearly tossing her onto the bed. Hagen cried loudly, his displeasure evident. But neither of them noticed as they hurriedly removed the clothes from one another.

***

Three days later the two Dygon Guards returned from Tanwen. The news they brought was bleak, providing little evidence as to who the killer was, or why Endler had been killed. His body was found on the castle wall, his throat slashed so severely that his head was hanging on tenuously. There were signs of a fight, but little else. The bodies of two other guards had been found nearby. Clearly the assassin had dealt with them first before closing in on his real target. The killer must have been skilled, killing the two guards quietly without alerting Endler. That was speculation, but it seemed plausible.

Jarak had argued briefly with his councilors, their desire to keep him safe overriding any diplomatic reason to visit Tanwen. But Jarak had disregarded their council, pointing out that his presence would bring a sense of stability to a town that had just lost their regent in a heinous way. He wanted to be there, to show his strength, as well as to symbolize to his people that he was not afraid. Not to mention he wanted to personally look into his friend's death and be there for the funeral. If he was honest with himself, he was hoping to be a part of capturing the killer, and declaring and participating in the assassin's sentence. So despite his councilors' consternation, Jarak, Cat, Hagen, Baccus, two other Dygon Guards, a handful of servants, as well as twenty sentinels, rode out two days later for Tanwen.

***

It was the second day into the trip, well into the night, when Jarak awoke with a start, a stinging pain shooting up the side of his neck. His body went ridged under their sleeping furs and his eyes bolted open, wide with shock and pain. Ice cold agony shot up and down his neck, paralyzing his body. He could not move a muscle, but his eyes worked, pivoting around, adjusting to the darkness of the night. Their sleeping tent was large, in the center a soft mattress of feathers, heavy furs and cotton blankets covering them. Several small tables occupied the rest of the space, along with a few chairs, as well as several candles on the tables burning softly, their flickering orange flames casting little light throughout the travel tent.

There was a dark form standing above him, his features invisible in the shadows. "Good evening King Dormath," the form whispered. "It is nice to see you again."

Jarak couldn't move his body, but his eyes darted to Cat, who was lying still next to him. His mouth barely responded to his desires, his voice box nearly frozen. But he managed a few words. "Please...don't...hurt her." Jarak's heart was pounding and his paralyzed body was in such pain that he could not concentrate enough to even turn on his towd. He doubted he could draw any energy from the man, but he had to try. Closing his eyes, he tried to concentrate on the man's aura, or even Cat's, but nothing but racking pain came to him.

"I'm sorry, Jarak, but you will not be able to draw any energy. But do not worry, the poison will not kill you, or your wife. And no harm will befall your son. I am no monster." TorGynin paused, as if thinking about his words. Then he lowered himself to his knees at the edge of the bed, which was placed directly on the carpet covered ground. They had not brought a frame for the bed as it was too much to pack and carry on the trip. As it was, Jarak thought the extravagance too much for the journey, but his retainers insisted, especially since Cat and the young prince would be accompanying them. "I am the one who killed Endler Ral. And you are not yet privy to what I'm about to tell you, but Serix Rilonan, your friend, has also been slain."

Jarak was panting hard as he tried to battle the pain and the man's words. Still he could not move. But his wide eyes were a clear reflection of how he felt. "Why?" he managed to croak. By this time Jarak's eyes had adjusted to the darkness and he could further make out the assassin. The man wore a black hooded cloak, and some sort of dark mask that covered his face, all except his eyes.

TorGynin blinked before answering. "Revenge," he said simply, with little emotion. "They made a mistake long ago, and they have now paid for it. You are in a similar predicament, and your folly has now caught up to you. For your crimes, I will be taking your wife with me." Jarak's eyes widened in fright, but he could not move or speak. He could barely breathe. "I cannot kill you, as I did the other two, but you must pay. Your queen will be taken away, and you, and your people, will never see her again. Thank you for bringing her along by the way. You have made my task much less complicated." He reached out with a gloved hand and touched Jarak's arm. It was gentle, and almost loving, but his words eerily did not match the gesture. "The pain that you will feel every waking moment of your life is your sentence," TorGynin whispered softly. "Every time you look at your son, you will be reminded of her, and many years from now, when you are aged and bed ridden, you will wonder what has become of her. The aching loss you will feel is your punishment."

TorGynin blinked, and in that instantaneous moment he had stood and moved towards her, reaching down and flinging her body easily over his shoulder. Jarak's eyes followed him, a feeling of dread overwhelming him, causing his paralyzed body to shake. Cat was being carried off, and he could do nothing. His heart pounded and he managed to grunt unintelligently, unable to move or talk as the poison overran his body. The man paused, looked down at him, and then he was gone, disappearing in the shadows like a wolf in the night. Jarak screamed inside his mind, and luckily for him, the poison spread quickly, causing shadows and a hazy cloud to interrupt his vision. The painful thought of losing Cat to the assassin drifted from his grasp, darkness quickly overwhelming his consciousness.

***

Two days later Jarak lay still in his bed. Two bodies had been found that night. One was Gorvannin, one of the Dygon Guard, as well as one sentinel. There was a small cut in the back of the tent and it was there the sentinel body was found. Gorvannin's body was at the perimeter of the camp. It was hard to tell exactly what had happened, but by the looks of it, the man had killed the sentinel that was guarding the back of the tent, entered there, and perhaps during his escape had encountered Gorvannin. Both had been killed by a small dart in the neck, clearly laced with some poison, a different sort than what still afflicted Jarak.

Pain still racked Jarak's body, but he could now talk, his eyes frantic with worry. Baccus sat next to him in a chair. He was despondent, the loss of their queen falling heavily on his shoulders. Jarak clearly could not travel, so for now the camp was armed and had spent the morning preparing for staying another night, or leaving quickly, which ever came first.

They had been talking all morning, trying to figure out a plan. Do they send their scout and a small force away to go after Cat? Or do they wait until Jarak can travel himself? Jarak was adamant about sending soldiers after her now, but Baccus was not so sure. Whoever had done this was highly skilled, and he didn't think a small force would be able to find him. Not to mention if they sent a small force after the Queen, then it would leave the king much less protected. Who knows, that could be the intent of the assassin to begin with. But that seemed unlikely based on what Jarak had said about the assassin. After all, if Jarak's death was the goal, then the man could've easily accomplished that task two nights ago.

"Sir, perhaps we should send A'rakis after him to at least find his trail. We could then locate him when you are fit to travel," Baccus suggested.

Jarak's face was haggard and his eyes were rimmed red, moisture, like a veil of sadness, glistening from them. "It was my fault. I should have said no to her accompanying us."

Baccus shook his head. "No sir, the fault lies with me. And you know as well as I, that telling the Queen what to do is generally as successful as trying to swat a fly with a stick."

The flap opened and A'rakis, their scout, entered. The man was technically part of the legion, and he wore light leather armor over chainmail, a short sword dangled from his hip. His shoulder length dark brown hair was very curly. A red cotton head band was tied tight around his forehead to keep the hair from his eyes. He too looked haggard, his face reflecting his disappointment. "I'm sorry, Sir," he said to Baccus, before turning to Jarak, "and to you, my King. I apologize, but I've searched for miles around the camp and can locate no sign of his passing. Even the ground directly around the tent shows no trace of him. I cannot believe it as any man carrying a person would leave deep imprints. But there is nothing."

Jarak closed his eyes, the pain flooding his body was nothing compared to the pain leaching from his heart. Tears dripped down the side of his face. A'rakis shuffled on his feet uncomfortably, not sure what to say. He looked to Baccus, who nodded and indicated for him to leave.

A'rakis bowed and stepped away. "I am at your service, my King." Then he left quickly.

Jarak opened his eyes and shifted his gaze to Baccus. The sadness was still there, but something else stirred deep within their depths. It was tenacity, dripping with barely controlled anger. "Take fifteen sentinels and escort the prince back to Cythera. When I can stand, Cowin, A'rakis, and the four remaining sentinels will accompany me to the nearest town. I want the best warriors with me."

Baccus stood. "My King, you cannot send me away. My place is beside you. Let Cowin escort the prince back to Cythera."

Cowin was the other Dygon Guard, a veteran who was one of the few remaining from the Saricon Wars. He had just said he wanted the best warriors with him, and Baccus was the best of the Dygon Guard. "Very well, see to it."

***

Tongra Orgul turned to face ReeOnen as she entered the council room. There were two other Saricons present and they both sat at the table as the Tongra looked up at the black tapestry, a white depiction of Heln expertly stitched into the fabric. The heavy black cloth was massive, covering the entire wall behind the main conference table. Over ten years ago the room had been graced with ornaments displaying the grace and majesty of Argon and Felina, the dominant gods of both Kael and Dy'ain, and most of the southern coast of Corvell. But no more. Kael had been conquered, and Dy'ain nearly so, the invading Saricon armies wiping out any existence of the two gods. Now two statues of Heln flanked the tapestry, and the walls were covered with Saricon shields and weapons, the faces etched or painted with Heln's red symbol, the horned helm.

ReeOnen walked confidently past the two guards, moving quickly to her Tongra. Her poise faltered briefly as she saw the look in the Tongra's eyes. She glanced at the other two men, both

Talgrins, the Tongra's high councilors. She saw nothing in their stoic expressions.

"What news of the DarPool program?" he asked, his voice baritone. Saricons were typically large in comparison to the men and women of Corvell and Belorth. But Tongra Orgul, even compared to her father, was colossal, his strength and Fury legend among the Saricon. His head was shaved except for a length of hair starting from the top of his head and growing to mid-back, the tail wound in vertebrae taken from his victims, each one representing a people or land he had conquered. Winding scars graced his scalp and the side of his shaved head, the artist having expertly carved the symbols into his flesh.

"It goes well. We have two Ora'ky in play, and a third is progressing well." Ora'ky was the Saricon word for assassin.

Tongra Orgul stepped closer. "How long before the third is ready?"

"At least three years. His constitution seems strong enough to support the change. Next is his training."

Tongra Orgul nodded, his eyes narrowing as he looked down at ReeOnen. "Word has reached us that King Dormath's Queen has been kidnapped."

ReeOnen swallowed hard but kept her gaze on the Tongra. She could not show any weakness, or any doubt that she had had something to do with her disappearance, which of course she had. "King Dormath has many enemies."

"Including you," the Tongra hissed. Then his hand came up fast, the back of his mighty fist striking her across the face so hard that she was launched sideways, falling hard to the ground. He stepped towards her, anger rising in his eyes as lavender fire flashed across his irises. It was his Fury, and it wanted to be released.

She looked up at him with as much confidence as she could, as anything else could mean her death. "I had nothing to do with it."

He pointed his thick finger at her as the lavender flames flickered across his eyes once again. "You had better not!" he stormed. "The Gratatuit will be honored! You have nine more years before your revenge, our revenge, can be satiated! If I learn you have stepped on our honor, then I will kill you myself. Do you understand?"

She slowly stood and wiped the blood from the corner of her mouth. "I understand, my Tongra."

Chapter Five

The Gashwin alley was dark, pregnant gray clouds all but eclipsing the moon's glow. The wagons came to a halt next to a thick timbered warehouse built on stilts along the wharf, the water from Whistling Bay slowly lapping against the pilings below. The bay was aptly named, as on tumultuous and thunderous days the screaming wind blew through a rock formation jutting up from the southern side of the entrance into the harbor. The strange round opening created a whistling sound that could be heard all around the busy trading town. But it was a calm day on the ocean this night.

The slavers went about their jobs with practiced efficiency. Bronas and a few others lifted open the flaps and dragged Thea, Jana, and Emy from the wagon, guiding them towards a steel door hooded in shadow. The alley was narrow, the ground rough, the old worn pavers having been hammered by hoof and rain for many years. Tall stone buildings rose up around them, further casting the alley in darkness. It stank of the briny sea and refuse.

Orna banged twice on the door. Moments later a metal panel, about eye height, slid open. "It is I, Orna."

There was a shuffle behind the door and suddenly it opened, a fat, round bellied man with receding hair standing before them. His face glistened with sweat and he smelt like tobacco smoke and fish. He glanced behind the large women and nodded. "I see you have them."

"I do, now let me in little man."

The man stepped aside and Orna entered, followed by the three women, Bronas, and the rest of the slavers. The room was very large with ceilings at least fifteen paces high. It was a warehouse, with several large double doors that opened to the opposite side facing the docks. There were crates stacked up about three paces before the doors leading to the docks. There were an additional two doors on the right, and four on the left.

Thea, Emy, and Jana were still gagged, their hands chained together. They were dirty and exhausted, fed only once a day for the remainder of the trip. Their hair hung in greasy tangles matching their haggard appearance. But so far they had not been touched, minus a slap or two. Each one was worried that was about to change.

The fat man stepped before them. "I am Palin, and this here is my warehouse," he added with a flourish. "I have been paid handsomely to keep you here. But have no worry, you will be fed and bathed. I am no monster, and besides, I have a rather strong proclivity for the more masculine type," he added with a wink, glancing at Bronas.

"Is the ship on schedule?" Orna asked.

Palin frowned. "I'm afraid not. Brutal storms have hammered the coastline and our ship was forced to harbor. The last word I received was she was three days behind schedule."

Orna frowned. "You do know who these women are?"

"I do. But what can we do? There is no other ship heading that far north that is willing to take the cargo."

"He will come for them," Orna added.

"Let us hope that our benefactor was able to stall him. We should have the other package by the end of the day tomorrow."

"Which was when de ship was supposed to be here," Orna added, clearly frustrated. "When the other package arrives, idleness will get us killed. We need to be leav'in, and soon."

Palin put his hands out. "No sense worrying bout what we have no control over."

By this time the other men had departed through the two doors on the right, leaving Bronas alone with Orna and Palin. Those doors led to rooms that had been set up as temporary sleeping chambers for the slavers, as well as Palin's permanent offices. It was late, but the men would likely refresh themselves and head out to local drinking establishments located along the wharf. One in particular suited them nicely, an old watering hole for rats such as them. It was called the Swaying Pig, but many of its patrons referred to it lovingly as the Piss Hole.

"Let's get dem locked away, me mouth is parched and I need sum ale to ease me worries," Orna added.

Palin nodded and walked to the doors on the left. Each one had a sliding bolt, clearly designed to lock from the outside. It was obvious that the three were not his first human cargo. He slid one door open and Bronas pushed Jana inside. The room was small and square, with a dirty mattress and old blanket in the far corner. In the opposite corner was a small hole cut into the floorboards.

The big slaver guided her to the far wall by the mattress and locked her chain to a bolt on the wall. Then he removed her gag and she took in a deep breath. The air was dank and musty, but fairly clean from the salty ocean breeze drifting in from the hole in the floor. "Don't bother screaming," Bronas added. "No one will hear you." He stepped back to join the others at the door.

"Dear girl," Palin added. "The hole there is for your personal business. Once we get the others set up in their new accommodations, I will bring you some food. Tomorrow I shall bathe you. Now get some rest."

They left and put Emy in the room next to them, and Thea in the third, leaving the fourth for this package that was supposedly arriving tomorrow. Thea could only guess that the package would be another woman.

Bronas locked Thea to the bolt on the wall and took off her gag. Immediately she gathered what moisture she had left, and spit it in the slavers face. "You are going to die," she added vehemently. "Brant will carve you into little pieces...all of you."

Bronas smiled and took two of his fingers, slowly wiping the spit from his cheek, and licking it off them, savoring her spittle like it was honey. "We were told not to harm you, but remember you lovely piece of flesh, that I, unlike fat Palin here, crave that which only a woman can offer. I have ways in which I can quench my desires without damaging your flesh." Then he shrugged casually. "Well, perhaps there will be a little damage, but I can hide most of it." Bronas stood up from her. "Be ready, I will be coming for you." Then he shut the door behind him, leaving Thea to her dark thoughts.

To Thea's relief, Bronas did not come for her that night. But the thought of it alone nagged at her mind and she got very little sleep. The next day Palin was true to his word and offered each one of them a warm bath. They bathed individually, and not without two of the slavers watching over them, their lustful stares soaking up their bodies. But Thea cared little, her desire to be clean overriding any sense of unease. He dressed them in moderate but well-made dresses of soft spun cotton. That day they ate a simple breakfast of oats and water, followed later that evening with warm beans and bread. They were not treated well, but nor were they harmed. They were fed individually in their rooms and had not had the opportunity to talk with one another.

Thea's body hurt all over, but she was regaining her strength. It was late that night and she was lying on her simple bed, her eyes staring at the shadowed ceiling. Her mind drifted to Tobias and fresh tears streaked the side of her face. She wiped them away and told herself to stop crying. She had to be strong for both Jana and Emy. She thought of Brant. Where was he? Was he even still alive? What were they doing with them? She had asked Palin that very question when he had taken her upstairs to the drawn bath in his own private quarters. He was still donning his dirty clothes and smelt strongly of sweat, drawing forth the thought of whether he ever used the bath himself.

"I do not know, my dear. My part in this endeavor is to house you until the ship arrives. That is all I know."

She had proceeded to ask him about the ship, but he would say nothing more.

She was just getting sleepy, her drifting thoughts finally dragging her eye lids down, when there was a commotion in the empty room next to her. She heard some screaming and a loud thump as someone slammed into the wall separating them. Then she heard a door slam.

Earlier that day she had noticed a knot on one of the thick boards was loose. Working it slowly, she was able to remove the knot, exposing a small hole into the empty room next to her. But obviously it was empty no more and she got up from the bed, the chain embedded in the wall just long enough for her to reach the spot. She slipped the knot free and looked through the hole. It was dark and she could see nothing.

"Hello," she whispered. "Is anyone there?"

There was some commotion on the other side of the wall followed by a voice through the hole. "Yes, who are you? Where are we?" The voice seemed frayed and frantic, which was to be expected.

"I'm Thea. Who are you?"

"Ca'tel, Queen of Dy'ain, wife to Jarak Dormath."

Thea gasped. "Cat, its Thea, Brant's wife." They were not close friends, but because of Brant and Jarak's friendship, they had met many times over the last ten years. They didn't see each other more than a few times each year, but Thea considered her a friend nonetheless, looking up to the Queen immensely.

"Thea," Cat whispered, trying hard to speak low through her excitement. "Where are we?"

"I don't know. These men attacked me at our home while Brant was in town. They killed

Tobias," she added, her voice cracking as she voiced the horror.

"Oh Thea, I'm so sorry. Do you know who they are or where we are?"

"I do not. They took Jana from town and another girl. We've been on the road for five days and locked up here for two."

"We must be on the coast," Cat reasoned, smelling the salt air. "What of Brant?"

"I do not know what has become of him," Thea said, new tears streaking her face.

"We are going to get out of here," Cat said, trying to sound confident.

"How did you get taken?" Thea asked.

"Jarak and I were traveling to Tanwen to investigate the murder of Chamberlain Ral. We were both poisoned and I was taken from the tent on the second day of our trip."

"What! Jarak is dead?"

"No, the poison was some sort of paralytic. He was not killed. I have no idea why I was taken but the man had said something of revenge. I've been unconscious and in great pain for much of the trip here. I hurt now immensely and can barely move. The poison is still running through my blood."

Thea got a surge of hope. "If Jarak is alive, then they will be coming for us."

"Yes, if they can find us."

"And if Brant lives, I know he will find us."

"Do you know why we are here?" Cat asked.

Thea sighed. "All I know is a ship is coming to take us away. It's already late due to storms and its making the slavers nervous, which makes me think that Brant is still alive. They worry he is on their trail."

"I imagine so." Cat paused. "We cannot get on that boat," she warned. "If it takes us, then Jarak and Brant will have no way of finding us. It will be like looking for a rice grain on a white sandy beach."

"What are we going to do?" Thea whispered in despair. "The boat is to arrive tomorrow." Just then she heard a commotion outside her door. "Shhhhh, someone is coming."

She jumped back to the mattress as her door unlocked and swung open. Palin was there with a glass of water. "Here you go, my dear, one glass before bed." She took it and smiled, thankfully swallowing the cold liquid. It tasted different, slightly bitter. Then she saw his expression and her heart pounded with fear. "I'm sorry," he said, and stepped away, revealing Bronas as he stepped around the entry and sauntered into the room. Palin left without another word.

"I told you, bitch, that I would get to enjoy your flesh. Luckily for you, tonight is the night."

Just as he spoke her vision blurred and her head swam, feeling instantly like her mind was ready to shut down, to enter a deep sleep. "No...," she whispered, "please don't," she added, her words already slurring, her body feeling like it weighed a thousand pounds.

Bronas walked towards her and somewhere in her consciousness she saw him unbutton his pants, the nervous voice of Cat yelling through her consciousness. Her body slumped as she tried to fight the pull of the drug he had given her. He knelt on the mattress, the smell of stale sweat and ale overwhelming her. She screamed to move, to fight, to get up, but her body would not respond. She felt his great weight on her, his rough hands spreading her legs. She screamed in her head, and just before she lost consciousness, Bronas snickered, the heat from his breath, and the wet warmth of his tongue on her neck the last sensation she felt.

***

Brant and Gorrin pushed as hard as they could, but the poison was still pulsing in their veins, tiring them quickly and cramping their muscles. By the third day Brant was back to normal, but Gorrin was still dragging behind. Brant was frustrated by their pace, and Gorrin could tell.

"Go on without me," Gorrin said as he stopped to stretch his tired muscles. There was something in the poison that had leached into their muscles, sucking the energy from them. But Brant had an advantage over Gorrin, and despite his frustration, he wasn't going to hold their slow progress over his head. Even though Brant had not fought in many years, he still trained daily, keeping up his endurance as well as his strength. He was also a Merger, and Angon, a Kynan, old keepers of the earth magic, had taught him how to fully access this ability. Brant had continued to practice the skill every morning, allowing him to access more and more of the earth's energy. Angon had shown him that everyone's auras were always pulling energy from the earth, and when one gifted in the Way used their auras, or another's, they were simply pulling indirectly from the true source. Angon had cracked the door for Brant, and over the years he had greased the hinges, and pushed the door further open. Over the last two days, as he walked the path, he concentrated on slowly pulling energy from the earth, filling his body and pushing the poison out. Gorrin was not capable of this, and he was not about to leave him because of it.

Brant shook his head. "We will continue together," he said, handing Gorrin a leather of water.

Gorrin nodded and drank deeply. "At least their tracks are clear," he added, eying the deep wagon ruts. It had rained some, but not enough to wash away the deep ruts caused by the laden wagons.

"Let's just hope those are their tracks to begin with. I hope Caelin was right and they were heading to Gashwin." Brant looked up the road. He glanced back at Gorrin, his eyes hard. "Ready?"

Gorrin tossed the leather water container back to Brant. "Lead on."

By the fourth day Gorrin was nearly free from the poison's grasp. The first half of the day they walked through rolling hills of tall grass, the green blades undulating in the breeze like they were underwater. Around midday the grasslands had melted into pockets of trees, the tall trunks and swaying branches forming thick walls of foliage around them. Caelin had told them that once they hit the forest that they would be near the coastal town.

Brant was pushing hard, with Gorrin five paces behind him. They were not jogging, but moving at a brisk pace, Brant's mind occupied by visions of Jana and Thea, chained, scared, and hurting. He was so focused on what he would do to the slavers who took them, that he didn't even notice the men standing before him until he was ten paces from them.

"Whoa traveler, what's your hurry?" The man that spoke was tall and wearing a gray cloak over black leather breaches, a long sword at his hip and the glint of chainmail beneath a matching black tunic. Two other men flanked him, both holding crossbows.

Brant pulled up short as Gorrin moved beside him, his bow in hand, an arrow nocked but not drawn. There was a rustle behind him as three more men emerged from the brush, each brigand brandishing silver steel. It was a typical ambush by marauding thieves. But these men were well dressed and carrying decent steel. They were clearly good at what they did.

Brant glanced back slowly before returning his tense green eyes to the man that spoke. "You've picked the wrong men to rob." His voice was hard, dripping with confidence that he should not feel surrounded by six armed men.

The man felt his anger, and his confidence, and seemed to falter some. He glanced at the two men beside him but they just shrugged, showing little concern, clearly confident that they outnumbered the two trail burners. "Let's just make this simple and there will be no blood shed.

Hand us your weapons and anything you have of value and you may continue to Gashwin unmolested."

"I have another suggestion," Brant said as he pulled energy from the earth, filling his aura until he could hold no more. "You walk back into the forest and leave us be. That choice alone the only one that sees you walking away from this. You have ten heartbeats to decide," Brant growled.

The man was taken aback and did not know how to respond. Unfortunately for him, the man to his right decided his fate for him by raising his crossbow. "Let's just take him," he said.

"No!" the leader yelled. But it was too late.

Brant reached up, and in a blur had his blade free from the scabbard on his back, blue fire bursting from it as he shot forward with incredible speed. Both crossbows twanged, but Brant swatted both bolts away with his flaming blade, his enhanced state allowing him to see the bolts at a much slower rate. He was on them in a flash. Brant's sword cut down through the first man's crossbow as well as his torso, cutting him in half from shoulder to hip. Spinning by the gruesome spray of blood, his sword disemboweled the second crossbowman, continuing the blades momentum he spun it around incredibly fast, stopping it short of the leader's neck, who had stepped back from the initial attack. The blue flames were now dissipated, the cold Kul-brite steel barely touching the man's flesh. The leader had not drawn a weapon, as if that action alone would keep him alive. And perhaps it did, as that was why Brant had stayed his blade.

Gorrin had reacted when Brant had, although not as fast. Turning on his heel his bow came up, the first arrow striking one of the brigands in the chest, dropping him to the ground. The other two charged him, but luckily they were ten paces away, and Gorrin had time to draw a second arrow and fire it at point blank range, catapulting a second attacker to his back, a white feathered arrow quivering in his neck.

"Stop!" the leader yelled, Brant's blade held at his throat. The third attacker stopped in his tracks no more than four paces from Gorrin. The man's eyes were wild with fear as they took in the scene. Brant had killed two of his comrades within three heartbeats, and Gorrin the other two. Gorrin had dropped his bow and drew his long sword. They were both still, waiting for the other to attack.

Brant stepped in closer to the man, his green eyes burning with power. Aura energy still flooded through him, eager to be released. "You are alive now because you drew no steel."

"Who are you?" the man whispered, clearly frightened.

"It matters not," Brant growled. "Tell your man to stand down or you will both die."

"Stephus, stand down!" the man said forcefully.

The brigand facing Gorrin slowly backed away, lowering his sword. "What now?" the brigand asked.

"Well, boyo, that depends on you," Gorrin said. "What do you want to do?" he asked, looking back at Brant.

"If we kill them," Brant growled, "they will hurt travelers no more."

"True enough," Gorrin said as he walked back to stand closer to Brant, putting more distance between him and the sword wielding thief. He gently laid his hand on Brant's shoulder, causing the swordsman to look at him. "But my guess is they have connections in Gashwin...a place to hock their wares, a dark hole where his kind hang out. Perhaps they have some information for us, in exchange for their lives of course."

Brant looked back at man, leaning in closer. "What is your name?"

"Lorander," the brigand answered, his eyes pivoting towards Brant. "Please, sir, I can help, just as your friend suggests."

"Let us play a quick game," Brant said. "Your answers will determine whether you live or die. Yes?"

Lorander nodded his head. "I will answer truthfully, and help where I may. Please don't kill me."

"Let us say that a group of slavers passed through Gashwin a few days ago. If so, where would they go?"

Lorander looked excited for the first time. "Yes, yes, of course," he muttered. "There is a secret place. It's called the Swaying Pig, located along the wharf. It is a dangerous place, a drinkin' hole for pirates and other unsavory folk. A good place for slavers I think."

"Is there someone there I can speak with...someone who knows about the coming and going of these unsavory folk?"

Lorander nodded his head. "Yes. His name is Palin. He frequents the place often."

***

It was dark by the time Gorrin and Brant entered the streets of Gashwin. The town was small in comparison to Cythera, but for a coastal trading town it was one of the largest on the Dy'ainian coast. Grain and other foods were brought in by small and large farmers alike, sold to merchants who then shipped the products up and down the Bitlis and Dark Seas. Sometimes, on rare occasions, the Dygon Guard would bring shipments of Kul-brite from close by mines, transporting the precious metal by ship to Cythera and Tanwen, two cities that housed Scion Forgers, the only men skilled in the Way who could manipulate the precious steel into weapons.

The stone buildings were two to three stories high in most places and they flanked narrow roads and alley ways, creating a spider web of paths through the town. Each town in Dy'ain had a regent whose job was to rule the city in the king's name. Brant had no idea who the regent of Gashwin was, and he hoped he would not need to meet him, or the town's guard. If he needed to, he was confident he could use his reputation, and his position with King Dormath to enlist their aid. But right now he wanted to work outside the law. He wanted to find Thea and the others, and kill every last one of the slavers, and he didn't want the town's guard to get in the way of that. The law had a way of slowing down retribution.

It was well into the night and most of the streets were empty, with a few flickering lanterns and candles seen inside various windows. A few people were about, their cloaks pulled tightly about them as they walked to the various nightly establishments throughout the town. After all, those were the only places open this late at night. Brant and Gorrin were looking for one in particular.

Gorrin nodded down the main road. "The wharf should be that way."

They walked briskly, hoods pulled low, hands on the pommels of their blades. Gorrin looked over at Brant. "Brant, what's the plan when we get into this place?"

"We find this Palin, and we see what he knows."

"And if he knows nothing?"

"We find someone else who does."

They found the wharf easy enough, the tall masts of the ships gently swaying above the many buildings that flanked it. The wharf was more or less a very long dock, built on stilts that ran the entire expanse of the city along the harbor's west coast. Many long docks were connected to it, stretching out into the harbor where they housed hundreds of boats, some small, two-man fishing boats, and others wide hulled merchant vessels with tall masts rising into the dark night. The water side of the buildings along the wharf was juxtaposed by a narrow alley, the old worn cobble stones just wide enough for a single wagon. Branching off it were many other narrow paths. It would be easy to get lost in the vast network of alleys and narrow roads.

There were less people about, this side of town being the not so welcoming section. You had to be of a certain sort to be walking the narrow alleys along the wharf late at night.

Two men were walking towards them, their hoods masking their faces, their cloaks pulled tightly around their bodies to ward off the cool breeze from the harbor. Brant stepped before them. "Was wondering if you could point out the Swaying Pig for us? We be lookin for a spot to wet the tongues."

The men looked up and one said, "Piss off," as they moved to walk around him. Brant was in no mood for subtleties. The man who spoke was shorter than Brant, but seemed stocky in his thick wool cloak. Brant shot his arm forward and gripped his thick neck in his iron grip, yanking him hard to the right and slamming his body against the side of a building. Pushing a little energy into his arm he lifted the man off the ground and leaned into him.

The man's partner was so shocked by the speed and power of the attack that he stood dumbfounded as Gorrin quickly drew his blade and placed it at his neck. "Don't move," my friend, "and you'll walk away."

Brant leaned in close as he held the man a foot off the ground with one arm. He was flailing and gasping for breath, but he could not free himself from Brant's vice-like grip. "I'll ask you again. Where is the Swaying Pig?"

The man tried muttering something, but he could not speak through Brant's powerful grip. Brant eased up some, allowing him to talk. "Third alley down, turn right," he gasped. "There be no sign...look for a black door with a lantern hanging next to it."

Brant dropped the man and he nearly fell over, gagging. "Thank you." And he turned and walked into the darkness, with Gorrin sheathing his blade and following.

It didn't take them long to find the place. True to the man's word, the establishment had no sign, just a sturdy black door and a lantern hanging above it. Brant looked back at Gorrin before he took hold of the handle. "Be ready for anything," he said, his eyes tense. "I will do anything to find my girls. You understand that, right?"

Gorrin nodded, his face equally stern. "I'm right behind you."

Brant opened the door and they stepped into a misleadingly large room. Immediately they were hit with the smell of sea salt, wood smoke, ale, and sweat. It was like someone had taken a sailor's coat that had never been washed, rubbed it in charcoal, and shoved it in their noses. The room was spacious but dark, with soft glowing lanterns along the edges of the room and candles flickering on the table tops. There was a huge stone fireplace on one wall, one of the biggest Brant had seen. The giant round stones covered the entire wall, rising all the way to the high shadowed ceiling. Thick logs burned brightly, the stones around the fireplace aged with black soot. The far wall was occupied by alcoves, each one a cozy booth adorned with soft red cushions. But by no means was it opulent. The cushions were worn and frayed, and the wood tables were scarred and chipped from use. Black soot stained the walls above the lanterns and the floor was dirty and worn from the tread and scrape of filthy sailors' boots.

There were over twenty men spread about the room in pockets of two and three, with a few groups of five. The occupied tables were boisterous and loud while the few groups in booths talked quietly over spirits and food. The noise quieted for a moment when they entered as eyes turned on them. They were appraised quickly, the cacophony returning as Brant strode to the bar as if he were a regular.

A large man at the bar turned from a wooden keg when they approached. His body was colossal, and at one time it may have even been muscle. But his fat did little to take away from his austerity. Black sigils wound around his right arm ending in a demon's face expertly depicted on his huge bare shoulder. He wore a black sleeveless shirt stained with a mixture of grime and what looked to be flour. Silver rings dangled from his ears and his round face was dominated by a black goatee, two strands on either side woven into twin tails.

He placed two full mugs on a tray while a small dark-haired serving girl snatched it away without a glance at them. "Don't recognize ya...you in the right place?" he said gruffly, his voice deep and full of contempt.

"Two ales," Brant said, ignoring him.

The man narrowed his eyes, looking at them both. He quickly decided that they fit the part and grabbed two new mugs, filling them from one of the three kegs on the far wall. He set them down roughly and ale sloshed on the counter. "Four tiggs."

Brant reached into his belt and produced his coin purse. Reaching inside he set five tiggs on the counter, grabbed the mugs, and turned away without a second look. He handed one to Gorrin and they moved to an empty table on the far wall. Sitting down, they drank their ale slowly and looked about the room more closely.

A few moments had passed when Gorrin broke their silence. "The group in the second booth looks questionable. And the man sitting alone at the table by the fire has looked at us several times."

Brant had purposefully sheathed his blade at his hip, hiding the pommel with the edge of his cloak. He doubted he would be recognized, but his sword was unique and quite famous. He had already noticed the group in the booth. There were six of them, each one with the look of a predator. Various weapons and pieces of armor could be seen even in the dim light. They were definitely not sailors. The man at the table however looked very different. He was short and lithe in statue, with glossy straight black hair and a swarthy complexion. He looked as if he had some Schulg in him, but in the shadowy room it was hard to tell. It looked as if the man was wearing hardened leather armor with a short sword leaning against the stone fireplace nearby.

"Look at the bottle he is drinking," Gorrin said, indicating the man by the fire.

Brant did, not recognizing the label, which was a swirling pattern of black and white against a black bottle. "I'm not familiar with it," Brant said.

"It's an expensive liquor called Tan'wa'kee," Gorrin said. "It's distilled from a unique fruit found only in Enoreth far to the south. The man must either be wealthy, or important."

"Which means he might know something," Brant said.

"That's what I was thinking."

Brant looked at Gorrin. "When we approach him, I want you to do the talking. You are more versed in this type of dialog. Sit close to him."

"What will you do?"

"I will sit opposite him, further away."

"You want to be ready in case things turn violent?"

Brant nodded. "Ready?"

Gorrin stood. "Let's find out what he knows."

They both walked towards the table and when they neared the man looked up from his drink. Just as he did so the three men sitting at the table to his right stopped talking and stood, eyeing Gorrin and Brant, their hands on the pommels of their blades.

He casually raised one hand and motioned for them to sit, which they did. The man looked bored, his eyes tired and seemingly in some far-off place. He didn't say anything, but simply raised his eyebrows as if to suggest, *what do you want?*

Gorrin stepped to the side of the man's table. "Sorry to interrupt ya, but was wondering if we might have a few words."

"Everyone has a few words," the man said, his speech succinct and clear. "But most have no words worth hearing."

"That may be true," Gorrin said without skipping a beat. "But how do you know the value of a man's words unless you've heard them?"

A gradual smile graced the man's face. "True enough. Please," he said, "have a seat." He looked at Gorrin and Brant, his eyes appraising them equally. As Brant suggested, Gorrin sat close to the man, while Brant sat in the chair across the table from him.

"My companion and I have just come into town. We are lookin for a group of men and wondering if you have the eyes and ears of this town?"

The man's dark eyes flitted back and forth, continuing their appraisal. "And what makes you think, amongst all the others in this fine here establishment, that I would have the eyes and ears of the town?"

Gorrin eyed the bottle. "Not many can afford a drink such as that. Safe to say you are someone worth speakin to."

The man smiled and looked at Brant. "Do you speak?"

"I do," Brant said quietly. "But I find we all have our skills."

"And if I may be so bold, yours is more attuned to steel." Brant tilted his head in acknowledgment but said nothing. "You see," the man continued, "when one is continuously surrounded by cutthroats who would sell their own sisters to a whore house, he develops a certain proclivity in recognizing those who have seen violence. And you, well, it drips from you like freshly melted wax."

Brant leaned forward and placed his scarred and muscled forearms on the table, his intense green eyes aimed at the man like an archer's arrow. "Let me cut to it," he said slowly. "We are looking for a man named Palin. We have word that he may know something about a group of slavers traveling through town."

The man's expression turned to stone, his dark eyes narrowing. "Who are you?"

Brant flexed his hands, making it look as if he was barely keeping in check the violence that was pounding against his will power. And it fact he *was* barely controlling his frustration. He didn't want to play this verbal game. Every moment they wasted reduced the chance that they may find Thea and the others. He needed answers, and now he firmly believed the man before him had them.

The man noticed Brant's discomfort, and sat back from the table, his movement causing the men at the table nearby to stand again. This time the man didn't tell them to return to their seat.

"Who we are does not concern you," Brant said, glancing at the men next to him as if they mattered little. "What does concern you, is that we believe a group of slavers may have come into town. We want to find them, and now. We have coin. Can you help us?" Brant asked.

"And why does it concern me?" The man asked, nodding to the men at the booth that Gorrin had noticed earlier.

The room had suddenly quieted as the men at the table stood from the booth and walked towards the man's table. Brant didn't need to look to see that they were surrounded. He looked at Gorrin, whose face said, *what now?*"

"It concerns you," Brant said slowly, his tone cold, "because I believe that you know who this Palin is, and where I can find him. And since this is true, if you do not tell me, I will rip your throat

out with my bare hands after I kill every man here
that stands against us," Brant said confidently,
every word an unveiled threat. "You see, these
slavers took from us both," Brant added, glancing
at Gorrin. "I will find them, with or without your
help. The question is, will you still be alive when I
do?"

The man paused, looking at Brant, gauging
his every word. Finally he sighed and spoke. "I
would love to help you, as you seem genuinely
sincere. But you see, Palin is an associate of mine.
We occasionally work together. Now, how would it
look if I sold out my business partners?"

Brant opened the door to the earth's energy
around him. They were not on open ground, thus
the conduit was restricted. But still, he felt the
energy below the floor boards, and sucked it up
into his already throbbing aura. "It beats being
dead," Brant answered.

The man smiled. "Kill them!"

Brant reacted before the last syllable left the
man's lips. He flipped the table up with his left
hand to protect Gorrin, simultaneously his body
pulsed in blue fiery energy. He had never used his
aura energy in such a way, but ever since Angon
had awakened in him the connection to the true
source of power, his use of his Merger abilities had
broadened. He had not practiced the tactic, but
the idea came to him in a flash as the power
flooded through his body. It wanted to be
released...it seemed to beg for it. And he answered
its call, the bright fiery flash a devastating result.
The fire hit the table, which in turn struck Gorrin
and knocked him away from the fight. The man
before him moved with great speed, jumping back
from the flames, the power and intensity of the fire,

however, searing his clothes and flesh and catapulting him into the stone wall behind him. The men at his rear and flanking him shielded their eyes just before the power knocked them off their feet, the men in the front taking the full brunt of the fire. The distraction had worked.

Before the man even struck the wall, Brant's sword was out and he moved through the surprised men with a speed and intensity that they had not expected. He Fuzed as he cut into them, the blue fire erupting from his blade causing them more confusion. The three men in the front were down before the rear assailants could organize an attack, their blood splattered across the stone wall behind them. By this time, Gorrin had flung the table off of him, drew his blade, and entered the melee.

Brant spun like a dancer, his enhanced speed sending him across the floor where he met a man moving towards him with his sword drawn. Frantically, the man lifted his blade before him, but it did little to stop Brant's Kul-brite steel. Blue fire pulsed as it cut through the metal like butter, causing equal devastation to his face as it cut his astonished expression in two. Another man was on him, and attacking at a rate nearly as fast as Brant. He was a Merger, but not a very talented swordsman. Their blades met several times before Brant's powerful stroke cleaved his sword in half, his strong forearms snapping his blade quickly into his throat, withdrawing it just as fast. Never stopping, his anger fueling the power inside him, he cut down the others before him.

As he ripped his blade across the stomach of the last man, he spun to face the fireplace, his bright steel marred with dripping crimson. Gorrin pulled his blade from the body of the man he had killed and met Brant's gaze, both of their eyes scanning the room for more assailants.

Some of the patrons had left, and the others that had jumped out of harm's way were standing against the wall and the bar's edge. Several had hands on blades, but none attacked. They were obviously not with the mysterious man and his cronies, but they were hard men, and violence was no stranger to them, their eyes making that apparent.

The leader was no longer leaning against the stone wall and Brant spun his gaze towards a commotion by the door. The leader was nearly at the exit, patrons near him jumping aside eager to be nowhere close to the man. Reaching for the knife at his hip, Brant drew the blade and snapped his arm forward, the silver blade somersaulting across the room. The hunting knife was nearly as long as his forearm, with a weighted tip designed for throwing. He was no expert, but ever since Jarak had given him the Kul-brite knife as a gift for his birthday three years ago, he and Tobias had practiced many times, often turning the practice into contests. It was the one area where Tobias could beat Brant.

But Brant's aim was true and the heavy tip struck him in the shoulder, the Kul-brite biting deep, the power of the throw knocking him into a table where he stumbled to the ground. Brant was on him in flash, grabbing him hard by the back of his cloak and ripping the knife from his flesh, dropping it onto the ground. The man screamed as Brant hoisted him with one hand, slamming him hard against the near wall, his dripping sword still in his other hand.

The man screamed when he hit the wall, the wound in his shoulder causing him great pain. His clothes were charred in various places and some of the flesh around his neck and chin were red, several blisters already forming. "I'll tell you what you want!" he screamed. "Don't kill me."

"Where is this Palin?" Brant said again, his voice low and dripping with power.

"He has a warehouse...the southern end of the wharf! It's large and built of stout logs! A steel door marks its entrance!"

Brant let go of his tunic and placed his powerful hand around his throat. "Good," he said softly. "What's your name?"

"Sigorin," he stammered.

Brant leaned in closer. "I want you to know that I am a man of my word." Then he squeezed with all his might, aura energy firing through his forearm, his hand like an iron vice on his throat. Sigorin's eyes bulged and then Brant ripped his throat out, fresh blood spraying him in the face. The man gurgled something incoherent before he slumped down the wall, his lifeblood pooling on the floor boards.

Brant picked up his knife, sheathing it before turning to face Gorrin who was standing ready behind him, his eyes unreadable. The room was deathly silent as he walked past Gorrin to the barkeep standing behind the bar. Reaching into his money pouch, he set five gold dracks on the counter, using his sleeve to wipe the fresh blood from his face. "For your troubles," he said, turning around and heading for the entrance. Gorrin followed and they left quickly, hoping to melt into the shadows. He doubted the town guard would be called to a place such as the Swaying Pig, but the last thing they wanted was a confrontation with them. They needed to get away, and fast.

Chapter Six

Thea was shoved hard through the double doors at the rear of the warehouse. Her mind was reeling, a heavy weight of grief settling on her back, pushing down any sense that they might be rescued. Before last night there was a spark of hope within her. But now, snuffed out by Bronas, the light shone no more. Last night the slaver had raped her, and even though the drug he had given her had knocked her out, there was something deep in her conscious that she remembered. She wasn't sure if it was real, but she could still smell his stale breath, feel the weight of his muscular body and the scratch of his beard along her neck. Disgust dripped from her, but it was despair that gripped her heart. She was gagged and shackled at the wrists and ankles, nearly tripping as Bronas guided her along the wharf toward one of many docks that spanned out into the harbor.

Jana, Emy, and Cat were similarly bound, following just behind her, guided by Orna and the other slavers. Palin stayed behind; shutting the double doors of his warehouse once they were gone. It was late at night, the stars and moon veiled by plump dark clouds. A storm was coming, its ominous forthcoming matching Thea's troubled heart.

Looking up, Thea searched her surroundings, looking for any way to get away. The long wood dock before them was the home of many boats, but there was one that drew her attention. Docked at the very end was a huge black ship, its tall masts rising higher than any boat in the harbor. The sails were charcoal gray; a black symbol resembling a skull graced each massive stretch of cloth. Men in black and gray raced across the deck preparing to depart. A long wood bridge stretched from the ship's deck to the dock below, ten warriors in dark armor and small shields standing at the base. Who were these men?

A barrel-chested man in a long wool cloak stood before them. He nodded as Orna stepped past them, standing before the man.

"Got the coin?" the man said, looking about nervously. It was late at night, and dark, and they were the only ones around.

Orna said nothing, holding the small chest with one hand, she reached into her cloak and produced a bag of coins. She handed it to the man who smiled, stepping aside.

It was the dock manager Thea thought in disgust. Slavery was illegal in Dy'ain, but clearly it mattered little to him as long as he got paid. Orna continued walking down the long dock with Bronas, Thea, and the others following.

Thea stepped closer to the edge of the dock. Perhaps jumping in and drowning would be better than stepping aboard that ship and disappearing into the unknown. Bronas read her thoughts and grabbed her roughly, yanking her back to the center of the dock.

"You won't be getting off that easy, lassie," he laughed. "Your journey is not yet over. Do not fret, you and I will have much more time together." He laughed again, shoving her forward as Orna guided them closer to the dire looking ship.

A tall pale man in dark soft spun cotton and wool stepped from the small throng of warriors.

Contrastingly, this man wore no armor, a black cloak wrapped around his broad shoulders. Twin short swords were strapped to his back and a black leather wrapped knife was cinched tight at his waist. His hair was nearly white and cut short, accentuating a sharp white beard at his chin. A scar stood out along his right cheek just adding to the man's baneful appearance. His eyes were surrounded by shadow, the contrast with his pale skin making him look quite sinister.

Orna stopped before him. "You are late."

The man smiled and held his arms to the side in mock placation. "It could not be helped," he replied. His accent was similar to Oran's, but much stronger. "Annaset was angry and her wrath was awakened on the seas."

"Let us hope she was not angry with us," Orna said.

"Oh no, she is eager for her prizes," he said, looking at Thea and the others. Thea noticed that his accent was the same as the slavers, putting parts of the puzzle together. She had never heard it before, but clearly they were all from the same far off land. And who was this Annaset? Some unknown god? She had so many questions but the answers eluded her, and good thing, as she was afraid she would not like them. "Remove their gags," the man ordered.

Bronas unbuckled Thea's while several other men did the same to Jana, Emy, and Cat. Thea looked at the man. "Who are you?" she asked. "Why are you doing this to us?"

"Who I am matters little," the man said. "But I shall offer you my name, as it would be rude to do otherwise. You may call me Quill. As for the other question, well, you are being taken as an offering to Annaset. It is a great honor." He looked past her to the other three. "Which one is the Queen?"

One of the slavers pushed Cat forward to stand next to Thea. She looked defiantly at the man. "My husband will find you. You are as good as dead," she said vehemently.

The man smiled. "Your spirit is strong. Annaset will be pleased."

Cat glanced at the swords on his back. "Lend me a blade and I shall show you my spirit."

"I know of your reputation, thus we will keep steel far from you. Now," he continued, looking to Orna, "where is the gold?"

Orna handed Quill the chest. "Our benefactor has paid us well."

The man held the chest, as if testing its weight. Then he smiled, handing the chest to a warrior who brought it up the plank to the ship. "Let us go, I already tire of this heathen place," he said with a sneer.

Orna nodded and followed Quill up the plank, Bronas, Thea, and the others following. The soldiers had stepped out of the way and flanked them, looking about, ever vigilant for some unseen threat.

***

Brant and Gorrin had run hard up the alley adjacent the wharf. At the far end, just where the man had said, they found the heavy steel door marking the entrance to Palin's warehouse.

"What now?" Gorrin asked, looking around for another entrance. "We could just find the entrance to the docks and see if the warehouse has a rear door, which it must."

"I'm sure it will be locked as well," Brant reasoned, his tone tense as he realized how close he might be to finding Thea.

"True, but in my experience, the front door is always more fortified than the back."

Brant thought for a moment. "I have an idea," he said hastily, pulling forth his coin purse from the pocket on his tunic. "Let's just knock." Without waiting for a response, Brant pounded on the metal door.

They heard nothing in response. "You sure about this?" Gorrin asked, now holding his long sword, his bow strapped around his chest.

Brant shrugged and knocked again. This time there was some commotion beyond the door and the metal shutter in the center slid open, revealing dark and wary eyes. "What do you want at this time of the night?" It was Palin.

Brant lifted up the coin purse so Palin could see it. "Sigorin sent me over to give you the coin he owes you. And don't be cross with me, I was deep in a lasses love when he sent me on this little trip. So do you want the coin or not?"

Palin frowned through the door. "I don't recall him owing me anything."

"Fine!" Brant snapped in mock annoyance, lowering the coin. He glanced back at Gorrin who was standing behind him, barely visible. "Guess the whores and drink are on me tonight."

"Wait!" Palin yelled through the door. "Now that I recall, he does owe me some coin."

Brant stood firm before the door, drawing energy into him from the cobblestone ground. The lock mechanism disengaged and the heavy bar on the other end was removed, the steel door swinging open on squeaky hinges. Palin stepped forward into the shadows of the alley just as Brant snapped his right foot forward with tremendous power.

Palin's eyes widened in shock just as his foot struck him in the sternum. Bones broke as the fat man was lifted off his feet, catapulting him backwards into the room where he slid across the floorboards to crash against stacked crates. Brant and Gorrin stormed inside with blades drawn, Gorrin shutting the door behind them.

Looking around quickly, the room seemed empty. Brant ran to Palin who was sitting up against a crate, his face pale, his chest rising up and down erratically. He was breathing, but the wheezing told Brant that he had done some terrible damage, probably breaking ribs and shoving them through the man's lungs.

"Where are the girls?!" Brant growled as he kneeled next to him.

He was unmoving, his wide eyes filled with the fear of imminent death. "They... are gone," he wheezed, struggling to breathe as his lungs filled with blood.

Brant reached down and grabbed the collar of his tunic, yanking him close to his face. He moaned in pain, his eyes fluttering. He didn't have much longer. "Death finds you now, and Argon knows you deserve it. Do something good with your last breath. Where did they go?"

Palin's eyes fluttered, nearly rolling back in his head. But he held on, focusing his gaze on Brant. "They are on the docks...right now," he spat, the last of his breath leaving his body.

Brant dropped him and turned to Gorrin, who already had his bow in his hand and an arrow knocked. "The doors!" he said, running to the double doors at the rear of the warehouse with Brant on his heels.

Gorrin lifted the bar locking them and Brant pushed them open, running onto the wharf with frantic haste, his eyes scanning the darkness. Thick clouds drifted across a tumultuous sky, blocking most of the moon's light. But it mattered little, his eyes drawn to a line of lanterns lit along the nearest dock, their meager light cast across the long planks of the dock leading to a huge black ship rocking gently in the harbor waters.

Brant took in the scene quickly. There were nearly twenty men crowded around a plank leading to the ship, many sailors readying the ship for departure, the sails ready to be unfurled. Lanterns lined the ships railing and Brant could see many men scurrying around the ship like monkeys. The boat was leaving, and now.

"Brant, look!" Gorrin said, pointing to the top of the plank where it met the ship. Brant's eyes followed his finger, and he could just make out, among the subtle lantern light on the railings of the boat, four women being pushed aboard.

"Thea!" he screamed, power from his tarnum adding to the strength of his shout. Everyone on the boat turned towards the wharf at once, and that's when he knew it was her. He would recognize her face anywhere. Standing nearby were Jana and Emy, and to his dismay, Cat was next to them.

Thea could barely see the two figures on the wharf, the shadows of the night obstructing her view. But she could tell from his voice that it was Brant. "Brant!" she screamed, putting everything she had into that cry. Bronas struck her hard in the face, knocking her to the ground. She looked up defiantly, blood dripping from her nose. She was smiling. "I told you...Brant is going to kill you all."

Quill reacted quickly, ignoring Thea. "Take them below," he ordered Orna and the other slavers. Then he looked to a pale man to his right, his long greasy brown hair held back by a black head band. "Typus, get this boat moving!"

"On it Captain," the man said, racing to distribute the orders.

Quill turned to the railing and looked down at the men below. They were already forming a defensive position, two men wide by five deep. "Men, a great honor is before you!" he yelled to them below. "It is time for you to meet the dark angel! Hold the dock!" In unison the armored warriors banged their swords against their shields. Quill turned to several nearby sailors. "Pull in the plank."

Brant had never felt so much emotion overcome him at one time...relief, joy, happiness, all coalesced within him, followed quickly by his friend, anger, when Thea was struck by the man beside her. Every ounce of his being was channeled into power, the joy he felt in seeing her, the anger that rose to the surface, all of it was harnessed in his tarnum, and it exploded with more power than even he thought possible.

Gorrin blinked, and Brant was gone, running down the dock in controlled rage, blue fire erupting from his blade. He covered the length quickly, leaving Gorrin far behind, an arrow drawn back, the fletching close to his face. "For my son," he whispered, releasing the shaft. The arrow flew high, arcing down to strike a man standing next to Quill. He had aimed for the leader, but the boat was now moving, throwing off his aim.

The man next to Quill fell back, a white feathered arrow jutting from his throat. Narrowing his eyes, Quill looked back to the wharf, barely seeing the bowman. "Goronda, bring your bow!" he shouted.

Moments later a massive form stepped beside him. Despite the chill of the night he wore no shirt, his thick gray skin protecting him from the elements. His frame was stocky and lined with bulging muscle, his abnormally long, strong arms, hanging past his knees. He was a bullgon, very rare, typically only found high in the mountain peaks of Corvell. He stood two heads taller than Quill, and his neck was so thick that it grew from his shoulders directly to his head. The creature's features were human-like, but much more angular and rough, like a sculpture's unfinished work. But it was the thing's eyes that were the most unnerving. They were bright yellow, like a cat in the night.

The bullgon was carrying an enormous bow, a quiver of arrows strapped to his muscled back.

Each arrow looked as long as a spear. He looked at Quill. "Yes Captain." Goronda's voice was deep and powerful.

"See that bowman?" Quill said. Just as he pointed, another arrow struck the bullgon, penetrating several inches in his shoulder. Goronda didn't move or cry out. He didn't even blink.

"Yes."

"Kill him."

The bullgon reached back quickly and with practiced ease nocked the giant arrow, drawing it slowly back. The great bow was as big around as a man's wrist and the black wood creaked as Goronda's muscles stretched with the power necessary to pull the bow back. He sighted the arrow for a moment, and released.

Gorrin was just getting ready to snatch another arrow from his quiver when he changed his mind. The boat was slowly withdrawing from the dock and the range, combined with the darkness of night, was already making the shots difficult. He figured he would be better off following Brant, getting closer where he could better put his bow to use. Holding his bow, he raced down the dock.

He ran three stepped when something struck him a glancing blow to the shoulder. A sharp pain shot down his side and the power alone nearly spun him off the wharf. A loud thud resounded behind him and looking back he saw a spear-like projectile jutting from the wall of the building, the metal head buried deep in the damaged wood. Gritting his teeth he reached up to touch the top of his shoulder, his hand coming back red. It hurt, but the bleeding was minimal. It looked like the huge arrow had grazed him by a hair.

Brant's heart dropped when he saw the sails unfurl and the boat start to drift from the dock, ten men left behind to face him. They were sacrificing their own men to get away. He knew he couldn't let the boat slip into the darkness. Growling, he took in the men before him just before he attacked. They wore dark armor, the chest plate embossed with the shape of a black skull. They carried swords and small shields and held their formation like disciplined warriors. Each man's face was hard, but behind their dark eyes was an eagerness to face death.

He was moving fast and would be upon them in mere heartbeats, but despite his rising anger fueled by desperation, he saw the subtle move as two men in the rear threw something. His enhanced vision picked up metal objects flying towards him just before he struck.

The objects hit the dock sounding like hundreds of hail stones, and before Brant realized what they were sharp pain shot up through the bottom of his right foot. Skidding to a halt, Brant realized what had happened, his eyes quickly scanning the wood planks of the dock behind him. He had run through a bunch of small metal spikes, each one shaped in such a way that no matter how it landed, one of the spikes would be standing straight up. Luckily, he had avoided them all, except for one that was now embedded deeply into his right foot. Then the men charged.

Brant looked up and saw the boat was now ten paces from the dock. Realization struck him that he would not be able to reach the boat. Screaming with a rage that he did not know he possessed, Brant released the coalescing energy that was boiling within him. Like in the bar, but this time with no restriction, he exploded in a blue-white fire, the aura energy flashing from him in a great pulse.

The fire struck the first four men, killing them instantly and catapulting them backwards into the others, the initial fire followed by a wave of heated air powerful enough to knock the others to the dock.

Brant drew more energy, and although the link was tenuous as he was not standing on the earth, he was able to draw it up from the shallow water. His sword burst with fire and he attacked, ignoring the pain in his foot the best he could.

The men before him were professionals, and the first two he encountered fought from the ground as they struggled to get their footing. There were four others in the rear who had survived, and they quickly stood as Brant fought the two on the ground.

Their swords swung at his ankles as they held their shields above them. But Brant did the unexpected, leaping up and over the sword swings, he placed his left foot on one of the shields and with enhanced strength he pushed off, leaping high and over the four men behind them. They were so caught off guard by the move and the speed in which he executed it, that they did not have time to react as Brant cleared them all, landing with a thud and rolling forward to his feet. Spinning like a top, he turned on them, his sword cutting into the backs of the rear warriors. The flaming Kul-brite steel cut through their armor, killing them quickly, their bodies falling to the wood planks.

Two others turned, lifting their shields to meet Brant's attack. Metal rang and their shields nearly caved in from Brant's power. One man's arm broke but he fought back the pain, his sword sweeping for Brant's belly. Executing a Kilting Way move, Brant parried, his blade snapping forward like a bent branch, the razor edge cutting into his jugular before snapping left and finding the crease between the other man's pauldron and cutting deep into his left shoulder. The man howled but did not relent; his right hand bringing his sword down towards Brant's head.

But the blade never made it as the man jerked forward, stumbling off the edge of the dock with an arrow stuck in his back. The two men who had fallen from Brant's initial fire attack were unmoving, arrows rising from their cold flesh. Gorrin was thirty paces away and moving towards him fast.

"Wait!" Brant yelled. Gorrin stopped in his tracks. "Look on the ground."

Gorrin looked down and noticed the metal spikes. Slowly, he moved through the steel traps. Once clear, he ran to Brant's side who had yanked the spike from his foot and moved to the edge of the dock, leaving a trail of blood behind him. Soon, the town's guard would arrive, the violence of the fight not going unnoticed.

"What are we going to do?" Gorrin asked, his voice low as they watched the black ship disappear into the night, its lanterns nearly invisible as the shadows sought to swallow their meager light.

Brant felt sick. For the first time he didn't know what to do. They were gone, on some unknown ship sailing for some far off land. "We need to find that ship." But Brant knew that that would be no easy task.

Gorrin turned from Brant and walked to the dead men on the dock. He squatted down and inspected one, a deep frown following. "I've never seen men such as these."

Brant turned at his voice. His defeatist attitude was gone, replaced again with grim determination. "They are very pale," he commented, standing above him.

"They look like Northmen," Gorrin added, inspecting their armor and clothes more closely. "But the design of the armor is unique, as well as this symbol," he added, pointing to the black skull on their cuirass. "I've never seen anything like it."

"Nor I. I'm beginning to wonder if these slavers are of the same lot. Do you remember how pale they were as well? I took notice, but thought their coloring was connected to their home in Vyalia."

Gorrin was shaking his head. "I do not believe that the people in Vyalia are this pale, but I could be wrong."

"I wish Kivalla was here," Brant whispered.

Gorrin looked up. "Who is this Kivalla?"

"He is the Keeper of the Records in Cythera, advisor to the king," Brant answered. "He is the most knowledgeable man I know. I believe he would have some answers for us."

Gorrin stood. "We could use them."

There was a commotion on the wharf as torches flared brightly followed by the town guard, heavily armed legionnaires. There looked to be ten in number and they searched the wharf before a

soldier in the front spotted them and the bodies.
Within moments they were running towards them
with weapons drawn, a single warrior in the front
holding a shield and spear.

Brant had long ago sheathed his sword and
he stepped before them. "I'd hold that advance!" he
said. "There are metal spikes on the dock!"

The leader stopped and held up his fist, the
men behind him halting abruptly. The man was
clean shaven and bald, the only hair on his face a
black and gray mustache. He looked down and
noticed the metal spikes, looking up and
reappraising them. "I'm Kryus, Captain of the
town guard. Who may I thank for the warning?"
His tone was thankful, but on edge, still trying to
figure out what had happened.

"Brant Anwar, and this is my companion,
Gorrin."

The man blinked and tilted his head,
wondering if he had heard him correctly. Not
everyone in Dy'ain knew who Brant was, but many
knew of his various other names sung in songs
since the Saricon War. But if you were a soldier,
you knew of the name 'Brant', as it was spoken
often with great reverence. "You are *the* Brant?"

"I am."

Kryus lowered his sword, but did not sheath
it. "What happened here?"

"It is a long story, Captain. I'd rather tell it
once to the regent. Can you take me to him?"

Kryus hesitated. It was very late at night,
and Regent Morrellis would not be happy to be
woken at home. But if this man was truly Brant
Anwar, then what choice did he have. Kryus
glanced up at Brant's sword, noticing the handle

protruding from behind his back for the first time. It looked like the blade of legend. He decided to trust in his instincts, after all, the man before him fit Brant's description. "Yes, sir," he said. "Follow me."

Brant nodded and he and Gorrin carefully made their way through the spikes as Kryus gave orders to a few of his men. Five men stayed behind to record the scene as well as remove the bodies while the others stepped in behind Brant and Gorrin and escorted them to the Regent's quarters.

They arrived at the regent's personal quarters soon after, a four pace high stone wall surrounding the two-story home. Everything was made of thick gray stone and the entrance was blocked by an iron gate. It looked more like a fortress than an aristocrat's palace, and if it wasn't for the green leafy vines growing up the front façade of the structure it would look quite cold and unwelcoming.

The gate was locked but a large bell hung from an iron hook embedded in the stone columns flanking it. Kryus hesitated for a moment before ringing the bell. They waited in uncomfortable silence, the soldiers clearly not happy with having to wake up their boss.

A few moments later and a man opened the front door of the home. He was holding a lantern and he slowly walked the ten paces down the stone paved path to the gate, his gaze finding Captain Kryus immediately. He wore a white long sleeve shirt with a black tunic over it, long black cotton breaches finishing his ensemble. He was very dark, tanned to the point that he looked like a

Schulg nomad. His green eyes were unreadable, but his posture suggested annoyance. "Captain Kryus, you do realize the hour?"

"Of course, Balfis," Kryus responded. "I would not be standing here if it was not important." He gestured to Brant and Gorrin. "This is Brant Anwar and his companion Gorrin. They requested to see the regent and by the bodies and blood scattered across the docks, I thought it prudent to wake him."

Balfis looked at Brant and frowned, as if he did not believe it was him. He paused for a moment before fumbling for the keys at his side. "Very well," he replied, unlocking the gate and opening it. "Follow me."

They followed the servant into the home, leaving the legionaries behind at the door. Kryus, Brant, and Gorrin, followed Balfis inside where he led him to a large library to the right of the foyer.

"Help yourself to refreshments," Balfis said. "I will fetch Lord Morrellis."

Balfis left, leaving them alone in the study. The house was solidly built of stone, the window sills and joints lined with dark wood. Hundreds of books lined dark wood shelves that covered every wall of the study except where the large fireplace was placed, the blackened wood inside cold and unlit. A large cushioned couch and various chairs faced it, with expensive ornate wood furniture complimenting the opulence of the room. One table behind the couch was occupied with a silver platter, several bottles filled with various spirits sitting amongst a collection of glasses.

"I need a drink," Gorrin said, moving to the bottles and filling a glass with three fingers of amber liquid. He downed it in one gulp, his expression one of surprised content. "Now that warms the body in a most pleasant way."

Kryus was staring at Brant. "Are you really Brant Anwar?"

Brant nodded. "I am."

"What happened out there?"

"They took my wife," Brant answered, pausing as if he was going to continue. But he didn't, saying no more. His expression told Kryus not to press the issue, and he didn't.

Moments later a man wearing a red robe lined with black felt entered the study. Despite the fact that he was just woken up, he looked refreshed, even smiling when he saw his guests. Lord Morrellis was perhaps sixty, his hair white in contrast to his tan, wrinkled skin. "Captain Kryus, welcome, and do not fret about the hour, after all how often does a man get to meet a national hero." Lord Morrellis winked at Brant as if he knew the title was irritating. He walked to him with his hand out. "Welcome Brant Anwar. I am Lord Morrellis, regent of Gashwin."

Brant shook his hand. "I'm sorry for the hour, but our news is quite urgent. This is my companion, Gorrin."

Lord Morrellis shook Gorrin's hand. "Well met and I'm glad you found the spirits."

Gorrin held up his empty glass. "Much needed, and appreciated."

Lord Morrellis nodded. "Please, have a seat."

They followed the regent to the couch and everyone sat, Brant sitting adjacent on a brown leather chair. "Lord Morrellis," Brant begun, his voice tense, "I am not one for pleasantries even on the best of times, so I will cut right to the issue. My wife and adopted daughter, as well as another young woman from Amorsit, were taken by slavers. I tracked them here and found them in a warehouse at the wharf. They were being loaded onto a black ship when we arrived. Gorrin and I killed them, but the boat got away."

Lord Morrellis sat back in the couch, taking in the abruptness of Brant's words. "Slavers in these parts are very rare," he said with concern. "I can only assume that the grab was not random."

Brant nodded. "I believe that to be true. I seem to be the target. But there is more," Brant added. "I saw a fourth woman before the boat left the dock." He paused and looked at each man, building the tension. "Ca'tel Dormath, Queen of Dy'ain was there, captured, and held prisoner with my family."

This time Lord Morrellis leaned towards him, his diplomatic face losing the battle to obvious worry. "Are you sure?"

"Yes, it was her. Obviously, the king and I are being targeted. Someone is trying to hurt us through the ones we love."

Lord Morrellis rubbed his temples, trying to work out the sudden headache. He got up and poured himself a glass from the decanter with the amber liquid, downing it in one gulp. "This black ship," he began, looking at Kryus, "have you heard of it?"

Kryus shook his head. "I have not."

"Go get me the harbor master," Lord Morrellis said. "I want answers."

"Yes sir." Kryus stood and headed for the door.

"Kryus," the regent added.

Kryus stopped at the door and turned. "Yes."

"Bring men with you. I suspect foul play."

Kryus narrowed his eyes. "Yes sir," he added.

The captain left and Lord Morrellis looked at Brant. "Any idea who these men were that you killed on the dock?"

Brant looked at Gorrin. "They look to be Northman," Gorrin added. "They were very pale, but they wore armor and carried weapons of a design I have not seen before."

"There was a symbol on their cuirass of a black skull," Brant added. "Do you know of it?"

Regent Morrellis looked dire. "I believe that I do."

Suddenly the door burst open and Lord Morrellis nearly fell over the edge of the couch. Brant was up and his sword appeared in his hand, the Kul-brite steel sparkling even in the dim light. Standing at the entrance of the study was Jarak Dormath, his Kul-brite armor and clothes dusty and dirty from travel. His sweat streaked face was covered with black stubble and his green eyes, normally sparkling with life and mischief, vibrated with a sense of urgency that Brant had never seen before.

The King looked at Lord Morrellis, his tense gaze flitting to Brant, surprise causing him to move back a step. "Brant, what are you doing here?"

"The same reason as you, I believe."

Chapter Seven

King Jarak went straight to Brant, clasping arms hand to forearm, placing his other hand on his shoulder. "Brant, I am very happy to see you," he said, his eyes distraught. "I need your help."

"And I yours."

"What has happened?" Jarak asked, releasing his hand, obviously wondering why he was there.

"I have been targeted, just as you," Brant began. "Men came to the farm while I was in town." Brant's eyes glistened in the gloom of the room as he thought about Tobias. "Tobias was killed, and they took Thea, as well as Jana and another girl from town."

King Jarak shook his head and ground his teeth. "I am so sorry, Brant." Jarak knew Tobias and liked him very much. But it was the knowledge that Tobias was Brant's son, if not by blood, than by deed that made his heart ache for his friend. He knew how much the boy's death would impact Brant, and it crushed his heart knowing the pain that Brant must have experienced when he found the boy's body. But they could not linger on the dead; there were still the living to find. "I do not understand what is happening, but Cat was taken from me as well. Are the disappearances linked?"

Brant nodded his head. "They must be," he said. Then he took a few moments to tell Jarak of the mysterious man who had poisoned them on the road, and his description got a reaction from Jarak.

"It was the same man who came to me," Jarak added when Brant was done. "I could not move, and even now I feel the poison in my blood. What happened to us must be linked."

"I believe there is little doubt. Jarak," he added, pausing as if he didn't want to tell him. "I saw Cat. She was on board a ship, leaving the dock just before you arrived. She was with Thea and the others."

Jarak's eyes shone with a mixture of worry and hope. "You saw her?"

"Yes."

Jarak looked at Lord Morrellis, walking towards him with his hand outstretched. They shook hands as Lord Morrellis bowed his head. "Lord Morrellis, I'm sorry I could not send word of my arrival, but as you can see things have been most desperate."

"I am here to serve, Your Grace."

"Do you know anything about this ship?"

Lord Morrellis frowned. "I'm afraid I might. Please, your Highness, have a seat and I will have servants bring us food and drink and we can talk of a plan." The king was just about to interrupt when Lord Morrellis continued, placing a placating hand on the distraught king. "King Dormath, I have men right now bringing the harbor master to me. We will get to the bottom of this, but let us do so with a sound plan."

Baccus had entered with Jarak and was now standing just inside the door. Balfis had entered behind the king and awaited their orders. Jarak urged Baccus forward. "Lord Morrellis, this is Baccus, commander of the Dygon Guard. Have you met before?"

Lord Morrellis stepped before him and offered his hand. "Only by reputation," he said, shaking the warrior's massive hand. Then they all made the other introductions, specifically with Gorrin who knew none of them. "Please, everyone, have a seat and rest," Lord Morrellis said when they were done. Then the regent looked at Balfis. "Balfis, please bring us cold cuts and beverages." Balfis bowed deeply and left without another word. Regent Morrellis turned to the men as they sat. "Now, let us talk about this ship."

They spoke hurriedly over cold cuts of meat, cheese, and bread, washing it down with a chilled sweet wine and water. Refreshments were brought to the sentinels who had accompanied the king and were now waiting in the foyer.

"So you think this black ship belongs to the strange clan of Northmen that we have heard about?" Jarak questioned. Rumors have been whispered about a clan of marauding Northmen who have crossed the Varos Mountains and built small settlements along the eastern edge of the Bitlis Sea. Technically, those lands were not within the borders of Dy'ain, so thus far nothing had been done. But word of piracy and raids far to the north had reached Jarak and his ruling council. They had yet to be substantiated, but by the sound of it, doubt was no longer a reason to sit idle. Most of what they've heard so far had been conjecture, stories told by merchants and traders bringing their wares from Rygar along the Sar'am River into the Bitlis Sea and Dy'ain.

"It seems reasonable," Lord Morrellis replied. "According to Brant and my own men, they were definitely Northmen. And the symbol on their shields corroborates what I've heard of them."

"Which is what?" Baccus asked.

Lord Morrellis frowned. "What we know about them is limited," Lord Morrellis began. "But it is said they worship a dark god, one who requires blood sacrifices."

Jarak glanced at Brant who balled his hands into fists, the knuckles turning white. "But why go so far out of their way to take our loved ones? It makes no sense."

Just then the door opened and Kryus shoved a man forward, his hands tied behind his back and his nose bleeding. It was the harbor master. "I'm sorry to interrupt," Kryus said, holding the man before them. "But I think you will want to speak with harbor master Kriel. As you said, Lord Morrellis, he tried to flee."

Jarak was up in a flash and moved to stand before the frightened harbor master, the man's eyes wild. "Do you know who I am?" he asked sternly.

The man gulped, looking at his bright Kulbrite armor, his family crest embossed expertly on the cuirass. Kryus was also taken aback by the king's presence, bowing deeply but staying close to the harbor master. "Mmmm, my King," Kriel began, mumbling, "I'm sorry..."

"Don't say another word," Jarak growled as he drew energy from the Mage Stone at his belt. He wanted answers, and he needed them now. Blue energy erupted from his right hand and he snapped it out like a whip, the magical rope wrapping around Kriel's body several times before lifting him a foot off the ground. Kryus's eyes widened and he stepped further back. The harbor master's eyes bulged as Jarak tightened the magical rope. "With but a thought I can slowly burn you alive, or squeeze you until you teeter back and forth between consciousness and death. You might walk away from this if you tell me exactly what I need to know." The man nodded frantically, but said nothing, his eyes pleading. "Good, now, who took the queen and the others?"

This time the man looked confused. "The Queen?" he sputtered. "I- I – I just thought they were slaves."

"Slavery is illegal in Dy'ain," Lord Morrellis said angrily. "You broke the law to fill your own purse. If King Dormath does not kill you now, then you will be punished for your crimes."

"Please don't kill me," he spat. "I didn't know the Queen was one of the women."

Brant stepped forward with his hand on his sword, but before he could draw the blade, Gorrin placed a placating hand on his shoulder. "We need to know what he knows," he said softly.

Brant narrowed his eyes but removed his hand from the pommel of his sword. "One of the women taken was my wife, the other my adopted daughter. You will tell us what happened."

The harbor master saw the death in the eyes looking at him and knew he had little choice. "They paid me a lot of gold to look the other way," he blurted. "They were Northmen, some tribe they called the Caskas," he said hurriedly, hoping Jarak would not kill him on the spot. "I think it means Black Skulls or something ur rather. I don't know," he cried, tears streaking his face. "I was just trying to earn a liv'in."

Jarak tightened the fiery rope, the flames so far not burning him. "You get paid for what you do," he said, "which is more than you deserve. Where have they taken them?"

The man was shaking his head. "I don't..." he began, but could not speak as the air was being squeezed from him. Jarak loosened up on the rope. The man took a deep breath. "I only know that they have some base in the Worm Holes."

The Worm Holes were an intricate network of waterways along the northeastern end of the Bitlis Sea. Many rivers flow from the Varos Mountains, the Sar'am being the largest, and together they formed a huge network of sloughs and river systems so intricate that on a map they look like hundreds of worm holes dug into a rotten log.

"I have heard of no such base," Lord Morrellis replied.

"It's new," the man said. "Seems they are lookin for fresh blood to appease their dark god. I don't know," he cried, "I'm only tell'in ya what I've heard. Please don't kill me. That is all I know."

"Why did they take my wife," Brant growled, stepping closer, "and the queen? What vendetta do they have against us?"

The harbor master was shaking his head. "I told ya, I do not know. I did not know who the women were. They approached me with gold, more than I've ever seen, to allow the ship to dock and export the cargo. They mentioned some benefactor. That is all I did."

"Benefactor?" Brant asked.

"I overheard them speak of some wealthy benefactor who paid the Northmen to take the women. But they seemed scared of him. Honestly, I'm so sorry, but that is all I know."

Jarak unwound the magical rope and the fiery apparition disappeared into his hand. "Take him away. I want him tried for treason."

Kryus yanked the man from the ground and pushed him towards the door, all the while he was screaming for mercy. After all, a conviction of treason was punishable by death. Jarak turned to Lord Morrellis. "We need a ship, and now."

"We have no military vessels in port," Lord Morrellis said, his tone dire.

"Wait!" Kriel said through the open door. "I know of a ship!"

Jarak turned back to the door. "Bring him back in." Moments later Kryus shoved Kriel back into the room. "Speak," he said. "I have little time and no patience for wasted words."

"I know of a man, a captain, who is nearby," Kriel hastily replied. "He is the best sailor I know of."

"Who is he?" Jarak asked.

"I will tell you, but I ask for leniency."

Jarak tightened his jaw but he had no time to banter words. "If what you tell me is useful, I will stay the executioners axe. But regardless, you will spend time in prison."

"Okay, okay," Kriel said quickly, happy with the terms. "The man's name is Tovar."

"Tovar!?" Lord Morrellis said. "He is a known smuggler."

Kriel was shaking his head in agreement. "Yes, but he is the *best* smuggler. His crew is experienced, and no one knows these waters better than he."

"Where is his ship?" Brant asked.

Kriel frowned. "I don't know."

"Then your information is no..."

"But I know where you can find him," Kriel blurted. Jarak stared at him to continue. "He is visiting a lady friend. I know where she lives."

"You better."

"King Dormath, if I may be so bold to offer a suggestion," Lord Morrellis said. Jarak nodded for him to continue. "It is very late and you need a few hours of sleep. You all have suffered greatly and need to rest. You will do no one any good if you cannot think straight. Why don't you get a few hours of rest and we can find Tovar at first light?"

Jarak looked at Brant and saw the same steel resolve he felt. But Lord Morrellis was right, and besides, his body still ached everywhere from the poison and hard travel. And despite Brant's iron will to leave immediately to find this Tovar, it was clear that the warrior and his companion needed some sleep. They were splattered with blood and dust from the road, not to mention that Gorrin's shoulder and Brant's foot needed mending.

"You are quite right," Jarak said, his eyes turning to the regent. "We need a healer for their wounds," he added, looking at Gorrin and Brant. "Also, I want supplies collected and ready by first light. We will find this captain, and by midday tomorrow I want to be leaning on the railing of his ship as we sail north."

Lord Morrellis nodded and called for his servants.

Kriel was true to his word and led them to a series of small stone cottages stacked neatly together, each one sharing a wall with the other. The cottages were parallel to similar dwellings separated by a narrow cobblestone road. Orange and pink hues were barely poking through the hazy, wool gray of morning, and despite the early hour a few of the cottages already had smoke rising from their chimneys. Jarak sent the four sentinels to the rear of the cottage to check for an exit, and if one existed, to make sure it wasn't used. Jarak and Brant stepped close to the door while Gorrin hung back with Baccus in the shadows. Lord Morrellis was still preparing supplies for a quick departure.

Brant looked at Jarak who nodded. They had discussed the best way to intercept the smuggler, and thought that perhaps announcing that the king was at the door was not the most effective. So they had agreed to a more expedient introduction. Brant drew power from his aura and channeled it into his legs and hips. Stepping back, he kicked the door as hard as he could, the power of the kick busting the lock and nearly breaking the door from its hinges.

They rushed into the small cottage and saw a startled raven-haired woman preparing a fire at the hearth, another sleeping form lying amongst disheveled furs and blankets in the far corner. The women screamed and the man bolted out of bed. He was completely naked.

Brant had his blade out and he Fuzed, not because he thought he needed it, but to scare the man into inaction. It worked, the astonished smuggler stood frozen, his eyes flitting to a long sword and belt leaning against the wall. But seeing a Merger stand before him, along with a man wearing Kul-brite armor, deterred him from moving towards the blade.

Jarak stepped towards him. "We are not here to hurt you," he began.

"Sure looks otherwise," the man said, his eyebrows raised questioningly.

"Tovar!" the woman said, clearly frightened, "what's going on!?"

The smuggler raised his hand to keep her from moving, obviously wary of the blue flaming sword. "Stay where you are, Erwina."

"Neither of you need fear us," Jarak continued, looking to Brant. "Brant, lower your blade." Brant dispersed the flames and did as he said. "I am King Jarak Dormath and I have come to ask for your help."

Tovar was lean and his long arms and legs were wrapped in sinewy muscle. His face was a dark brown, much darker than the skin below his neck. Obviously he was a man who spent a lot of time in the outdoors, the sun and wind aging his face beyond his years. The aged leather look of his face made him appear tough, and neither of the men doubted that he was. His short hair was jet black, with just a few wisps of gray, although there were more silver streaks in the sharp goatee that graced his pointy chin. His black eyes appraised them both, his expression unreadable as he took in the two men before him.

"You have a strange way of asking for help...my King," he added last minute. He didn't say it like he forgot Jarak's title, more like he was unimpressed.

"Please, put on some clothes," Jarak said.

The man bowed, and although it was subtle, it seemed mocking. He slipped on his breeches and tied them at the waist. "Please, have a seat," he said, gesturing towards the small humble table in the middle of the room. "Erwina, would it be too much trouble to get your king some tea?"

Erwina was of medium build with an ample bosom, her face gracefully aged with thin lips and large oval eyes. Presently, she was standing in shock, her big brown eyes wide, looking at Jarak standing in his glistening Kul-brite armor.

"Erwina?"

She broke from her trance and looked at Tovar. "Oh, yes, I'll fetch some presently. I'm sorry, my King, but all I have is lavender."

"I thank you, Erwina, but do not bother yourself," Jarak said, sitting down opposite Tovar.

"We will not be long," Brant added as he stepped closer, but did not sit.

"No offense, but I hope not," Tovar added.

"We need you and your ship," Jarak said bluntly, skipping the pleasantries. "Our need is dire, and we have no time to barter. So name your price."

Tovar leaned forward. "You are the king Dy'ain, that I have no doubt," he said, looking over Jarak's armor, his inquisitive gaze moving to Brant and back. "And I reckon your companion is Brant Anwar. You could simply conscript my men and ship, take both by force. Tell me, why are you willing to pay any price to use a ship that you could take for free?"

By this time Erwina had sat at the table, unsure what to do with herself. She seemed nervous in the presence of the king and the man that killed the Saricon Tongra ten years earlier.

Jarak leaned forward, his eyes intense, but pleading. "Tovar, Northmen, for reasons we know not, have taken the Queen, as well as Brant's wife and adopted daughter. They took them on a black ship this very night. We were told you were the best sailor here...please, will you help us?"

Tovar sighed and sat back in his chair. He looked to Erwina, her face empathetic to the King's cause, as well as his openness. "You know I am a smuggler," Tovar said, this time his tone softer.

Jarak nodded. "I do, but I care not. I need a ship and an experienced crew, and I need them now."

"I know of this black ship," Tovar added. "I saw it once, far off in the distance. They had just raided a small coastal Schulg village. This village," Tovar continued, his eyes sad, "was known to me. I have been trading with them for over five years now, and when I arrived, the men and boys over twelve were slaughtered, the young women taken away. All that was left was young boys and aged old women. I will tell you that I have no love for the Northmen."

"Do you know where this ship docks?" Jarak asked, clearly excited that Tovar knew of the strange Northmen.

"Unfortunately, I do not." Jarak seemed to deflate at that. "But I have some ideas."

Brant had sheathed his sword and stepped closer. "Will you help us?" His tone was beseeching, which was rare for the swordsman.

Tovar's gaze flitted to Erwina, who nodded subtly. Then he sighed heavily. "I am sorry for your losses, both of you. But I will help you. I will need payment for my ship and crew."

"Done," Jarak said without a thought.

"As well as compensation to the families of any crewman killed in your service," Tovar continued.

Jarak stood. "I will have Regent Morrellis draw up a contract. When can we leave? Supplies are being readied as we speak."

Tovar stood as well. "My ship is anchored in a secret bay ten miles north. It will take me a day to call in the crew and resupply the ship. We can leave at sunrise tomorrow. The sun will be up soon. Meet me at the main gate at sunrise."

Jarak reached out and shook the smuggler's hand. "Thank you, Tovar."

The small contingent of men reached the hidden bay at mid-day, the narrow steep path to the tranquil inlet was arduous, making the bay a perfect location for a smuggler's ship. They had to carry the crates of supplies down the narrow rock-strewn path, the sides overgrown with brush and trees, the branches bent inland from many years of heavy winds blowing in from the sea. In several spots they had to lower the crates using ropes, but the experienced crew had clearly done it before.

A handful of the crew was in Gashwin, and Tovar had grabbed them before they left, adding to their ranks. He sent a few runners out to a small village just south of their location to bring in a few more. There were others already on the ship, making the total crew sixteen in number. They were a tough looking lot. Men who had spent their entire lives on the sea, toughened by the unforgiving waters they called their home. Most carried short swords and knives and had that look in their eye that they had used the weapons often. They had proficiently gone about their business loading the ship, their wary eyes often glancing to Jarak and his sentinels. They were smugglers, criminals, and their misgivings about having the King onboard were quite obvious.

Once everything had been loaded onto the ship, Tovar brought several men over to meet Jarak, Brant, and the others. The ship was of a unique design, one that Jarak had not seen before. It looked like a sleeker version of a military frigate, with a wider beam and massive main mast, taller than any he had seen before. There were two other smaller masts, a foremast and a mizenmast. They met on the main deck at the bow of the ship.

One of the men was tall, his face hidden behind a hooded gray cloak. He wore worn wool breaches with aged black boots laced to his knees. He was one of the few men who carried a long sword at his hip. None of the men wore armor.

The second man was short and stocky and looked like he was sculpted from stone, his body muscular and full of rough and deep edges. His woolen clothes were that of a sailor, loose and comfortable draping a cotton undershirt. His dark eyes were sunken behind a pronounced brow, black short hair covering his blocky head. On his back was a short broad sword, its black leather handle aged with use. Silver loops hung from his ears and three rod piercings lined the bridge of his misshapen nose, which clearly had been broken several times.

"King Jarak, Brant, I would like you to meet my ship's officers. This," he said, indicating the tall man still wearing the hood, "is Rizza. He is my master at arms."

The man reached out to shake their hands, seemingly unperturbed about the King's title. He wore a black leather glove with open fingers. Jarak reached out, but hesitated briefly when he saw the man's fingers. Each digit was scarred, like the skin had been burned, leaving behind a mess of discolored flesh.

His grip was like iron. "Well met, Rizza," Jarak said.

The man noticed his hesitation and slowly removed his hood, exposing a bald grotesque head. The man's skin was either gone, like his fingers, or it had changed into something different. It looked like a scar after a burn, but it covered his whole head, and Jarak was beginning to wonder if it didn't cover his entire body. The man's eyes were eerily silver in color. "Do not worry, King Jarak, I am not diseased."

"You are a Mage," Jarak figured.

Rizza hesitated, unsure if it was truly safe to admit it. Despite the King's lift on banning commoners with the Way, many still doubted their safety; lifetimes of subjugation not so easily erased from the minds of the people. "I am, results of ignorance when I was younger."

"I understand," Jarak said. "Is there a channeler on board?" Jarak was excited with the prospect as they had no channeler with them. He had chastised himself daily for not bringing Orfeen, his channeler, with him on the journey to Tanwen. It was a stupid mistake and they had no time to send for him.

"Unfortunately there is not." Rizza turned and shook Brant's hand as well. "I've heard a lot about you," he added. Brant nodded but said nothing.

"This is Balor," Tovar continued, introducing the short man on his right. The man's eyes looked angry, but he shook both of their hands, saying nothing. "He is my first mate."

Balor looked at Tovar, ignoring Jarak and Brant. "We are ready, Captain."

Tovar nodded. "See to it." Balor left without another word. Tovar turned to Jarak. "You will have to forgive him. He has no love for authority outside this ship. Many of these men have lived a hard life, and unfortunately they blame the government, and that's you."

"Well, make it known that if they help me get our women back, that they will have enough gold to live happily for the rest of their lives. I can promise them that."

Tovar nodded. "We will depart in moments," he said as he turned and left.

Brant stepped next to Jarak. "You think we will find them alive?"

Jarak looked at Brant, the morning suns light reflecting off his wet eyes. "We have to."

"Either way," Brant added, his voice like steel. "I will kill every last one of them."

***

All four of them were locked in a small room somewhere below the quarter deck. The door was bolted from the other side and the room was empty except for blankets and a chamber pot. They could not see the daylight and therefore had a difficult time knowing how many days they had been at sea. But their best guess was three.

The Northmen had more or less ignored them. The only contact had been to bring food once a day and remove the chamber pot. They were all frail looking, having lost weight since their short but trying ordeal. They were dirty and gaunt, their overall appearance that of a malnourished poor farmer. Their dignity had been stripped away, their hope faltering with it.

Thea was lying on her back on a dirty wool blanket, her eyes fixed on a knot hole in the ceiling. Beyond the hole was the unknown, her mind drifting to Brant. She could see him plain as day standing on the wharf, his scream echoing in her mind. Jana and Emy were sleeping in the corner, both too weak to fight back the exhaustion. Besides, what was the point? There was nothing to do in the room but sleep.

Cat got up from her blanket and sat cross legged next to her. Reaching out, she touched Thea's arm, her eyes warm despite her dirty and disheveled appearance. "You okay?"

Thea shifted her eyes from the knot to her queen, a gentle smile forming. "I think seeing Brant has made it worse. I want him to hold me so bad that my heart hurts."

A tear dripped from Cat's right eye. "I do not know if Jarak even lives. And my boy, well, I cannot bear the thought of not seeing him again."

Thea sat up and placed her hand on Cat's thigh. "I'm sorry, Cat. I cannot even imagine the pain you are feeling."

She nodded, both taking comfort in one another's empathy. "The other night," Cat began, "back at Gashwin...that man, I heard..."

Thea squeezed her thigh. "We don't need to talk about it," she interjected. "Besides, what I have endured is no more than a common soldier who puts their life on the line to defend their country. I was violated, but he can only hurt me, here," she said, pointing to her head, "if I let him. I will get through it."

"Are you going to tell Brant?"

"What would be the point?" She sighed. "No, I will not. It would only hurt him."

"Do you think he will find us?"

This time she smiled. "There is no doubt. I just hope we are alive by the time he does."

"That would be nice," Cat added, smiling with her.

"Either way," Thea added, her smile disappearing. "He will kill them."

"And that saddens you?"

Thea's eyes crinkled in thought, her lips tight. "No, it does not. What worries me is what will happen to Brant if I die. There is a violent storm within him, and thus far we have lived happily, the storm held in check. But if I die, I'm afraid of what he will become."

Cat didn't respond, thinking about her words. "Just because the weather turns stormy, does not mean it will forever be so."

Thea responded with a warm smile. "Thank you, Cat."

Cat reached down and held both of her hands. "We are going to survive this," she added, her tone adamant.

"I hope so." But she felt very little hope.

***

Brant was leaning over the railing, vomiting his breakfast of dried ham and bread into the Bitlis Sea. It was midday on their second day at sea and Brant was still looking for his sea legs.

"Still sick I see."

It was Gorrin who had moved to stand next to him at the railing. Brant wiped the corner of his mouth with his sleeve. "I will survive," he said.

"For some reason it affects me little." Brant looked at him and scowled. Gorrin smiled sarcastically. "I'm just happy to see that under all that muscle and grit, that you are human. It makes me feel more substantial."

"I'm glad I can help." They were both silent for a few moments, looking out at the expansive sea. The wind was minimal and the waters were presently a gentle roll, but it was enough to turn Brant white. The ships three triangle sail configuration and sleek hull was quite efficient, and despite the mellow winds they were moving at a decent rate. After a few moments of silence, Brant turned to Gorrin. "I'm sorry for the loss of your son," he said. "I've been so wrapped up in my own pain that I had forgotten about yours. Taryn was a good man."

Gorrin nodded, still looking out at the blue waters. "You know he spoke of you often."

"I did not know that."

"He wanted to impress you."

"He did," Brant said. "If he did not, I never would've agreed to him marrying Jana."

"That's what I told him."

"If I lose Thea, or Jana, I don't know what I'm going to do," Brant said.

Gorrin sighed. "We will move on, survive...what other choice do we have?"

"I'm not sure if I could move on. I can't imagine a world without them."

Gorrin gazed out into the open sea, his mind adrift with thoughts. "It will be hard, there is no doubt. I was just thinking, if I survive this, of going home to my Inn...imagining it without Taryn, imagining life without my boy. The sorrow wraps around my heart with every thought. I don't want to think of it."

"There is so much anger within me."

"Yes," Gorrin agreed, "For me, it's the only thing breaking through the veil of heartache. I hate to say it, but I think we're going to need this anger."

"That's what I'm afraid of."

There was suddenly a loud horn, two short bursts, and Gorrin and Brant turned from the railing. The crew had reacted to the horn immediately, each man moving quickly, going about their task with practiced proficiency. The horn had come from the man high up in the crow's nest. The question is, what did it mean, and why did the crew seem so alarmed?

Balor was at the wheel and behind him, shouting orders, was Tovar. Brant glanced around and saw Jarak, Baccus, and his sentinels near the bow of the ship, also looking about, wondering what was happening.

Rizza ran by Brant heading towards the foremast at the bow. "What is happening?!" Brant yelled at him as he ran by.

"Blue serpent coming in fast!" he yelled back as he continued past him.

"What's a blue serpent?" Gorrin asked.

"I don't know, but by the looks of it, it can't be good," Brant responded.

Brant ran towards Tovar, and it looked as if Jarak had the same idea, arriving there moments after. "Tovar!" Brant yelled over the excitement. "What is going on? Rizza said something about a blue serpent."

Tovar looked concerned. "They are dangerous killers capable of sinking ships."

Suddenly the ship jerked under them as she instantly picked up speed. Within a few heartbeats the boat was moving nearly double its speed. Tovar lifted his eye glass and looked to the port side of the ship.

Brant looked towards the bow and saw Rizza standing before the front sail, his arms out wide, his body in a braced position. The front sail was billowed tightly as if a micro wind storm had struck it. Brant suddenly realized what was happening. Rizza was a Mage, and he was using his powers to fabricate a huge amount of wind, causing the boat to accelerate quickly.

"Jarak!" Brant yelled. "Look!" he said, pointing to the bow of the boat.

Jarak was already beside him. "He's conjuring wind."

"Damn it!" Tovar explained as he lowered the eye glass. "The beast is still gaining on us. It must be a big one."

"Can we fight it?"

"Don't worry. We are prepared for this. Nils, get the ballista ready!"

A young deck hand that was standing near Tovar was already running towards the port side. The boy was maybe thirteen winters with unruly long dark hair. The boat's weaponry was four ballista, each capable of launching huge spear-like projectiles. There was one on either side of the main deck as well as one positioned on the bow and stern.

Tovar followed Nils with Brant and Gorrin close on his heels. Jarak grabbed Brant by the arm to turn him around. "I'm going to see if I can help Rizza!" he said. Brant nodded and the King ran off, with Baccus and his four sentinels right behind.

Nils had the Ballista cranked back and was reaching inside a long rectangular box sitting next to the railing. Brant noticed there was a bolt rack near the weapon holding six spear-like bolts, the sharp tips pointing towards the sky and wrapped in oil skin. But Nils wasn't reaching for them, and Brant wondered what was in the box. Looking inside, Brant saw Nils gently remove a long ballista bolt. Inside the box was one more projectile, the entire bolt surrounded by old pillows of what was probably cotton. Analyzing the bolt more closely Brant could see that just below the sharp steel tip was a circular object built into the spear. It was about as big as an oil lamp. Nils gently placed the bolt into the weapon and stepped back for Tovar.

"Do you know what a Tynell is?" Tovar asked as he grabbed the handles and looked out into the expansive waters. So far they could see nothing.

Brant did. "It's a Saricon weapon that explodes when thrown and shattered."

"Exactly. Inside the weapon are two compounds, that when mixed together, cause a fierce explosion. We have retrofitted the weapon to fit the base of the spear. On impact, the clay jar shatters...and boom."

Brant just then noticed that the object below the heavy tip was indeed clay, wrapped in a thin oil skin. "How many do you have?"

"Just these two," he said. "They are expensive, hard to find, and even more difficult to work with. We have to buy them on the black market as no one yet knows how to make them."

"Look!" Nils yelled as he pointed and leaned over the railing.

Everyone followed his finger and saw something large burst from the water a hundred paces to their right. It was nearly as big as the boat and moving fast.

"That thing is huge," Gorrin muttered.

"It's a big one," Tovar agreed. "Balor!" he shouted. "Hard starboard turn!"

Suddenly the boat jerked hard as the sailors screamed out orders, Balor spinning the wheel to the starboard side. Men jumped around like monkeys adjusting sails and expertly working together to maneuver the boat.

"What are you doing?!" Brant yelled. He hated not being able to help.

"They like to swim next to the boats before they attack. I think they think it's a game. When they tire of the game, they ram the boat with their incredibly hard skulls. Then it's just a matter of cracking it open like an egg and feasting on the prize."

"You mean us?" Gorrin asked, although he already knew the answer.

Tovar didn't respond knowing it was a rhetorical question. "I'm hoping the hard turn will bring the beast next to us. Then I kill it."

Jarak skidded to a stop next to Rizza, wind howling around him as he spun it in a vortex and pushed it towards the sail. He must be pulling energy from the auras of the crew members, which would be a dangerous thing to do. Pulling tainted energy had a very adverse effect on the Mage, and over time can cause physical abnormalities as well as mental. The auras of the crew were not necessarily tainted as they were just elevated in excitement, but Jarak was sure that some were scared, and when you started to get into auras laced with fright, anger, jealousy, and pain, then it typically didn't end well for the Mage. It was possible that Rizza knew which auras to draw from, thus lessening the impact of drawing from negative auras, but sooner or later, his power well would run out. You could only draw so much energy from a person at a time without causing them to tire quickly. The boat suddenly shifted to the starboard side and Jarak nearly fell. But Rizza seemed to expect it, his legs planted firmly on the wood deck.

Jarak had the power stored in his Mage Stone, and he was somewhat reluctant to pull from the auras of the men. But he was very powerful, and experienced, and shuffling through auras and finding clean energy was something he had mastered long ago.

"How can I help?!" Jarak yelled.

"More speed! Join with me!" Rizza yelled without looking at him, concentrating heavily on the task. To pull energy from many men while ignoring unclean auras, while holding a spell required great concentration. Jarak had no doubt that this particular spell was not the first time the Mage had been forced to use it.

Over the years Jarak had grown in power, and along with the increase in strength Jarak had improved his spell repertoire. Using wind to fly, or channeling it in a particular direction, was fairly novice. Turning on his towd, he reached out and searched the auras around him. Bouncing from man to man, he was surprised to see focused and tense auras, but very few that were actually afraid. It seemed these men were hardened sailors, or perhaps they had great trust in their captain, either way the auras were fairly clean. Drawing small amounts from man to man, Jarak concentrated on the spell, weaving the energy into a vortex. Within a few heartbeats he pushed it forward into the foremast sail, the mast creaking from the strain as the boat jerked forward faster.

"Not too much!" Rizza screamed. "We don't want to break the mast or rip the sail!" Together they concentrated on keeping the boat moving at an incredibly fast rate. Whatever Captain Tovar was up to, they better do it quickly or they would run out of energy.

Tovar looked towards Rizza and Jarak, taking notice of the sudden increase in speed. Then he looked back to the water just as the serpent surfaced off the port side, no more than thirty paces away. "Get ready!" he yelled. Hold tight on to the railing!" he ordered. "They like to nudge the boat and see if they can toss anyone overboard! The speed helps as sometimes they tire of the chase and leave for easier game."

Brant looked at the creature that was moving fast just under the water. Its body was long and thick, a nearly turquoise shimmer under the blue water. It looked to have a long tail and flippers that were each as long as a man. It was very streamline; the long neck tapering to what Brant only guessed was its head.

Suddenly the serpent veered hard towards the boat.

"Hold on!" Tovar yelled just as the creature crashed against the hull, its heavy body causing the boat to jerk under their feet. Brant gripped the railing like an iron vice, but to his horror he realized that Nils had not got a firm hold on the railing before the creature struck. The sudden shift in the boat caused Nils to tumble over the railing, a scream of terror escaping his lips as he fell towards the dark depths.

Without thinking for his safety, Brant pushed aura energy into his body and flung himself over the railing, his left hand still holding onto the wood edge, his right swinging out and reaching for the falling boy. Brant's body was a blur as his fingers found the boy's shirt, and using his momentum he heaved with all his enhanced strength and tossed the boy back over the railing where he tumbled across the main deck.

"Brant! Look out!" Gorrin yelled, nocking an arrow to his bow and leaning over the railing.

Brant was holding on with one hand, his grip so strong that his fingers had dug into the wood railing. Looking down into the water he saw the creature bolting back towards the boat with incredible speed. He didn't think...he just reacted and drew his blade from the scabbard on his back, all the while dangling like bait over the side of the boat. He Fuzed just as the creature jumped from the water. Time slowed for Brant as its huge head, covered in some thick exoskeleton, shot from the water, its maw open wide revealing row after row of razor sharp teeth, each the size of the dagger at his belt. The creature's mouth was so wide that Brant held no illusion that it could swallow him whole in one bite.

An arrow zipped past Brant's head and thudded into its open mouth just as Brant's sword arced down, the fiery blade cutting through the beast's armor that was covering its snout. At the same time Brant lifted his body up, his grip nearly cracking the railing, raising his legs at the same time.

The creature jerked back with a roar from the blade and arrow, its mouth snapping shut, barely missing his feet before crashing back down into the water. Moments later several hands reached down and helped Brant lift his body safely over the railing.

Tovar, with his hands still on the weapon, was staring at Brant with amazement. Gorrin helped him up just as Nils joined them at the railing. "Thank you," the young boy said, his eyes wide with shock.

Gorrin looked at him with wonder. He had witnessed Brant's speed and strength before, but nothing quite like that. "That was close," he said.

"Too close. Nice shot by the way," Brant added as he patted the man on the shoulder.

"Here it comes again!" Tovar yelled as he readied the weapon. "I think you made it mad!" The creature moved in closer, swimming side by side the boat, no more than twenty paces away, a trail of red streaming behind it. "Looks like you wounded it pretty good!"

Tovar had the weapon aimed at the creature but it was still too deep under the water. He couldn't risk missing, or having the impact on the water causing the tynell to explode without contacting the creature's flesh. The explosion might injure it, but perhaps it would just further enrage the beast. They needed to make their shots count.

"We need some more bait!" Brant yelled. He glanced at Nils, who still looked in shock from his near-death experience. "Can you get me a length of rope?" Nils nodded and ran off, eager to get clear of the railing.

"Brant," Gorrin said, very much concerned. "You sure you want to do that again?"

"Actually, no, I'm not," Brant responded. "But if that thing sinks this boat, then we have no chance. I won't let that happen." Just then Nils skidded next to him carrying a length of rope. "Good, now tie that end off," Brant ordered. Then he turned to Tovar, who was eyeing the creature, waiting for the thing to surface. "Tovar, be ready. When it comes for me, shoot it."

Tovar looked at him like he was crazy. But he nodded in understanding. "When I fire this thing, you're going to want to get as much distance between you and it as possible."

Tovar didn't have to explain what he meant. Obviously if Brant was too close to the creature than the explosion might kill him, or knock him off the rope, which meant he was as good as dead. Brant nodded in understanding and gripped the rope tightly; pulling on the end to make sure it was secured. Then he looked at Tovar as he readied himself. "Ready?"

Tovar gripped the handles of the weapon more tightly, his eyes saying good luck. "Ready," he responded.

Without a second thought, Brant leaped over the edge, using the rope to quickly descend, stopping about three paces above the water line.

"Here it comes!" Tovar yelled as the creature shot towards Brant. This time the serpent was coming in fast, clearly hoping to not only swallow Brant, but to crash into the boat with all its strength.

Brant channeled energy into his arms, and using his strong legs he held his body off the hull of the ship, glancing back out into the water. His heart was pounding as the creature shot towards him like a bolt from a crossbow, and in a massive splash of water the huge beast exploded from the water, its giant armored head angled right at Brant. "Now!" Brant screamed as he used his incredible strength and speed to scurry up the rope. In his enhanced state, he heard the click of the trigger on the ballista and felt the bolt fly past him. Just as he reached the edge of the railing, he heard the explosion, the stunning sound followed by a concussion of air, the strength of it lifting him high and tossing him over the railing and ten paces beyond. The boat shook as something, likely the thing's body, struck the hull. Brant crashed onto the deck and tumbled into water barrels that were strapped to the decking. Instantly after he hit the barrels, a rain of blood and chunks of flesh coated the boat, sprays of crimson splashing the deck like a massive wave.

"We got it!"

Brant heard Tovar's shout, but his head was still ringing and he could barely stand. Strong hands lifted him and held him up. It was Gorrin. "You okay?" he asked with concern.

"I think so. Just a little dizzy."

"I should think so," he added, letting go of him as he regained his footing.

Tovar joined them, his face splattered in gore, but none of it dampening the smile on his face. The boat slowed as the crew finally paused in their tasks to yell and cheer in excitement. Even Balor nodded in Brant's direction, clearly impressed. They had never seen anything quite like that, and it didn't take long for the whispers of Brant's exploits to reach the ears of the entire crew.

"Well done, Brant," Tovar said, standing before him. "I've never seen anything like that."

Brant held himself up, finally able to think past the ring in his ears. "Let's hope you won't have to again," Brant said softly, his languid smile showing his own surprise that he had survived.

Tovar continued to smile as he placed his hand on his shoulder. "And thank you for saving Nils. We owe you a debt."

"You owe me nothing. You would not have been in danger if it weren't for us."

"True enough," Tovar added. "But just the same, not many men would've done what you did, and for that I thank you."

Brant nodded, his head still spinning.

"I think you need to lie down," Tovar said, seeing his unease.

"On that, we can agree," Brant added.

Chapter Eight

A week later and Thea felt the boat slow and heard commotion above, the scrambling of sailors running across the deck and the shouts of orders echoing in the tight confines of their room. She glanced over at Cat who sat up from her blankets, her expression one of worry and excitement. Were they going to get off the dreadful boat? If so, what did that mean for them? Trepidation of the unknown was covering them like a wet wool blanket. Jana and Emy stirred, rising from their sleeping blankets on the floor.

Thea cried inwardly, seeing the defeated expressions of the younger girls. They were skinny and malnourished, their faces gaunt and eyes sunken and rimmed in shadow. Their simple cotton clothes were dirty, matching the tangles and knots in their once glistening hair.

"What is happening?" Jana moaned.

"I think we are stopping," Thea answered. "Remember, whatever happens, be strong. They cannot take your dignity unless you let them."

Cat nodded at her words but said nothing.

It wasn't long before the door opened and Orna entered with Bronas and another sailor that they did not recognize.

"Let's go," Orna ordered, stepping aside to give them room.

Cat looked at Thea with uncertainty. They had not been let out once since the ship left Gashwin over a week ago. They were excited to feel the sun on their skin again, but they had no idea what was waiting for them outside of their small room. It was a frightening thought. It looked as if they were not going to bother to tie their hands. Did they think so little of them? If possible, Cat was going to show them differently.

Cat left the room with the others close behind her. They were escorted up the stairs through a hatch to the main deck. Immediately they had to cover their eyes from the sun, the bright light nearly blinding, the strong fresh odor of sea air an overwhelming change compared to the dank, smelly room they had endured. Once their eyes adjusted to the light, they were able to see that it looked to be about mid-day.

The boat was moving at a slow speed entering a narrow passage, the inlet lined with huge rocks and short wind-blown trees growing from the densely packed stones that rose up from the deep water, forming cliffs on both sides. It was ominous and beautiful at the same time. They had no idea where they were.

Cat quickly scanned her surroundings as they were taken to the Captain. The men glanced their way but gave them very little notice as they went about their jobs. They were clearly Northmen, their pale skin and bright blue eyes making that apparent. But why were they here? As far as Cat knew, the Northmen lived far north of Rygar. They were a fierce race and some thought that the Saricons could be somehow related to them. She looked around trying to get a bearing on where they were at. Nothing looked familiar, which was to be expected. Although she had little idea of where they were, she knew they were nowhere near the lands of the Northmen. Have they come south to raid? And what is their role in this charade?

Most of the men carried short swords or small knives. Instantly she made her mind. She would not be pushed around like some weak aristocrat's wife. She was a legionnaire, and one of the best swordsmen in Cythera. The great lengths they had endured in capturing her told her that she was important enough to keep alive. She was going to test that theory and show them, despite her present weak condition, what she was capable of with cold steel in her hand. She glanced back over her shoulder and saw the soldier escorting her was close, his eyes looking out at the surroundings around them.

Without a second thought, she faked a stumble, falling towards the man, her hand reaching for his blade. Instinctively he caught her, realizing too late that she had gripped his sword, the sound of steel sliding on steel drowned out by the commotion of the ship as she drew his blade in one quick motion. Regaining her footing quickly, she sliced the blade down and across the man's inner thigh, cutting his femoral artery before darting off towards the ship railing.

The man tried to chase her, but suddenly felt light headed as waves of crimson gushed from the horrible wound to drench is right leg. Looking down, he saw his life's blood pool on the wood planks, falling over as dizziness quickly claimed his consciousness.

Orna and Bronas were not prepared for her sudden attack and she was half way to the railing before men around them noticed what had happened. "Don't let her jump!" Orna yelled, moving fast to catch her.

Two sailors close to the railing heard the alarm and stepped before her, one carrying a short sword and the other a thick bladed knife.

"Don't kill her!" Orna yelled.

Cat smiled at that, knowing they would have to hold back their attacks. Taking full advantage of that knowledge, Cat engaged them like an angry animal. She had little energy, and she used it all on a series of viscous attacks. Her right foot snapped out, the impossibly fast and powerful kick connecting solidly with one of the sailor's noses, snapping his head back violently in a splatter of blood. The man stumbled backwards held up only by the railing behind him.

The other man tried to grab her in a bear hug, his knife still held in his right hand. But she was a whirlwind. Her sword came up quickly, cutting the man in the bicep as he reached for her, her fleeting form gliding past him where she continued her momentum and whipped her blade across the nearly unconscious man's throat that was leaning against the railing. Blood sprayed from the deadly wound and the sailor fell backwards over the railing into the water below.

The shore was close and she placed her hands on the edge, prepared to leap over and land in the frigid waters below. She held little hope that she would get away, but she had to try. Glimpsing the blue water below, she was perched to jump over when thick arms grabbed her legs and yanked her back hard, tossing her over his shoulder to the deck below. But it wasn't a *he* at all, it was Orna.

Cat skidded on the deck, her sword still held in her right hand. Leaping up, she crouched, preparing to continue the fight. Orna stood before her, her own sword out. Six other men surrounded her, three of which wore dark armor and carried long spears. She was surrounded.

Captain Quill stood before her as well, his stolid expression unnerving. "You will make Annaset very happy," he said, no hint of anger at killing his crew members apparent. "Now drop your sword or we will hurt the other women."

Cat glanced and saw other men surround Jana, Emy, and Thea, who were all looking on with stunned expressions. But she didn't drop her sword, wondering if taking out a few more of them before dying would be preferable to what awaited her.

The Captain nodded at Bronas and he punched Jana in the side. She groaned and crumpled to the deck, writhing in pain. "It can get a lot worse," Quill continued. "Drop your sword." Suddenly Quill lifted his right hand and blue icy snow materialized from nowhere, swirling around his fist. "Do you know what it feels like to have your fingers and toes freeze and fall off?" he added with a sanguine smile.

What was he, Cat thought? *Was the Captain a Mage?* She figured it wouldn't be prudent for her, or the others, to entice him further. So she relaxed her stance, dropping her blade to the deck. "If I get the opportunity, I'm going to kill you."

The Captain smiled, the swirling blue cold disappearing in a flash. "Of that I have no doubt. Now, let us forget these un-pleasantries and enjoy the sun's warmth. Take it in now," he suggested, "for it won't be long before the cold mountain snows are going to be your only companion. Behold," he said, pointing to the huge snowcapped mountain range far in the distance, "the Varos Mountains."

Cat forgot the recent fight and stared at the huge mountain range rising up behind the rough stone surroundings and splattering of wind-blown trees. So they had been taken north towards the Sar'am River. The Varos Mountains were a huge range, so big that she thought them un-crossable, which is why she knew nothing of the lands beyond. Did these Northmen somehow live in the inhospitable mountains, or did they come from the unknown lands beyond? She feared her answers would be forthcoming.

***

Brant, Jarak, Baccus, Gorrin, and Captain Tovar stood around a flat wood table staring at an intricate map. The room was the Captain's room, a rectangular table filling most of it, a door leading to his sleeping quarters on the starboard wall. Shelves lined the walls filled with charts and books and a four-lantern chandelier hung above the table. Spread out on the table was a map of the Bitlis Sea and the lands beyond, and everyone was looking intently at the detailed portion in the northern section of the parchment.

"Where did you get this map?" Jarak asked. "I have never seen one so detailed." The map was hand drawn, neatly done, with intricate details few of them have seen.

"I made it," Tovar said.

Jarak looked at him with amazement. "You've been to all these places?" he asked, pointing to the Worm Holes, the area of concern.

"Yes," Tovar replied. "For a smuggler, secrecy is sometimes necessary. These inlets," he said, pointing to the intricate network of waterways so called the Worm Holes, "are great places to hide if necessary. Over the last fifteen years I've mapped every nook and cranny of the Bitlis Sea."

"Which is probably why these Northmen have picked it as a base," Gorrin added.

"The question is," Brant said, "will we be able to find them?"

Tovar leaned forward, sighing heavily. "We are two days from here," he said, pointing to the southern portion of the Worm Holes. "I'm not going to lie, finding them, especially without being seen, will be nearly impossible. It would be easy for someone, even a large ship, to get lost in there. The best plan would be to start there," pointing to the first finger of water, "and work our way north. I am knowledgeable enough of the waterways to know which ones are navigable, and which ones are not. That will help minimize the search. But even then, it's like finding a grain of salt in the ocean. We will eat up many days exploring the various inlets. And if we do find them, they will surely know of our presence before we know of theirs."

"There is no sense worrying about what we cannot control," Brant said softly, his eyes scanning the map carefully.

"How many days do you think they have on us?" Jarak asked in unmasked frustration.

Tovar stood and poured himself a glass of wine from the decanter on the table. "I don't know much of their ship, but I'd bet we are the faster vessel. They had nearly two days on us," Tovar shrugged, thinking. "We might have gained half a day at the most."

"What if we find a heavily defended garrison?" Baccus asked. "They must have some port, or staging base tucked away somewhere in one of those inlets. The question is, what are their fortifications, and how many men do they have?"

This time it was Jarak's turn to sigh. "We have no army," he said. "It is us, and my four sentinels." Jarak looked at Tovar. "I will not press your men into service, but do you have any men who would be willing to fight?"

Tovar squinted and pursed his lips in thought. "As you know, most of us have no love for any sense of authority...but, some of the men are fighters, and they might toss their steel in if they got something in return."

"Put the word out to your crew," Jarak said, making up his mind. "If we need men, I will pay an extra twenty gold dracks to each man who fights with us, payment due to their family if they were to fall." Jarak paused and looked around the room, his green brilliant eyes making eye contact with each man. "I will see our women rescued, or die trying."

A day and a half later and they reached the first inlet of the Worm Holes. Captain Tovar sailed past it, informing the others that it was shallow and not suited for a large ship. Luckily for them the day was clear and calm, the inlets easy to see. The remainder of the day they entered and explored the first navigable inlet, a particularly long finger of water. Tovar said it went back nearly ten miles and was deep enough for a large vessel throughout most of it. Not finding anything, they ended up anchoring on the way out as night halted their search.

Brant found Jarak leaning against the ship's railing, looking out as the moon's bluish glow painted the white peaks of the Varos Mountains.

"Do you think they are out there somehow?" Jarak asked after a few silent moments.

"They have to be," Brant replied softly. "I cannot fathom anything else."

Jarak looked at his friend. "I'm sorry about, Tobias."

Brant nodded in acknowledgment but said nothing.

"I wonder if Cat, or Thea, is looking up at these mountains right now, wondering where we are...wondering what will happen to them." The King wiped a lone tear from his right eye. "Why do you think they took them?" he asked, looking at Brant.

Brant was clenching his jaw, barely holding back the flood of emotions. "I don't know. We have made enemies over the years. Perhaps it was a Schulg plot, to pay us back for what happened to Tangar." Tangar was the Schulg chief's son who had bought Brant when he had been arrested at Amorsit for accidently killing the magistrate's son in a bar fight. Tangar had trained him for two years, all the while forcing Brant to fight in the Schulg pits. He had become Ull Therm, which in the Schulg language meant master killer. But Brant had escaped, along with his giant friend, Uln. But Tangar pursued, eventually finding them at Kaan's cabin where he was confronted by Kulvar Rand, the famous swordsman and leader of the

Dygon Guard. Kulvar had killed the Schulg warrior in three sword strokes.

"But I had little to do with Tangar's death," Jarak reasoned.

Brant shrugged. "He was killed by Kulvar Rand, a representative of the royal family. To the Schulg, that means you."

"Perhaps," Jarak whispered. "The plot seems too intricate for them. I feel like we are missing something. Why would the plot include the murder of Endler and Serix? And who was that man who had entered my tent, taking Cat away into the night? And why sell them off to these Northmen?"

"I cannot answer your first questions, but I'm afraid that they were sold to the Northmen to take them far away from us...to punish us. This dark god of theirs makes me nervous."

"You think they were taken for sacrifice?" Jarak looked haunted, the thought of his Cat being executed to some grisly god clearly frightening him.

"I don't know. We have to find them." Brant's tone was adamant.

Jarak reached up and squeezed Brant's shoulder. "I'm glad you are here."

Brant smiled weakly. "And I you."

***

It took them a quarter of a day to sail up the inlet, the black ship anchoring fifty yards from a flat sandy shoreline that gently sloped up to a small base made up of a dozen wood buildings of various sizes and shapes. An earthen redoubt was built around it with big logs laid on top of each other forming the upper portion of the protective wall. The small encampment was built against a large rock formation on the eastern side, the earthen and wood wall built right against it. There was a wood gate on the southern side of the small base that was open when they arrived. A second smaller ship was anchored in the tranquil deep waters.

Taking no chances, the four women had their hands tied in front of them, a long rope wrapped around their necks connecting them together so they would not run. They were put on a smaller boat and rowed to shore, escorted under armed guard to the small camp. As they neared, Thea noticed for the first time a stone carving over three paces high jutting up from behind the earthen wall. It was roughly done, but still it was obvious that the form was a tall woman in flowing robes, a hood pulled low over shadowed features. It was ominous in appearance and she shuddered when she walked by it.

Near the shoreline was at least ten Northmen building a boat that looked to be about half the size of the big black ship. The boat was half way finished, the frame resting and secured on logs embedded perpendicular into the ground forming a rail system to slide the boat into the water once complete. But it wasn't the boat that drew her attention; it was the two giants that were carrying massive logs from a pile to the workers to be split into planks. Thea had never seen anything like them. They were at least a few heads taller than the Varga, a giant breed that once lived freely throughout Dy'ain and Kael. Through thousands of years of war, conquest, and disease brought by the Dy'ainian ancestors, their numbers were reduced significantly, and they were now relegated to the Heyrith Forest. But these creatures were much larger, and they were not green like the Varga, their skin more blue-gray than anything. They looked more or less human, with bigger noses and wide mouths, their eyes spaced further apart under a strongly pronounced brow ridge. White scraggly hair grew down to their back and they wore mismatched pelts across their huge chests and legs, their muscular arms exposed to the elements.

"What in Argon's name are those?" Thea whispered to Cat.

"I don't know," Cat said, her eyes wide as she watched the beasts easily lift the thirty foot logs, each one as big around as man's leg.

Orna yanked the rope hard and nearly jerked Thea from her feet. "Don't say your weak god's name before Annaset!" she barked, indicating the stone statue. Then she smiled. "And those are bandabars," she said, her cold eyes flitting to the giants. "In our language it means peak dwellers. Now let's go."

Once inside, the smell hit them first. Various men milled about a center courtyard performing daily tasks, their expressions wolfish, while some were indifferent. They were Northmen, their pales bodies covered with furs and dark steel. The ground was trampled and muddy and smoke rose from fires lit around the clearing. Fish and a small stag cooked over fires, the smell of burning fat mixing with human sweat and refuse. Orna and Bronas guided them into a small building, the walls built from rough sawn lumber. Captain Quill walked by them without a second look.

Inside the building they were shoved against the far wall where they were secured to steel manacles, a long chain bolting them to the wall. There were three other women similarly secured, two lying on their side, the third sitting with her legs crossed and her eyes closed. They wore dirty and worn cotton clothes like their own. Each had a chamber pot close by and if the smell was any indication they had not been emptied in a few days. The two women that were lying down sat up slowly when the door opened, their expressions scared and despondent at the same time. The third woman's eyes flashed open, but she did not move, her moon blue eyes following them as they were roughly shackled to the wall.

Bronas locked the manacles on Thea, reaching down and massaging her buttocks before leaving her with a mocking laugh. Thea did her best to ignore him. The last thing she wanted was to give him any satisfaction at making her feel violated. She was closest to the woman with the blue eyes.

"Hello," she said softly after Orna and Bronas left the room. "Where are we?"

The woman's face was oval with a narrow chin and thin lips. She would have been nondescript if it weren't for her eyes. Her tangled brown hair hung to her mid back. "Your guess is as good as mine," she answered. She spoke well, with an aristocratic flare that was in sharp contrast to her disheveled appearance. "I believe we are east of the mouth of the Sar'am River but even that I cannot be sure."

Cat was next to Thea listening intently. "The Worm Holes," she said to herself. "That's where we are."

"What are the Worm Holes?" Thea asked.

"An intricate network of waterways at the northern end of the Bitlis Sea," Cat replied. "They form a border between the Sil Desert and the Varos Mountains."

"My name is Thea," she said to the blue-eyed woman.

"I am Morella."

"These are my friends, Cat, Jana, and Emy," Thea said, indicating each of them. Morella nodded, her expression stolid. "Where are you from?"

"Kreb," Morella answered. "You?"

"A small town north of Cythera," Thea added for them all, leaving out Cat's true identity.

Morella frowned, the only outward emotion she had yet shown. "Seems a long way for these savages to travel for fodder for their dark god."

"Annaset," Cat whispered, repeating what Captain Quill had said previously.

"Yes," Morella continued. "That is correct."

"We are to be sacrificed?" Jana mumbled, her haunted words glazed with exhaustion.

"That is my understanding," Morella replied.

"Why us?" Cat asked.

"I can only guess. I am a lord's wife from Kreb. Perhaps my aristocratic blood pleases this Annaset. I do not know. These young women," she continued, indicating the two girls next to her, "are beautiful, and maybe that is also desired. This is only speculation of course. As for you three, well, you are young and beautiful, or perhaps you are more than just modest villagers from a small town north of Cythera."

Thea looked at Cat but neither said anything about her identity. Jana and Emy remained silent as well. Thea looked back at Morella. "How long have you been here?"

"Two days," she said. "I've heard them talk and it seems they have been waiting for you."

"Waiting for what?" Cat asked

"We are to head into the mountains," she replied. "I believe that is where we are to meet this Annaset."

***

The next day Captain Tovar and his crew expertly maneuvered through two other inlets, finding nothing before anchoring in one for the night. It was the following day that they got their first break. Tovar was directing Balor through a narrow opening marking the entrance of a deep inlet when a cry came from a lookout on the port side. It was Nils, his face flushed with excitement as he lowered the spyglass when Tovar neared.

"What is it?" the Captain asked.

"Look." The young man pointed to the far edge of the inlet, the shore littered with rocks and drift wood. It was not far off and the Captain didn't need the spyglass. Nestled amongst the pieces of bleached wood was a body.

"Balor!" Captain Tovar shouted. "Prepare a boat!"

They had anchored the ship while a small boat loaded with Tovar, Jarak, Gorrin, and Brant rowed to shore. The weather had turned some; the clear blue skies now the color of damp cotton. But there was little wind and it didn't look like rain. They made it to shore easy enough.

The body was on its stomach and Brant reached over and grabbed the dead man's shoulder, turning him over.

"Well it's a Northmen," Tovar said. The man was pale in death, but he looked like a Northmen nonetheless. He wore the clothes of a simple sailor and by the looks of it his throat had been slashed. "He hasn't been dead more than a few days."

"His throat was cut," Brant added, stating the obvious.

"It was Cat," Jarak said, his face lit up with the first smile in weeks. They all looked at him with a *how do you know* expression. "I know she did this," he continued. "She would fight back any chance she got. You know how good she is with a blade," he added, looking to Brant. "He is clearly a Northmen. Who else could've done this?"

"It makes sense," Brant added.

"It's a good clue," Gorrin agreed. "If she killed the man and he fell overboard, they would not think to retrieve the body. It means we found the right inlet."

"Lots of unknowns here," Brant continued. "But even if it wasn't Cat it's the best clue we have."

"Just because the body was washed up here, doesn't mean this is the inlet," Tovar reasoned.

"I agree with Brant, a dead Northmen is the best evidence we have," Gorrin said. "My bet is this is the inlet."

Brant looked up from the body, his piercing green eyes finding Jarak. "Ready for a fight?"

***

Thea and the five other girls stood in a line in the middle of the courtyard, a rope tied around their necks and attached to one another to keep them from running. They were wearing warm furs over their dirty cotton clothes as well as leather fur-lined boots given to them by the Northmen. For once, they were somewhat comfortable, warm, with bellies full of nourishing stew they had been given the last couple days. They had regained some of their energy, and by the looks of it they were going to need it. It was early in the morning and the air was crisp and cool, the sun's rays barely peaking over the tall rock formations that surrounded them, not yet beating back the cool night chill.

Northmen were all around them preparing for what looked like a long trek. There were eight short, stout mules, each heavily laden and covered with long tangled white hair. They were a breed she had never seen, clearly bred for the cold mountain passes. There were at least fifteen men outfitted for travel checking their packs last minute for anything they may have missed. Orna, Bronas, the big bullgon named Goronda, and of course Captain Quill were among them. They were all dressed in warm furs, except Goronda, who wore a fur lined vest, his huge arms exposed, seemingly unaffected by the cool morning air. One of the giants she had seen earlier was also there, standing tall in its meager furs, a huge well carved club, the heavier end embedded with black steel blades. It was the size of a sapling and looked quite devastating. It seemed that Morella had in fact been correct. They were heading into the mountains.

Thea had lots of questions that she wished answered. Who were these Northmen and did they really live in the high cold reaches of the Varos Mountains? Or did they live beyond them? If so, why come to Dy'ain? And how did they get ships here? It was hard for her to believe that they actually built the boats along the shores of the inlet. But it was possible. She saw tools all about the shoreline as well as rigging and equipment that she had seen before at the ship yards in Cythera. If that were true, then these Northmen were an industrious lot. Were they really here for captives and plunder? Were they really to be sacrificed to this dark god Annaset? Looking carefully, she did notice a few crates stacked upon the mules. Two men had carried each one so they were definitely heavy. Was there gold and valuables inside, plunder taken from raids, or even Kul-brite steel, which she had a hard time believing as it was nearly impossible to find outside the reaches of the Dygon Guard. And the biggest unknown was why they were specifically targeted? There were plenty of easier captives, much closer than Cythera. She had so many questions, and besides lots of time to ponder them, there were no answers to be had.

Quill stepped before them wearing heavy gray and brown furs of what looked like a mountain wolf. He wore a pack and carried a sword at his hip. The big giant stepped closer to them, his silver-blue lighting eyes looking down at them with little expression. "The road you are about to travel will be arduous to say the least," Quill began. "We are taking you to one of our newest temples deep into the mountains. It is there that you will meet Annaset, goddess of warriors, ruler of ice and shadow, guide between the living and the dead."

"We care nothing of this Annaset," Cat spat defiantly.

Quill, who was normally void of rash emotion, snarled, his face transforming in fury as he stepped towards her quickly, the back of his hand glowing blue before hitting her across the face so hard that she nearly fell over. "Queen Dormath," he growled. "Do not speak ill words of Annaset. She likes your strength, there is no doubt, but impertinence does not please her." Cat licked her bloody lip, her stare sharp like a spear. The side of her face was marred with a long mark, the icy cold of his fist freezing the skin, causing it to turn a lighter shade, like a mild burn. But she said nothing, and Captain Quill continued. "The path we travel is treacherous and you will be tied together, so please, take care. We wouldn't want you to meet Her to early. Now, I'm curious, what do you know of our people?" It was a question directed at Cat.

But it was Morella who spoke. "You are descendants of Gargaelins from the lands north of Rygar, even beyond the Varos Range. You live for war...you rape and pillage...you are a pestilence to the races of men." Her voice was smooth and calm, devoid of emotion, which sounded strange considering her choice of words.

Quill smiled. "You are partly right, but I'm afraid you speak of our cousins. We do not rape, at least not typically. Annaset requires strength, and to rape the weak belittles her word."

"I couldn't agree more," Thea said, looking directly at Bronas. The big warrior shifted uneasily on his feet but said nothing.

Quill picked up on the tension but ignored her comment, continuing his dialog. "We are a small clan called the Caska with various settlements throughout the Varos Mountains and even beyond. We left our cousins long ago when we came to know Annaset, the true and only god. Our glorious god craves more blood, and that brought us here, to new lands, to new flesh. You are an intricate part of a great honor."

Cat spat at Quill's feet, her nose still bleeding. "Honor? You know nothing of it."

"Honor is not a stone structure, unmoving, it is a vast river...twisting and turning, always finding the easiest route. It depends on your perspective you see. For us, honor is whatever is necessary to appease our Goddess. And I'm quite sure that that concept conflicts with yours. We care little for *your* honor. You will all be some of the first non-Caskan to see this temple. And you will be some of the first to spill your blood before its altar."

Jana began to weep, and Thea's heart sunk. What was she going to do? Were they really going to die in some cold desolate place, sacrificed to some unknown god? She had no comforting words for Jana, as she had none for herself. Then suddenly a thought came to her, and she smiled. "You may kill us," she said. "But either way, nothing will stop Brant from finding you, and killing you. The day you took us, was the day you died."

Quill held his hands out wide in a placating gesture. "Perhaps," he agreed, "but the beauty of that is simple. My death at the hand of this great warrior would please Annaset greatly. I will sit in honor at her side. You see, either way, I win."

Morella laughed for the first time, thus far her only lapse in stoicism. "Your zealotry is comical. How many men, how many cultures, have died under the same guise? Everyone thinks they are right in their actions, and those actions are somehow sanctioned by their god. The history of those cultures alone proves that none of them were accurate in their beliefs. How can they all be wrong? How can they all be right? Mathematically it is not possible. Which proves that you to, just as they were, are false in your beliefs."

Quill took in her words before speaking. "Annaset will enjoy your blood as well. She feeds on all strengths, and yours is quite unique. It is a flavor she rarely tastes. Now, enough talk, prepare to march."

And with that, they were led from the small camp, leaving behind a garrison of thirty men. The trail was steep and strewn with rocks, the looming mountains before them rising like an attacking beast. That's how they felt, like defenseless pray led to the slaughter.

***

Thankfully Gorrin spotted the scout before the Northmen saw him. The man was perched high on a rock facing out towards the inlet, an unlit lookout fire prepared and ready to warn the garrison of someone approaching. Luckily for them the man was gazing out to the waters, expecting an enemy to come by ship, not land, and he never saw the small group sneak towards him.

Gorrin was ahead of them scanning the terrain for sign. A'rakis had peeled around the north side of the ridge, scouting further head. The land was inhospitable, covered with rocks and dense short trees and brush. At times they had to literally climb up outcroppings to find a clear path before them. Other than narrow animal trails, there seemed to be no paths traversing the steep hills flanking the inlet. Gorrin had snuck back to the main group informing them of the scout not so far off. Captain Tovar had said they would likely have scouts placed along the inlet. They waited a little while longer for A'rakis to return.

"Looks like you were correct," Gorrin whispered. "There is a scout near the top of the ridge beyond."

"Should we go around him?" Baccus asked. Their party consisted of Jarak, Brant, Gorrin, Tovar, A'rakis, Rizza, as well as Jarak's four sentinels. Their plan was to locate the camp and scout the location. They needed to know how many men were there, whether or not Cat and the others were their prisoners, and the basic defensive armaments. If necessary, they would return to the ship for more men. If not, they would devise a way to free the women.

"Can you kill him?" Brant asked.

"I think I can get a clear shot," Gorrin said.

"I did find a rough trail on the other side of the ridge," A'rakis said. "My guess is it's the path the scout uses to return to base."

They all looked at Jarak, who finally nodded. "I don't want a scout behind us," Jarak reasoned. "Take him out. Brant, you and A'rakis sneak around to the northern side of the ridge in case Gorrin misses or is spotted and he tries to run."

Brant nodded and ran off with A'rakis, carefully making their way through the short trees and boulders to the far side of the ridge. Gorrin left, silently working his way up the ridge face, picking his path carefully. The southern side of the ridge was steep, and the hunter had to skirt east to find a traversable path to the ridge's peak. With the patience earned from hunting his entire life, Gorrin crept closer and closer, using the rocks and sporadic trees and brush for cover. Finally the man was in sight, his back to him as he gazed out at the water's beyond. The hunter had to pause a moment as he took in the scene before him. The blue sky was dazzling, its beauty accentuated by the rocky cliffs and green trees, all looking down into clear calm waters the color of dark turquoise. It was stunningly beautiful, creating a strange dichotomy in Gorrin's mind as his eyes turned to the man before him that he was about to kill. It saddened him more than he wanted to admit, like the blood spilt would ruin the land's beauty.

Sighing softly he slowly nocked an arrow, rising above a low lying shrub as he drew back and lifted the bow. Exhaling slowly, he steadied his arm and looked down the steel tipped shaft. Releasing the arrow, the bow twanged and the man shifted suddenly to the sound. But it was just a twitch of movement before the arrow struck him in the back, catapulting him forward where he tumbled down the rocky embankment, somersaulting over the edge to fall the hundred paces to the rocky ground below.

Gorrin ran to the edge to make sure the man was dead. Once he was sure, he left and joined the others, all of them moving east around the ridgeline to meet up with Brant and A'rakis. The Dy'ainian scout found them as they traveled a narrow game trail to join them.

"Keep an eye out for more look outs," Jarak said, his green eyes finding Gorrin and A'rakis. "I doubt they have another, but let's play it safe."

Gorrin and A'rakis nodded and they ran ahead, Gorrin's strung bow in his right hand. Everyone else followed slowly, keeping low and moving carefully. They were not sure how far the camp was. According to Tovar, the inlet meandered close to ten miles from the mouth. They were prepared to spend the night if need be, but hoped it wouldn't be necessary.

The movement was slow going, their path dropping down to narrow gullies created by small streams dumping into the inlet, then back up to steep rock ridges that dropped straight down into the water. Sometimes there was no path at all. They talked briefly about it and wondered how the scout returned to base camp. They reasoned that he must have had a small boat somewhere along the inlet where the rough path had disappeared. A'rakis had followed the narrow trail to the water's edge, returning quickly with no evidence of a boat. But he did not look long and perhaps they had disguised the craft in the brush. Either way, they saw no continuing path along the inlet's edge. At one point, Brant had to climb a steep cliff and lower a rope, using his prodigal strength to help lift each man as they climbed, taking some strain off Brant's arms as they used their legs to scurry up the rock face. It was near dark when Gorrin and A'rakis appeared before them, the shadowy evening unable to mask Gorrin's bright smile.

"We found the camp," A'rakis said. "Follow us, and when we break free of the trees, stay low. We will crawl to the edge of the ridge. Make sure your armor is hidden so the remaining light doesn't reflect off of it." Everyone had made sure to minimize their armor, keeping just the necessary components for minimal protection and maximum movement. The sentinels kept just their chest plates, long dark wool tunics worn over it. Brant's armor was dark leather and steel and offered him little hindrance. Baccus and Jarak also kept just their chest plates, Jarak having a harder time hiding the brilliant Kul-brite steel. But he did not want to leave it on the ship. It was too valuable, and its lightweight and impenetrable protection was something he figured he would need. Tovar and Rizza wore light chainmail under their tunics and cloaks.

Clearing the tree line, the group followed the two scouts' lead and crouched low, slowly creeping across the rocky ridgeline, heading for what looked like the edge. Like a stalking cat, Gorrin and A'rakis dropped to their bellies and started to crawl over the rocks, the others following their lead. At the edge they stopped as the others joined them.

Below them was a natural gulch, a fast moving stream cascading down the valley amongst a network of fallen trees, brush, and moss covered boulders. Across the stream in a natural clearing was nestled the encampment, sandwiched between the water on the west and a large rock face on the east. From their vantage point they could see that the small wood buildings were surrounded by an earthen wall topped with stout logs stacked on top of one another. There was a closed gate made of thick timbers and inside cook fires flared brightly in the evening gloom. They saw a few shadows move about, and heard the distance voices of the occupants, but the distance and darkness proved ineffective at gathering more accurate information.

"It is going to get too dark to see," Baccus murmured.

"They are fortified," Jarak added, "that much we *can* see."

"Do you think they are down there?" Gorrin whispered, looking sidelong at Brant.

"There is only one way to find out," Brant replied, his gaze as cold as the evening breeze.

CHAPTER NINE

The morning came quick for the anxious group, the frosty night air licking at their skin and the tumultuous thoughts of what was to come eluding a solid night of sleep. They couldn't risk a fire so they found some narrow flat ground nestled against a rock edge, the other side shielded by dense trees and brush. The ridgeline blocked the wind coming down the inlet, so they remained relatively comfortable in their wool blankets and warm clothes.

Before the sun was even up the next morning, Gorrin and A'rakis had disappeared into the darkness. They had planned on the two scouts getting closer to get a better look at the encampment while the others watched the morning routine of the men below from the ridgeline.

It resembled a typical camp. Men were up cooking breakfast and preparing for the day. The first shock came when they saw a group of fur clad men leave through the gate to work on a half-completed ship near the water's edge. With them was a giant, a creature they had never seen before.

"What is that?" Brant whispered to Jarak, thinking he would know.

"That beast is bigger than the Varga. It can be only one thing, although I've only read about them," Jarak answered softly. "I think they are called peak dwellers, a distant cousin of the Varga that are very, very rare. It is said they live high in the peaks of the mountain ranges of the north, impervious to the cold."

"Won't be so easy to kill," Rizza muttered in awe of the great beast. "Look at how strong it is."

The big creature lifted a huge rough sawn beam by itself and placed it in position on the boat frame. The men around it looked half its size.

"If it bleeds, it can be killed," Brant said.

No one said anything, not feeling the confidence of the swordsman. They continued to watch carefully, trying to discern anything of value.

"I count twenty five different men," Baccus finally said. "I could be missing some in the buildings, but my best guess is they have between twenty and thirty men."

"I see no women," Jarak added.

"Must not be a permanent settlement," Rizza said. "Perhaps it's just a raiding camp."

They continued their observations, talking quietly of tactics and ideas, until Gorrin arrived. A'rakis appeared from the morning shadows soon after. It was nearly mid-day, and they were beginning to worry for the scouts. They congregated back at their sleeping area, away from the ridgeline and the ears of the enemy.

"What did you find?" Brant eagerly asked. All the waiting had gnawed at whatever will was keeping him from storming down into the camp with his blade drawn.

"I was able to climb to the closer ridge above their camp," he began. "I counted twenty seven men. And I can only assume you saw that giant," Gorrin added. "I've never seen anything like it."

"It's a peak dweller, very rare," Jarak added.

Gorrin sighed and shook his head in amazement. "Well the thing is strong, that's for sure. The wall around the camp is sturdy enough, but it would be easy to climb. I saw no sign of any women," he added finally. Brant was flexing his jaw, but he said nothing, waiting for Gorrin to finish. "I did find a worn path north of the camp. I followed it for a few miles and it seemed to rise towards the mountains. It had been recently traveled by a large group."

"How long ago?" Jarak asked.

"Best guess would be a day ago."

Baccus looked at Jarak. "You think they took the women away?"

"I don't know," he said in frustration.

"I snuck around to the northern side of the wall, where most of the buildings are built," A'rakis said. "I climbed the wall quickly to get a better view of the structures. There were half a dozen smaller wood buildings and a few larger ones. It would be a good place to start a distraction fire."

"What do you want to do?" Tovar asked, his eyes finding each man.

"I see two choices before us," Jarak began. "We attack the camp. Or we follow the path?"

"There is a third," Rizza added. "We go back to the ship and bring in more men."

Brant was shaking his head. "We do not have time for that. If they took the women into the mountains, we need to leave now."

"But we don't know if they did that," Tovar reasoned.

"Exactly," Brant said, his tone hard. "That's why we need to kill these men and then follow the trail. It's the only way to know for sure. Besides," he continued. "We do not want an armed garrison between us and the enemy that left into the mountains."

No one said anything for a few moments as they took in the swordsman's words. Finally it was Jarak who spoke. "I agree with Brant." His intense hazel eyes found each man. "We need a plan of attack."

It was near dark before they put their plan into action. Luckily for them, the garrison was not expecting an attack and lacked defensive procedures. Fires were lit in the courtyard where the men sat and ate, drinking from wine skins. The gate was closed, but it was obvious they were not expecting an attack.

Under the cover of darkness, Gorrin moved like a shadow to the camp's wall just to the left of the gate, climbing the dirt and wood structure easy enough. A'rakis did the same on the right hand side of the gate. By this time, night had descended, and again luck was in their favor as thick clouds covered the starry night. Gorrin stayed low on the rough wood planks that lined the inside of the wall, hiding in the shadows, watching the men below in the courtyard. He only saw a few bows amongst the boisterous lot, which was good. He couldn't see in the darkness, but assumed that A'rakis was in a similar position opposite him on the far wall. The giant was there, sitting on a huge natural rock that rose from the ground. There was no fire before it and the huge creature was gnawing on the carcass of an entire deer. The beast was fearsome looking close up, and Gorrin's heart pounded with adrenaline as he thought of the fight to come. None of the enemy were prepared for what was about to happen.

Hiding in the woods thirty yards before the gate was Tovar, Baccus, and two of the sentinels, Lamwin and a thick necked soldier called Tevus. Their steel was drawn and they waited low in the shadows. According to Jarak, the signal would be obvious. They had to hope that Gorrin, Brant, and A'rakis, could get the gate open.

Brant was pushing aura energy into his hands and legs as he worked his way slowly down the rock face. The wall was nearly unclimbable, but when Brant pushed power into his hands, he could literally hold onto any crevice or cranny, no matter how small or narrow. He picked a path down the rock face that dropped far away from any fires in the courtyard. If things went well, he would drop into the shadows behind a building. He had half way to go.

Jarak wiped the sweat from his brow as he looked at the camp's wall from the concealment of the tall grass at the rear of the settlement. They had to skirt along the water's edge to the back of the small garrison. The other two sentinels, Garrad and Thorgar, along with Rizza, crouched with him in the tall grass.

"I need to get closer," Rizza whispered. "I cannot feel their auras yet." Jarak however, was much more powerful, and he could draw on the Northmen's auras even at their present distance.

"When we get to the wall you should feel them," Jarak said. "Ready?"

They nodded and Jarak ran from the grass to the edge of the dirt and wood wall, dropping low into the shadows created by the looming structure. As planned, Jarak drew from the Northmen's auras, forming a current of wind under his legs launching him up into the air. He reached the top of the wall where he grabbed the log and climbed over. The wood buildings rose higher than the wall and the thatch roofs shielded him from the men in the courtyard beyond. But it was so dark that he doubted they would see him anyway.

His eyes caught movement to his right as a Northman strode towards him along the narrow wood plank path that lined the walls interior. Jarak swore, unsure how to proceed. They had seen no torches on the wall, thus assuming there were no lookouts. It looked like they were wrong in that assessment. If he was spotted, they would lose the element of surprise.

There was a spell that he had mastered several years ago but had yet used in combat. Thinking quickly, it seemed the right time to try it. He had already drawn a large amount of energy from the men, storing it in his tarnum. Each Mage's tarnum was different, a focal point within himself to store energy taken from people around them. For Jarak, his tarnum was the pit of his stomach, and as the lookout neared he pulled energy form that point, and used his mind to manipulate the energy into a physical construct. This spell allowed the Mage to coat his body with the energy, the energy taking on the appearance of the Mage's surroundings.

Within a few heartbeats Jarak's form disappeared into the wood and earth wall next to him. If one looked very carefully, you might see a shimmer, especially when the Mage moved. But sitting still allowed the Mage to be virtually invisible.

The Northman neared and Jarak slowly moved his hand to the knife at his side, drawing the blade slowly, the energy masking the silver steel just as it did his body.

Suddenly Rizza spoke from the other side of the wall, curious as to what was taking Jarak so long to throw the rope over the edge. Jarak swore silently. The Northman reacted with confusion, thinking perhaps he was hearing things. Just as he leaned over the wall to investigate, Jarak struck, leaping from his crouch with his knife flashing quickly. The man heard the movement and turned, but it was too late. Jarak's knife slammed into the side of his neck, and up into his brain stem, killing him instantly. Softly, Jarak lowered the heavy body to the wood planks.

Quickly, he pulled the coiled rope from his belt and threw it over the edge, wrapping one end around a wood piling sticking up from the wall. Within moments the three others had climbed silently over the wall.

Rizza glanced down and saw the body. "Oh," he said, a bit chagrined. "I didn't see him."

"I didn't either. Prepare yourself," Jarak said. "They should be in position soon enough."

Both of the Mages turned on their towds, drawing energy from the men in the courtyard. Jarak's was nearly full, and it took him only moments. Once Rizza was done, he looked at Jarak, his expression saying *ready*.

Rizza was not a powerful Mage like Jarak, but he had mastered several spells over the years, each a product of survival on the open seas. He could conjure and control wind, a necessary skill as a smuggler. Another skill was his ability to conjure fire, which when being attacked by pirates was quite helpful. After all, all sailors were afraid of fire.

Both of the Mages drew energy from their tarnums and focused it on molding it into explosive balls of fire. They were partly shielded by the buildings, but nonetheless did not want to be noticed too early. With a nod of Jarak's head they tossed their flaming spheres onto several of the buildings near the courtyard, the balls exploding in fire sending tendrils of hot flames all around.

Rizza and Thorgar ran off to the right along the wood planks towards the front gate while Jarak and Garrad ran left, stopping where the wall was built into the rocky cliff face. There was a set of rough stairs there and they leapt down with weapons drawn. By this time the fires were roaring and they could hear screaming as the Northmen were trying to figure out what was happening.

Brant dropped the last several paces to the ground just as the fires erupted nearby. Crouching low he ran to a pile of wood stacked high along the edge of the courtyard. The Northmen were so busy trying to figure out why two of the buildings suddenly exploded in flame that none were looking his way. He drew his sword and looked over the top of the split logs towards the main gate. The giant was standing now and looking towards the fires.

As the flames grew fiercer the light from the fire spread further like the rays of the sun in the early morning. Glancing up, Brant could just make out the shape of Gorrin on the wall's walkway. He was crouched, his bow drawn at full draw, the sharp point of the arrow aimed at the giant. Looking left, he noticed A'rakis shuffle low along the shadowed path along the wall near the gate.

That had been the plan. Once the fires started, Gorrin, A'rakis, and Brant would concentrate on getting the gate open and killing the giant, all the while Jarak and the others would converge on the confused Northmen.

Brant saw Gorrin crouch on one knee, his bow drawn back. The hunter's arrow struck the giant in the chest and the beast stumbled slightly, looking down at the quivering shaft trying to discern what had just stung him. Brant wasted no time and ran from the cover of the wood pile, his blade held low. Two Northmen were in his line and he cut them down quickly, angling for the giant's huge legs. Two more arrows struck the giant and that's when the thing roared and yelled something unintelligible, likely a warning in the Northmen's language, or the giant's own, Brant could not tell. A'rakis hung from the walls inner path and dropped to the ground below, his sword instantly in his hand.

The huge beast reached down and grabbed a giant club, the end capped in spiked steel. Brant came in fast, Fuzing at the last moment, his razor sharp blade cutting the tendons on the back of the surprised giant's knee. Roaring, the giant stumbled when its right leg gave out, simultaneously swinging the club around its body, swatting blindly at its assailant. Sprinting forward with great speed, Brant moved inside the swing, avoiding it entirely. He was so close to the beast that he could smell the thing, it's odor of sweat and its stinking furs nearly overwhelming.

It was then that A'rakis attacked the giant's flank, his sword sweeping in to cut the beast on his left arm, just above its elbow. His sword barely cut through the skin, but it was enough to enrage the beast, who snapped its left fist out, striking the scout in the chest. A'rakis flew several paces away to tumble across the ground and hit the rock wall, his head striking the stone hard.

Brant rammed his blade straight into the creature's fur covered lower back, the fiery blade sinking itself half way to the hilt. The giant arched its back and howled in agony, two more arrows striking its exposed chest. Brant yanked the blade free as the beast fell forward onto both of his hands, growling in severe agony. But it wasn't done yet, and with a great burst of anger the creature turned its huge body and roared defiantly, a cone of freezing frost shooting towards Brant. The swordsman was completely caught off guard, having no idea that the beast had such powers. Diving to the side he hoped to avoid the blast of freezing air.

By this time the Northmen had figured out that the fires were a distraction, and that they were being attacked. Weapons were brandished and they looked for their assailants, finding Brant's flaming blade easy enough as well as spotting Gorrin with his bow, the bright orange glow of the fires lighting the entire courtyard and the wall beyond. A'rakis was out of the fight, dead, or unconscious against the rock wall.

It was at this time that Jarak, Rizza, and the two sentinels attacked from the flanks, silently appearing from the shadows and cutting into the astonished men. Six Northmen died quickly before they figured out what was happening. Steel clashed as the invaders fought furiously to weaken the ranks of the defenders.

Gorrin saw the Northmen run closer to him, two with drawn bows. Without thinking he jumped off the wooden plank dropping three paces to the muddy ground below. Arrows thudded into the wood where he had been and he hit hard, dropping low and rolling over his right shoulder to try and lessen the impact of the drop. Pain lanced through his shoulder and his bow was ripped from his hand. Drawing his blade, he turned to face the defenders.

Jarak's Kul-brite blade cut through armor and flesh as he maneuvered through the Northmen. Garrad was just to his left protecting his flank, his sword slicing left and right as he fought furiously to stay next to his king. Each swing of Jarak's blade was fueled by the desire to see Cat once again. Maybe she was inside one of the buildings? That thought alone drove him forward. Growling, his ripped his blade from the chest of a dead Northman, barely getting the weapon back into play to block a powerful swing of a wide shouldered enemy. Jarak pushed energy from the mage stone embedded in the sword's pommel, directing lavender fire to erupt from the blade. The king was no Merger, but his Kul-brite sword, given to him by his father the night he died, enabled him to enact a spell similar to when a Merger Fuzes. It was short lived of course, at least until the stone's power was empty. The Northman's eyes widened and he stepped back in shock, not reacting fast enough as Jarak's blade reversed direction and cut him from his lower hip, across his body, to his right shoulder. The warrior fell over, nearly cut in half.

Freezing cold licked Brant's right foot but he was successful in avoiding the brunt of the blast. Rolling to his feet, he nearly fell as he realized his lower leg was numb. Growling in anger he pulled more energy from the ground through his feet, the cold instantly evaporating as new energy flooded his body. The giant thought he had a quick reprieve, hoping to get to his feet so he could fight. But his wounds were too serious and Brant's speed turned out to be his downfall. Brant took two leaping steps and jumped high, his blue blade arcing down towards the giant's head as the creature struggled to right himself from all fours. His blade flashed, the giant's huge head dropping to the ground just as Brant landed. A heartbeat later and the giant's colossal headless body thudded to the ground followed by a great gout of blood from the beast's severed neck.

"Brant!"

The swordsman looked to the gate and saw Gorrin fighting off two men, a third cutting across the courtyard to join his comrades. The hunter was in trouble. Brant's hand flashed and his dagger flipped through the air striking the running man in the thigh. He screamed and fell hard as Brant raced towards Gorrin, his sword cutting through the downed man's back as he flew by. Gorrin was hard pressed, a huge Northman pounding him down with powerful strikes, the second getting ready to finish him off by lunging in at his exposed flank. Brant cut the back of the attacking man's legs, his Kul-brite sword nearly cutting both legs off at the knee, his follow through cutting the second man's head off.

"We need to get the gate open!" Brant yelled as he ran to the gate with an exhausted Gorrin just behind. Brant heard commotion behind him and he turned to face three charging men. "Open the gate! I'll take care of these!"

Gorrin ran to the wooden structure and lifted the heavy wood beam from the locking position, all the while the sound of steel on steel echoing behind him. He pushed the gate open and immediately Tovar, Baccus, and the two sentinels raced inside.

The three men facing Brant were already dead by the time Baccus and the others were at his side. Baccus smiled at Brant, and together they charged ahead into the throng of amassing Northmen, the other four men trying to keep up.

Rizza fought with two short swords, his body moving expertly through the Northmen. Steel sought his flesh but he eluded its sting all the while delivering surgical cuts into the enemy. He had quickly killed two when suddenly he and Thorgar were faced with two men bearing crossbows. Thinking quickly he drew the last energy from his tarnum and reacted with the spell he knew the best, hastily flinging a huge gust of wind at the men. Their weapons jerked as the bolts were released. The wind struck the bolts first and then the Northmen, catapulting the two warriors to their backs. One bolt was knocked off course and narrowly missed Rizza's shoulder. The second bolt missed Thorgar's chest but struck him hard in the upper arm, the impact causing him to drop his sword. Rizza wasted no time and raced forward, cutting down both men as they scrambled to regain their footing and draw their blades.

Rizza looked up, blood and sweat dripping from his scarred face. If one didn't know better, he might be mistaken for a walking corpse, his damaged face covered in blood making him look quite forbidding. Four Northmen were around them and Rizza eyed them defiantly, moving back to stand next to the wounded sentinel. Thorgar roared and snapped the head off the back of the bolt, ripping it free from his flesh. Then he picked up his sword in his left hand looking at Rizza with fire in his eyes.

Brant and Baccus fought like enraged animals, their Kul-brite blades a blur of annihilating steel, the silver blades flashing in the fire's light as they dropped man after man to the bloody ground. Northern steel angled in at them, but they were always there to block and pivot, their own blades parting enemy flesh like a skilled butcher cutting his wares for sale.

Back by the fires Jarak sliced his blade across a man's throat, simultaneously drawing the last of the energy from his tarnum as he saw Rizza in trouble before him. Quickly, he formed a powerful fire whip with his right hand and lashed it out, the intense energy snapping the ten paces and wrapping around a man's neck. With a thought, Jarak willed the rope closed, pushing more energy into the magical appendage and popping the man's head off as a result, the gruesome wound cauterized by the intense heat of the rope. Jerking the whip back again, he snaked it out and wrapped it around a second attacker, all the while Rizza and Thorgar had already engaged the other two Northmen. This time Jarak didn't direct as much energy into the rope, not wanting to cut the man in half. Pulling back hard the power of the rope jerked the man across the ground to tumble at Jarak's feet. The rope was burning him badly and he was screaming in pain, the sound cut off instantly as Jarak snapped his foot forward, striking the man in the head and knocking him unconscious. Looking up, he saw Rizza and Thorgar had killed the last of the Northmen attacking them. Garrad pulled his blade free from a man's gut and moved next to Jarak, sweat and blood coating his face.

Looking about, they saw Baccus and Brant kill the last remaining men, a smattering of at least ten bodies scattered around them.

They met in the middle of the courtyard surrounded by the dead and the dying. The two buildings that were on fire were burning bright and it wouldn't be long before they were consumed by the flames destruction. Everyone was breathing deeply, their breath white steam in the cool night air.

Jarak was dragging the unconscious man by the magical rope. "Let's see to our wounded. Brant and Baccus, check the buildings for any sign of the girls." Then he kicked the Northman in the side. "It's time to get some answers."

Chapter Ten

Quill had been right. Thea had never been so tired. As the small party progressed closer to the spiky teeth of the massive Varos Mountains, the trail became increasingly more difficult. Rocky ascending paths flanked by sporadic trees turned into snow covered narrow trails surrounded by towering growths of ice covered stone. It was cold, colder than she had ever been. The Northmen pushed them hard, stopping for food and water, knowing that they needed the nourishment to continue the arduous trek.

The first night they had slept under a huge slab of stone, the escarpment offering some protection from the light scattering of snow that fell that night. Thea noticed that nestled up against the rock face was a large pile of split wood. Clearly the Northmen used this as a base camp and had prepared for such inevitabilities. Their morale was low and the women spoke very little, most too tired for idle speech.

Several fires were lit from the dry wood and the men went about their camp duties with practiced proficiency. It wasn't long before a meal of salted oats, hard bread, and water was served. Quill had ordered the removal of the rope as there was no where they could go. Besides, they had little energy to run off into the dark snowy night.

Orna sat down on a rock that had been placed by the fire. She spooned food into her mouth, her hard gaze looking at Thea. Jana, Cat, and Morella sat opposite her, along with three other Northmen she did not know. There were three other fires burning in the clearing with the rest of the men huddled close to the hot flames.

"Tell me of this Brant," Orna said.

Thea looked at her and saw that she was curious. "What do you want to know?"

"We heard he is Ull Therm. What is this term?" she asked.

"Do you know of the Schulg?"

"Nomads," she answered, "like us, but live in the grasslands."

"Yes. They fight for money and glory, in the pits. It's like an arena. Most often they take slaves and train them to fight. For every five you kill in the pit, you get a brand burned into your flesh. If you get six brands, you become Ull Therm. It means killer, or something like that."

"But he fights in the pits no more?"

"No. He farms."

Orna snorted like she said a joke. "He is still a killer."

"You shall find that out soon enough."

Her smile disappeared and she ate another spoonful of oats. Then she leaned forward, closer to Thea. "You really think he is following us?"

"Yes. He will never stop."

"Even when you are dead," she sneered, "your blood pooling at Annaset's feet."

This time it was Thea who leaned forward, her eyes equally hard. "Even then, more so in fact."

Orna sat back and smiled. "I am not so easy to kill."

Thea also smiled, trying to get under her skin by not showing her fear. "We shall see."

Cat had been listening to the conversation as she ate her food. When she was done, she set the bowl down and looked at Orna. "Why do you live here, in this inhospitable place?"

"To suffer is to win honor for Annaset. It is difficult to live here," she replied. "It makes one tough, like the mountain itself. Annaset laughs at luxuries. They weaken you. We live here to serve her, to be strong."

Morella was eating small spoonful's of the warm oats, trying to savor the nourishment and warmth in the freezing cold. But she nearly spit some out, chuckling at Orna's words. "Your ignorance is astonishing," she said, caring little of her harsh words. "You've created a god to justify your living conditions. It makes you feel better about suffering. Your god is a crutch. Her very presence keeps you here, living as you do, can't you see that?"

Thea was looking back and forth from Morella to Orna, half expecting the huge woman to lunge across the fire and beat her to death. But the warrior surprised her. "Annaset will enjoy your sacrifice. You have courage, a trait she admires."

"Are we really going to die for her?" Jana asked, speaking up for the first time. Her voice had lost her usual luster for life. She sounded as if her death was inevitable.

"There are ways to live through the trials," Orna added. "But they are not easy and require great courage." Then she looked at Thea. "I hope you survive," she added. "I want to buy you as a slave." She left it at that, her leering gaze making her intent quite obvious.

"You mean if we survive, we will still be slaves?' Cat asked.

"Of course."

Their prospects did not look good, and everyone stared into the fire, the heat emanating from it doing little to warm their chilled spirits.

***

Brant tossed a bucket of icy water on the unconscious Northman. The man was tied tight to a wood chair and he jerked violently awake when the water hit him. Brant and Jarak were in one of the structures that had not been burned, the interior lined with crude shelves stacked with dried food, jars capped with wax, bags of grain, as well as barrels of water and foul-tasting ale. It was a storeroom. The wounded were in another room as Tovar, who had some healing knowledge, saw to them. Rizza and Gorrin were searching the rest of the compound for anything useful.

They had searched the entire compound and did not find the girls. But the room in which they had been kept was still standing, the chains, manacles, and chamber pots making the buildings purpose quite obvious.

Brant wasted no time, knowing that the girl's survival was likely dependent on it. "Where are the Dy'ainian women?" he said, his tone like ice.

The Northman was thick necked with long reddish hair and pale skin. His eyes were black like coal, and he sneered at Brant with undisguised defiance. "They are gone." His accent was thick and the same as the woman's he had met way back at Bygon the night that Jana and Thea had been taken.

"We know that," Jarak said, stepping next to Brant. They had no time to waste and he was just as eager for answers as Brant. "I will offer you five hundred gold dracks and a pardon for your crimes if you tell us where they are."

Brant looked at him sidelong as if he was crazy. But he said nothing. Even the man paused for a moment. But it was only a moment. "You are weak," he spat. "Annaset spits on you." And then the man spit, his spittle hitting Jarak in the chest.

Jarak calmly responded. "I am about to cause you great pain. Prepare yourself."

The man's expression hardened as if he was preparing himself for the worst. Jarak raised his right hand and orange fire sprouted from it, fiery tendrils spinning around his fist. Then with a thought he sent a thin tendril from the vortex, the rope-like appendage undulating towards the man like a wiggling worm. As it neared the man it turned a dull orange color and Jarak paused it inches from his ear. "This is what's going to happen. I will send this thing into your ear, and as it digs deeper, I will slowly heat it up. Inch by inch I will burn holes throughout your brain. But you will not die. It will cause you more pain than you can imagine, and when I'm done, I will leave you a slobbering mess of the man you once were. You will need help to take a shit. Ready?"

The man's eyes were wide and he was shaking. He tried to violently move his head back and forth as the thin orange rope neared, but it found him nonetheless, shooting like an arrow right into his ear. The Northman screamed and thrashed about as smoke rose from his ear. "Now," Jarak said. "I'm going to send more energy into your head. I know it's hard to believe, but the pain will become more intense." More smoke gushed from the wound and the man howled, his entire body vibrating madly as if that action alone would dislodge the fire rope inching its way through his skull.

"I...will...tell!" he screamed. Instantly Jarak flicked his finger and the rope pulled from his ear to disappear into the burning globe around his fist. The man was sweating and spit dripped from his mouth as he panted with pain and fear.

He was hunched over and moaning when Jarak reached out and lifted his head to face him. "Tell me," he growled. "The damage I've done so far is minimal, although you will never hear from that ear again. But trust me, it can get much worse. Tell me."

"They went...into...the mountains," he mumbled.

"Where?"

"North...there is a trail."

"Where does it go?"

"To Rumorga."

"What is this Rumorga?" Jarak asked.

The man paused, trying to regain his senses. "Temple to Annaset."

"Your god?" Brant asked.

"Yes."

"How far?" Jarak asked.

"Three days."

"When did they leave?" Brant asked, leaning closer to the man.

"Yesterday morning."

Brant stepped back. "They have nearly two days on us."

Jarak paced in frustration. "We can't leave now. It's dark. We would get lost, or freeze."

Brant growled in frustration. "Let's get winter supplies. We leave at first light."

Jarak let out a deep breath, trying to calm his frantic nerves. All he could think about was Cat marching deep into the mountains, chained as a prisoner, surrounded by grim faced Northmen. "What do you want to do with him?"

Brant turned, lunging towards the Northmen as he drew his knife. Faster than a blink he rammed his blade up through the man's chin and into his brain. Quickly he withdrew the Kul-brite steel, blood gushing over the man's chest. Jarak just stared at him.

"I said I would kill them all, and I meant it." And with that, he left the room, his bloody knife still in his hand.

The next morning, before the sun's light began to warm the cold night air, they left at a slow jog. There were plenty of furs and food at the camp, and they each filled their pack with supplies they might need. Thorgar's wound kept him behind, despite his protests. And Gorrin's shoulder had swollen up and turned a nasty shade of yellow and purple. He couldn't even move it and he most certainly couldn't draw his bow or swing a sword. He was furious, but was resigned to stay behind with Thorgar. A'rakis had not yet woken and his shallow sporadic breaths worried the others. It was unclear whether he would make it. There was shelter and plenty of food and water to hold the three until they returned.

Brant and Baccus were leading as they pushed hard through the rocky terrain. It was mid-day when the temperature dropped and they started getting into snow, their footing more precarious as they moved forward at a steady pace. Not everyone could run like the two swordsmen, and soon Jarak and the others dropped behind, with the three remaining sentinels staying close by.

Brant was frustrated as he had the power and stamina to race ahead. But he knew that would be folly. He could fall and get hurt, or lose the trail and get separated from the main group. Not to mention that when he found the Northmen he doubted, despite his skill, that he could just waltz in their temple and kill them all. They needed to stay together. They continued on, Brant and Baccus scouting ahead, the rest catching up at a steady pace. The path turned treacherous, each step on ice and snow-covered rocks, huge vistas of stone and ice surrounding them at every turn. Several times they had to traverse narrow ledges to get back on the wider trail, the drop below ending in sure death. But they pushed themselves hard, taking a few rests to eat and hydrate themselves before pressing on.

It was near nightfall when they came across the campsite under the rock escarpment. They quickly inspected the area finding the continuing trail easy enough.

"What do you want to do?" Jarak asked Brant. The fires were at least a day old but they could not be sure. A light dusting of snow had fallen but lucky for them the days and nights had been cold and clear. The trail the Northmen had left behind was easy to see.

Brant looked up at the sky. "We still have a few hours before nightfall."

Baccus joined them along with Tovar. "This is a good location to camp. Do we risk getting caught out in the open?"

"Yes," Brant said adamantly. "Every hour counts. My guess is we have gained some time on them. There is no way that they could move at our speed with such a large group dragging the women with them."

Everyone was exhausted from the day's run, but a fire had been lit inside them and they were going to see their odyssey to the end, no matter how hard it would be. "The weather looks like it will hold," Baccus added. "I agree with Brant."

"We won't be able to save them if we freeze to death," Tovar added as he looked at the stacks of dried wood. "Out there," he added as he indicated the vast mountains around them, "we don't know what we'll find."

"It's a risk I'm going to take, by myself if I have to," Brant replied, his mind already made up.

Jarak sighed. "Well, lead the way then."

They ran on for another few hours, the encroaching shadows making it nearly impossible to see. By this time, the snow-covered trail had narrowed and they were picking their way through a tight path of fallen rocks and scree, the steep cliff sides around them giving them the feeling that they were walking a path that once was a small stream, that had, over hundreds of thousands of years, cut a path into the rocky mountain. The valley floor was no more than two paces wide and littered with snow covered rocks.

Brant paused and looked up, the last bit of sunlight disappearing behind the steep cliffs. "It's going to be dark soon," he muttered, wondering if he had made the right decision.

Everyone stopped behind them and took pulls from their water skins. Jarak was next to him looking up at the narrow patch of darkening sky. "I don't see any clouds," he added. "Perhaps the stars and moonlight will be enough to guide us through."

"Perhaps it's time for the torches," Tovar added as he came up behind them.

Brant was leery to use them, worried that they would be spotted if the Northmen had any scouts about. But they had little choice at this point. "I agree."

Each man had taken a few torches from the storeroom and now they removed one from their packs and lit them with a tinderbox.

The only real solace was they could easily see the worn trail left behind by the group before them. Lifting their torches high, they pushed on.

That night Brant had pushed the men harder than any of them had ever been, and for that tough lot that was saying something. Each man in their group was either a warrior of the highest order, or a man who had lived a hard life, their toughness testament to their survival. Relentlessly, Brant urged them forward, his strength and steadfast will giving them energy when they thought they had no more. They moved quickly over snow covered rocks, the trail lit by torches, the freezing embrace of the icy chill pulling at their resolve. They were trying to make up time. Brant knew that they had to gain on the group, and every hour might count in the end.

The sun had fully set after two hours and still there was no suitable place to camp. Despite the warm furs, fur lined gloves and boots they had taken from the Northmen at the base camp, they still felt the night's cold. It sought them relentlessly, licking their cheeks, working its cold fingers into every nook and cranny. Besides the oppressive cold, the darkness was thick, the moon light hindered by dense clouds that had moved in.

"Brant," Jarak said behind him, panting heavily. "We need to rest."

Brant stopped, knowing he was right. Their surroundings were dismal, offering little shelter. "Where?"

"There is nowhere," Jarak said somberly, "but we need it nonetheless. We will do them no good if we arrive so tired we cannot fight."

The others had caught up and were listening, taking long draws from their water skins. "We have no wood for a fire," Tovar added, "but I'm so tired I think I could sleep in this cold."

"The torches are nearly exhausted," Baccus added.

Brant knew they were right. "Rest here the best you can. I'm going ahead to scout. If I don't come back that means I'm either dead or I found them. Leave at first light either way."

Jarak looked at his friend, his expression draped with worry. "We should stay together," he said, grabbing Brant by the arm and pulling him further down the path, away from the others as they tried their best to lie down in the snow, wool blankets from their packs wrapped around them. They had put the torches out, the only light in the stone and snow gully was Jarak and Brant's torch. "Are you sure about this?"

Brant was grinding his jaw. "No, I'm not sure about anything. But all I can think about is Thea being dragged before some altar and sacrificed to some dark god as a way to seek revenge against me. I cannot sit here and sleep with those images in my mind."

"I understand," Jarak said, "but I can barely lift my legs. We need to be strong when we get there, or it will be all for nothing."

"I am stronger," Brant said, with no hint of boasting. "I have learned many things since we have fought together. I am able to draw power from the earth. It replenishes my strength."

"But you still need sleep."

"Yes, and I will have that luxury when Thea is once again by my side."

Jarak sighed in frustration but knew he could not change the swordsman's mind. "Fine, but be careful. And wait for us." He reached out and shook Brant's hand in the warrior's grip, looking him straight in the eye. "We will get them back, or die trying."

Brant nodded, released his friend's hand, and ran off into the night, his torch light slowly dwindling as he was swallowed up by the thick darkness.

***

It was near the end of the second day when Cat stumbled in front of Thea, dropping to her knee. Thea caught her by the shoulders and quickly Cat made eye contact. "We need to slow them down," she whispered as Thea helped her up.

Thea caught on quickly. They had no idea if Jarak or Brant was following them. But if they were, they needed to buy them time. If not, the only thing they knew for certain was they were heading towards their possible deaths. And it was not far off. If they could slow them down, then perhaps it would give them more time to prepare for an escape. That of course was very unlikely, but at least they would be doing something.

So she put Cat's plan in motion. Just as Cat had done with her, she did to Morella behind her, who followed suit with Jana. Taking turns, each one stumbled and fell, pretending to be exhausted, which wasn't hard as they all were. After half a day of frequent pauses as the men had to drag the women up from the snow, Quill finally stopped the caravan and turned on Cat.

"Do you really think your King followed you across the Bitlis Sea, found our camp, and is now tracking us deep into the mountains? Stop trying to stall the inevitable," he said. His icy tone clearly suggested his frustration.

"We are exhausted," Cat spat. "That's why we are stumbling. We need to rest."

Quill stepped close to her, his face a hand span from hers. "You will rest when you are dead and your blood drips from Annaset's teeth. Now move."

It was late the third day when they began to see signs of life. They had walked across a flat snow-covered ridgeline until they came to a huge stone wall. Thea looked up and was amazed at what she saw. The entire façade of dark stone was carved into the hooded visage of Annaset, her shadowed cowl at least twenty paces up. Her robed figure stood with her legs wide and crudely cut into the stone wall was an opening, the folds of her robe carved so they flowed into the passage. Every ledge of the statue was covered in snow and ice, adding to the ominous depiction.

"Welcome to Rumorga," Quill said.

Once inside Quill led them through various passages cut into the stone, the weight of the rock held up by huge logs and cross beams that spanned the walkways. Torches were lit once inside and as they moved further into the interior of the catacombs, they lit more torches that were embedded into the walls.

Quill parted ways with nothing but a smile and Orna, Bronas, and ten Northmen led them to a large room filled with iron cages, each big enough for two people. Torches were lit and within a few moments braziers were filled with wood and fired. Under the shadows of dancing flames, the girls were shoved into various cages, the doors locked behind them.

Orna stood before them. "Food will come soon," she said. "Get some sleep if you can. Tomorrow you're going to need it."

Then she left, along with the others, and
Bronas brought up the rear, his jeering smile
leaving them to their own dark thoughts.

The next morning they were fed a cold meal
of dried meat and cheese, then left alone until mid-
day when they were escorted by Orna and ten
soldiers through the cold catacombs once again.
Orna shoved them forward through a doorway, the
light of a cloud covered sun shining beyond.

They were pushed further into the hooded
light, and once there, Thea paused, her breath
caught in her throat. They were standing on a
smooth stone floor, every inch of it etched with
swirling designs. The floor was round and huge, at
least thirty paces in diameter. Rocks surrounded
them and loomed over them like attacking beasts.
Some were huge, so tall that if you fell from the top
you would surely perish. Others were short and
stout, with more rocks, small and large alike
jutting from the ground all around the manmade
perimeter they stood upon. All the rocks and cliff
faces formed a circle around them, the stone floor
they were standing on at the bottom. It felt like
you were in an arena.

Looking around her she became even more
frightened. Only Orna and six of the soldier's
remained, the other Northmen having withdrawn
the way they had come, the door shut and locked
behind them. The men stood behind them with
short recurved bows held low in steady hands,
white and black fletched arrows jutting up from
leather quivers on their backs. Another stone
statue of Annaset stood tall before them; the black
rock used to carve her polished and free of ice and
snow. The dark depiction was at least ten paces

high and the focal point of the exterior courtyard.
Thea noticed that the stone all around the statue
was stained red, the reasoning obvious and
causing Thea's heart to pound with fear. Once
they were shoved in the middle, over thirty
Northmen, and a few women, stood up from high
benches carved into the stone around them. Thea
recognized many of them as the same men that
had been with them since they left port in
Gashwin. Others were new faces, especially the
women, who looked just as fierce as the men, with
broad shoulders and long hair ranging from white
to red to light brown. Glancing around her she
saw that there was a veranda type structure ten
paces above the door she had used to enter the
arena, if that's what it was. Standing at the carved
stone railing was Quill, Bronas, and a few other
men and one woman, all staring down at her.
Quill smiled and nodded his head. Thea looked
away to the others surrounding her, her mind
thinking quickly, trying to find a way out of their
predicament. But there wasn't. They were
surrounded. None of the Northmen said a word,
their grim expressions eager in the morning light.
They stood on a raised dais that surrounded them,
the face of the circular wall carved into various
faces of men and women alike, their stern visages
nearly as sinister as the statue before them. The
giant that had traveled with them was there as
well, sitting comfortably on a stone bench double
the size of the others. It was large, made for three
or four giants. Today only one occupied the space.
Thea even spotted the huge bullgon, his gray tough
skin making him nearly invisible against the rocky
backdrop.

Jana began to cry and Thea reached over to hold her hand. "Be strong," she whispered. "Whatever happens, be strong. They cannot take that from you."

Two men emerged from doors flanking the statue, doors that Thea had not even seen before, their black openings blending in with the gray stone around them. They both wore soot colored armor and draped over their pauldrons were long cloaks made of glistening black fur, the hood pulled well over their shadowed features. Other than various knives at their belts, they carried no weapons. Stepping before them they raised their gloved hands in unison, removing their hoods at the same time.

All at once the Northmen surrounding them shouted "Kan'FaRoot". Then they sat down. The two men before her were so pale that it was hard to believe they were alive. Their heads were shaved bald and every inch of their flesh was covered with swirling scars, the intricate designs having long been carved into their flesh. Their lips were bluish in color, from the cold or hued paint Thea could not tell. Gray shadows surrounded their eyes giving them the appearance of a corpse's visage dug up after a week in the ground.

One of the men began to speak in their own dialect and Orna stepped closer to them, translating as he spoke.

"Another great day is upon us!" the man said loudly, his voice carrying easily to the men sitting higher up, the surrounding rocks reflecting his voice. "We have new offerings to Annaset. These women," he continued, pointing to Thea and the other five, "will bring us great honor. It is their strength that she craves, whether it be their courage, or their blood. Let us begin!"

The man who had not spoken stepped forward and looked at them all, his haunting eyes looking deep into them. He pointed to Emy and one of the other young girls that they had met at the base camp. Thea had learned that her name was Silowen, but she liked to be called Sil for short. She couldn't have been more than nineteen years of age.

Orna grabbed them and easily dragged them forward to stand before the man. He looked them over for a few moments before yelling, "Trial by blood!"

For the second time the men surrounding them yelled in their own tongue, the same phrase, "Trial by Blood!"

The door they had entered opened behind them as two men carried out a small wood table. As they passed, Thea looked to see what was on it. There were two knifes, two deep stone bowls, as well as a sand timer. They set the table in front of the two men who Thea could only guess were priests to Annaset. One of them walked back to the side of the huge statue and grabbed a round steel wheel. Thea had not noticed it before, the old gray steel blending in to the dark stone behind it. Slowly the man cranked the wheel and a stone door at the base of the statue shifted and lowered into the floor, creating an opening several paces high and the same wide, the darkness beyond foreboding to say the least. The door was cleverly disguised as the lower portions of Annaset's flowing robes and the seams were nearly invisible to the naked eye.

A few heartbeats later there was a massive roar followed by an explosive black form barreling from the opening, the rattling of heavy chains ripped across stone following closely. The thing was six limbed and reptilian, with a long gray scaled body and tail, the six powerful legs capped in black claws. The four back legs were short and muscular, while the front two were longer with claws that looked more like an eagles. The creature's head was huge and looked lizard-like, but the thing's maw was filled with hundreds of razor sharp teeth.

It ran incredibly fast towards them, its back claws gripping the stone with ease. Two heartbeats later and the chain went taut, stopping the thing in its tracks and jerking it back on its haunches, its upper body lifted in the air as its claws reached out, eager to rip into the flesh no more than eight paces away.

Thea and the others had jumped at the sudden attack, and they all instinctively moved backwards to get away from the creature. They ran into the men behind them, each now with an arrow nocked, just as the creature's chain went tight.

The man who opened the door walked wide of the creature, careful to not get too close. He moved before Emy and Sil. "One of you may live!" he began. "The one who fills their bowl with the most of their own blood by the time the sand stops will live. You will become a slave of the Caska, treated fairly for your courage before Annaset." He paused so they could take in his words, both girls shaking in fright. "The one that loses will be ripped apart and eaten alive by the Taresk," he said, indicating the beast behind him.

Emy began to cry and looked back at Cat and Thea, her entire body shaking. Thea's heart sunk, the reality of what was about to happen hitting her like a punch to the gut. It was Cat who spoke. "Do what you must!" she said, her words hard like stone. "Be strong."

The priest gave them no more time. He reached for the sand timer and turned it upside down, the white sand trickling through the narrow opening to the second chamber.

Both of the girls looked at each other like they did not know what to do. Sil was openly crying as well, her shaking legs barely keeping her standing. "I can't do this," she cried, looking around for someone to help her. Orna had pushed the other women aside as the six bowmen stepped closer, arrows ready if need be. The Taresk was growling and making horrible hissing sounds as if it knew that warm flesh would soon fill its belly.

Emy stumbled forward and grabbed the knife from the table. Tears streaked her dirty face and she looked back at Cat. "What do I do?" She stammered.

Cat was about to speak when Oran slapped her across the face, the power of the strike knocking her to the ground. "Do not speak!" she snapped, her huge body looming over her.

Sil saw Emy grab the knife and did the same, her expression one of horror and fear. She moved close to the bowl and placed the sharp edge on the meaty part of her hand. Then she hesitated, her body heaving with sobs as she looked with despair at the trickling sand and the rearing creature, its maw dripping saliva as it looked at the meat around it with a frenetic desire.

And that was what did it, the thought of the horrible beast ripping her apart giving her the courage to cut herself. She ran the blade across her hand and instantly blood spilled forth to pour into the bowl. She moaned in pain but held her shaking hand over the bowl, careful to not miss the container.

Cat stood up from the ground, her mind reeling and her head dizzy from the strike. Emy was looking back at them in horror, not sure what to do, the knife held low in her shaking hand. Cat could see that Sil was bleeding into the bowl and that there was less than half of the sand left.

"Emy!" she yelled, "cut here!" she added, gesturing to a line on her wrist running parallel with it.

Orna's hand came down again but this time Cat was ready for it, ducking under it she came in close, her palm snapping up into the women's chin. Orna's head jerked hard and she stumbled backwards a few steps. But she did not fall. In fact, she righted herself quickly and smiled, running her hand over the bloody part of her tongue that she had bit. "I like you," she said. "Perhaps I will purchase you instead of the other," she added as she glanced at Thea. "Now, do not interfere again or we will gag you."

Cat ignored her, her frantic gaze returning to Emy. Thea was gripping Cat's hand in disgust at what was happening. Emy had stepped before the bowl, the knife held to her wrist where Cat had told her. She paused, trying to get the nerve to do what needed to be done. There was less than a quarter of the sand left and blood was still dripping from Sil's hand into her bowl.

Emy looked up into the mountain clouds and screamed, not being able to look as she dragged the knife down her wrist. She was so frightened that she had pushed hard, and instantly fiery pain shot through her wrist as blood gushed in pulsing waves of crimson. So much spilled forth that some missed the bowl, and Emy nearly fainted from the wound, her legs buckling beneath her. Instinctively she braced her hands on the table to keep herself standing and the blood from her left hand drenched the table, pouring down the leg to pool on the stone floor.

"No!" Thea screamed, holding Cat's hand tighter.

Cat's eyes were wide with fright, but she said nothing, looking on with terror. Emy righted herself and leaned forward on the table, her left hand falling into the bowl where her blood continued to spill forth in great pulsing founts. The sand was nearly empty, and the two priests moved behind the girls, the crowd watching with silence.

Sil looked over at Emy's bowl and her eye widened with fright as more tears spilled forth. Her cries were incoherent as she grabbed the knife again. Howling in panic she placed the sharp blade on another part of the same palm and sliced it deeply through the flesh. Crying in more fear than agony, she held the blood drenched hand over the bowl, her frenzied eyes glancing back and forth to the timer and Emy's bowl.

Then the sand ran out and the two priests jerked the girls away from the bowls. Two more warriors had entered during the trial and they carried clean white bandages. They took the girls from the priests and handed the bandages to them, both hastily wrapping the strips of cotton around their wounds.

Emy could barely stand, the cotton on her wrists turning red as her wound continued to bleed profusely. Sil was holding her injured hand and looking at the bowls with fear. Hers clearly had less.

The priests inspected the bowls, quickly coming to a consensus. Together they faced the crowd, the growling beast behind them spurred on by the fresh blood. One man raised both hands. "The winner!" he said, lowering one and pointing it at Emy. "Her courage brings us honor!" The same man looked at the man holing Sil. "Annaset demands that she," he added, pointing to Sil, "must pay in blood for her weakness."

And with that the two priests stepped aside as the big warrior dragged the sobbing Sil forward. She was struggling and screaming but she could not free herself from the man's iron grip. The two priests joined the Northman, each getting a hold of one of Sil's arms and holding them out wide. Then without so much as a warning, the warrior behind her lifted his foot and kicked her with tremendous power in the lower back, simultaneously the two priests released her arms. Sil screamed and flew forward towards the creature. With great speed the Taresk lunged forward and lashed out with its long front legs, its hook-like talons gripping her flesh with ease and yanking her body into it. The creature was as large as a big wolf and probably double its weight. Its claws ripped through her flesh with ease, its great mouth clamping down again and again on her flesh, her dying screams echoing off the rock walls. Blood splattered the stones as the beast bathed in it, eating her flesh in great chunks. By the time the thing's mouth found her intestines, her body had stopped thrashing and her screams were no more, the only signs that she was living moments earlier was an occasional spasm of one of her limbs.

Thea and the other girls looked away and Jana almost fainted. Even the stoic Morella was shaking with fear and unable to keep her poise. Cat however, would not look away. She didn't want to forget the abhorrent act she had just witnessed, using it to fuel her own courage.

"Take her away with honor," a priest said to the man holding Emy.

Thea was disgusted at what she had just witnessed, and the fright that was coursing through her body was nearly overwhelming. What was next for them? The death was gruesome, but the most eerie part of the entire repugnant act was the fact that all the people watching had been completely silent. They hadn't cheered, howled, or cried. For some reason, that alone was nearly as bad as the bloody site before her.

One of the priests motioned for Orna to bring the others back into the middle of the dais while a few men took the table away. Again the priest looked at the four remaining women, before pointing to Thea, Jana, and Morella. Orna shoved them forward to stand before the man, the archers behind them with arrows still nocked.

The man walked before them, his eyes appraising them, looking them up and down. Then he spoke as Orna continued to translate. "Trial by pain!"

The crowd surrounding them yelled in response, "Trial by pain!" Then they were deathly silent again, watching, eager for whatever sacrifice was about to come.

Thea was visibility frightened. But when she looked at Jana all she could think about was what was going to happen to the young women. Thea had been her adopted mother for the last ten years and had developed a bond as close as any parent and child; at least that's what she assumed as she had no children of her own. But now she felt hopeless. What was going to happen to them? How could she save her girl? Tears streamed down her cheeks as Jana began to sob. Morella was visibly shaking as well. She had seemed so strong, so emotionless even, but now, facing a horrible death, all that fortitude was now blowing away, caught in a storm that even she was not prepared for.

Six men came from the rear passageway carrying three metal contraptions. They must have been quite heavy as two carried each one and despite their bulk and muscled arms were straining against the weight. When they got to the middle of the dais they set them down, positioning them in a triangle. Thea noticed that the base of the steel structures fit perfectly into a carved section of the floor. Looking at them more carefully they looked like metal weights with places for feet, thick leather straps dangling from the device in various spots. What were these things?

Orna shoved them forward and the six men grabbed them and lifted them into the devices, securing their feet with the leather straps. A long metal support rose up from the weighted section and a strap was secured just under their arms to keep their bodies upright. Once done they backed away and disappeared through the door they had come. Thea shook her feet and tried to move, but she could not. They were all three facing one another equal distance apart. The priests stepped forward again and this time one of them was carrying three long sticks, the ends caped with metal.

The man with the sticks looked at all three. "Annaset favors the courageous and resilient. The winner of this trial will prove her worth. These sticks are capped with steel. Embedded in each end are small razors, the width of the blade capable of delivering shallow cuts. You will beat each other with these until one is left. That one will leave the pit in honor, to be a slave to the Caska. The other two will be fed to the Taresk, whether dead or alive."

Thea looked at Jana and her face was pale. Morella was crying and Thea's heart was pounding in her chest. She looked up to the cliffs, tears streaming down her cheeks, looking for Brant. She needed him now more than anything. She knew that if he was still alive that he was searching for her. But it was now too late. She was alone. Jana was alone.

The priest handed each woman a stick and stepped away. "If you do not fight, you will all be fed to the Taresk." The sticks were long and flexible, the ends weighted by the steel. Even if the ends didn't have razors, they would do considerable damage over time.

Thea was nauseated by the game. It would take many hits to kill someone with the stick, all the while causing them great pain. But I guess that was the point... *Trial by Pain.*

"Thea," Jana said through her sobs, her face a mask of despair, "what are we going to do?"

Thea had no answers. But it was Morella who spoke. "You must kill me quickly," she said, some of her confidence returning. "You do not know me. In the end you will partner against me and I will die. I do not want to be fed to that thing alive. Please," she begged, "you must kill me."

"I can't do that," Jana sobbed. She looked at Thea. "How can we do that?"

Thea gained some strength from the noblewoman. "We must," she said, knowing the woman was right. Also knowing, however, that her death did not solve the problem in the end. Only one was walking away from the trial.

"If you do not start," the priest began. "We will remove you from the straps and feed you to the beast." His voice was calm, like he had said that very phrase hundreds of times. Perhaps he had.

"It will take many strikes," Morella said as she lowered her stick. "Hit me in the neck as hard as you can. Perhaps you can find an artery." She closed her eyes and lifted her head high, exposing her neck. Her lungs expanded as she took deep breaths, trying to calm her nerves, fresh tears making pink rivulets through her dirt smudged cheeks.

Thea lifted her stick. "I'm so sorry," she said through sobs as she brought her stick back, and with all her strength snapped it forward. The end hit Morella's neck and she cried out in pain, her entire body shaking. The weapon left a large mark, the shallow cut bleeding down into her dirty cotton smock. The longer she prolonged the inevitable, the more pain the woman would endure. So she quickly brought the stick down again, another cut appearing as the noblewoman jerked from the pain.

Jana was crying as she watched the horrible spectacle. The priest stepped closer. "If the other does not participate, she will be thrown to the beast."

"Jana," Thea said. "You must strike. She is suffering more now. We will end it faster together. Please, you must do it."

"Please, Jana," Morella cried, her eyes now open and pleading. By this time the upper portions of her smock were stained red and the side of her neck was purple from bruising.

Crying, Jana lifted the stick. Then she swung it as hard as she could, all the while sobbing profusely. Her stick stuck the women in the cheek, missing her neck. Then Thea stuck again, followed by Jana. Again and again they hit her neck. They were both yelling and crying in anger and what they were being forced to do. Hit after hit echoed in the pit, and thankfully it wasn't long before Morella stopped her painful cries. Her entire face was splattered in blood and her head hung limply, the weight of her body held up by the leather strap.

Finally they stopped and the pit grew silent, the only thing heard was the panting of the two women. If the noblewoman wasn't dead, she soon would be from loss of blood. Thea looked at Jana. The young woman looked exhausted, physically, and mentally, despair draping her like a rain-soaked cloak. What were they going to do?

"There can only be one survivor," the priest said softly, seemingly enjoying the difficulty of the task set before them.

CHAPTER ELEVEN

Brant had trudged ahead for most of the night, stopping to sleep for a few hours in a small cave he found. He continued to pull energy from the earth, giving him strength and endurance beyond what the others could achieve, but even he needed some sleep. Before the sun came up the rock-strewn gully opened up onto a flat snow covered ridgeline. It wasn't much longer until he found the huge statue carved into the rock face.

He heard Jarak's words in his mind...*you can't do this alone.* If he stormed in there now, he would likely die and the girls along with him. The only chance they had was to do this together. And so, reluctantly, he raced back to get the men, new hope surging through his body as he thought about how close they were.

Brant found them moving his way sooner than he thought. As it turned out they had only slept a few hours before getting back on the path. It was too cold to sleep well, and the urgency of their mission kept nagging at them. The sentinels as well as Baccus had sworn an oath to defend the Dormath royal family, and sitting in the cold trying to sleep while their queen was somewhere nearby in danger did not bode well with them. Tovar and Rizza didn't have a stake in the conflict, but they felt a need to do something. These Northmen had been raiding the Bitlis Sea, putting Tovar and his men in danger. Anything they could do to weaken them seemed like the right thing to do, and if they could save some people in the process then why not. Besides, they were being paid handsomely for the task.

After Brant told them what he found it seemed to rejuvenate them all, despite the grueling hike and lack of sleep. There was an end before them. They moved quickly through the narrow gorge and into the open ridgeline, nearly running across the frozen snow. As luck would have it, there had been very little new snow over the last few days, keeping the terrain much more navigable. It was almost mid-day when they neared the colossal rock face, the statue of Annaset gazing down at them from under the shadows of her cowl. They ducked behind a small series of boulders to discuss their plan.

"I need to say something before we discuss a plan," Brant said. "No matter what we find in there, I am going to try and free them, even if it means my death." Jarak was about to say something when Brant cut him off. "I need you to know this, as I do not expect the same from any of you. If my wife is there, I will wade through bodies and blood to get to her, even at the cost of my own life. I am not asking you to do the same."

Jarak looked at the unyielding faces around him. "I second that. I will do whatever is necessary to free my wife."

"My Lord," Baccus said. "Our lives," he added, glancing to the sentinels, "are yours. We swore an oath to you and your family, to protect you, to die for you if necessary. That oath, when I said it, might as well have been carved in Kul-brite steel for they are just as true now as before, more so even. I am honored to be here."

The other three sentinels, Lamwin, Tevus, and Garrad, simply nodded, their expressions saying it all.

Jarak looked to Tovar and Rizza. "I will not force you to join us. But I will say this...if you help us, and we survive, you will never have to work again in your life, that I can promise you."

"I'm in," Tovar said, "I'm getting to old for the smuggling trade anyway. But I will not force Rizza to fight, just as you would not coerce us."

Rizza looked at Jarak. "Count me in, besides, it's too cold out here. There is nothing like a fight to warm you up."

"Thank you," Jarak replied. Then he looked at Brant. "What's the plan?"

They could only see one opening into the cliff face at the base of the carved statue of Annaset. But Brant was pretty sure there was another way to access the compound. He alone had the strength to race up the mountain and check the rocks from above, climbing the snow-covered peaks if necessary. It was impossible to develop a plan when they had no idea what they were dealing with. They didn't have the lay of the temple, nor did they know how many men they would be up against. So, they agreed that Brant would try to enter from above, while the others infiltrated the compound from the front. Since they could foresee nothing, they agreed that they would storm the compound with blades drawn, using sheer force and power to shock the inhabitants. If they had more time, they might try to gather intelligence. But each hour they waited could result in the deaths of the captives. And that they could not let happen.

Leaving the main group, Brant ran up the snow-covered hillside, his powerful legs carrying him quickly through the deep snow. Opening the door in his mind, he pulled more energy from the earth around him, finding its flowing power almost instantly. Surging forward he ran like a madman, his legs pumping and his lungs heaving. When he tired, or got cold, he simply drew more energy from the earth around him. Once he neared the top of the stone façade, he looked for a foot hold to climb onto it. He found a niche in a crevice and started to climb the snow-covered rocks, leaping from boulder to boulder, moving higher and higher above the cliff face. Once at the top he started to meander his way down, climbing when necessary, pushing energy into his fingers to push away the cold and allow him to hold the tiny crevices and crags.

As he climbed lower he began to make out what looked like an opening in the steep rocks around him. Moving slower now, he picked the path of least resistance, jumping down a small cliff face he walked a narrow ridge to an outcropping that loomed over a gap in the stones around him. Once he got to the edge and peered over, his heart sunk in his chest.

Baccus led the group into the opening, hoping there would be no sentries posted. The sentinels were next, protecting Jarak, who was closely followed by Tovar and Rizza. Jarak's Mage Stones were filled, and he hoped to fill his tarnum with more aura energy before the real fighting started and it was then too late.

There was no one there to meet them and they continued down the long cold corridor. Various torches were lit along the route adding little light to the shadows. They entered an antechamber and noticed three corridors, one before them and one on either side. They heard voices coming from the right and the men quickly ran to the rock wall flanking the entry. Jarak reached out and pulled energy from the men heading their way. A third aura was frightened and he left it alone. "There are three, but one is scared," he whispered to his men. Baccus was on one side and Lamwin on the other, their swords held tight. The voices got closer and they readied themselves.

Moments later two men entered the antechamber holding a woman between them Baccus's sword came down and cut deep into one man's neck, blood spewing over the rock wall as well as his face. Lamwin's swing did similar damage, nearly cutting the other man's head off. Both stopped their follow up attack when they noticed the third person was a girl. She hadn't moved. She simply stood starring with wide eyes at the dead men and the silver blades inches from her. She had a blood drenched bandage on her wrist and she looked pale as snow.

"Please don't hurt me," she cried, barely able to stand.

Jarak stepped from the shadows to face her. "Who are you?"

"Emy," she stammered. "I'm from Bygon. Who are you?"

"King Jarak Dormath."

Suddenly she cried and slumped forward into his arms. Catching her, he dragged her to the side of the room while Baccus and the others pulled the bodies from the opening, piling them in the corner.

It was like all the remaining energy had left her, the sight of Jarak and the others offering some hope, at a chance to release the last remnants of will that had kept her standing. Releasing her, he gently pulled her away from his chest. "Where are the others?"

Suddenly the energy was there again, remembering her friends and what they were likely going through. "They are through there," she said quickly, pointing the way she had come. "Once you get to the next passage turn left. There is a door that leads to an exterior arena of some sort." She started to cry again. "They are doing horrible things to us. You must hurry."

Baccus joined Jarak. "How many of them are there?"

"I don't know. I was so scared."

Tovar joined them and took Emy's hand. "Emy, what do you do at Bygon?"

Her face crinkled in confusion, as if the question were strange considering their predicament. But she answered anyway. "I'm a server at a tavern."

"Think," he continued. "Were there as many Northmen as a busy night at the tavern?"

She thought carefully before responding. "Yes, I think so."

Tovar looked at the King. "Forty or fifty then," he said, his expression bleak.

"There is a giant as well," Emy interjected.

"Must be another peak dweller," Baccus reasoned.

"Emy, stay here and hide," Jarak ordered. "We have to go." He turned to Baccus. "Let's go."

This time they ran, knowing where they were going. They came to the turn and turned left like Emy had said, running down a shadowed corridor into another anteroom.

They were making a lot of noise and the three Northmen in the room noticed, moving towards' the door to investigate just as they stormed in. They hadn't expected an attack and they had not drawn their blades. Baccus and the sentinels cut them down in three heartbeats.

They ran to the closed door when Jarak stopped them. "If Emy is right, we are entering an arena. That means the enemy will likely have an elevated position." He looked at Rizza. "If we have a chance, we should fly to a high position and attack with fire."

"We will exhaust our tarnums quickly," Rizza added, stating the obvious.

"I will do whatever is necessary, and if that means I use tainted auras, then so be it. I will gladly accept the consequences if I can get Cat back."

Baccus was focused, his eyes glazed over in battle frenzy. He looked at Jarak. "It is an honor to die for you."

Jarak patted his huge muscled shoulder. "It will be my honor if you live for me."

But Baccus didn't hear him, already deep within his mind, thinking of blood and glory.

Jarak gripped the iron ring, looking back at them all one more time. Each face was resolute; their steely expressions clear in the dim room.

***

Brant didn't know what he was seeing. All he knew was that Thea was there, strapped to some device, facing Jana, while another girl was slumped forward in a similar device, her body held up by a leather strap. She was covered in blood. Jana and Thea held long sticks, the metal heads dripped crimson.

Brant slowly drew his blade, his hand shaking as the scene became clearer to him. Glancing around, he saw close to thirty Northmen, as well as another peak dweller. It was quite a drop below, but he thought if he enhanced his legs with energy that he could make it. He had no idea where Jarak and the others were, but he could wait no longer.

***

In the pit, Thea stared at Jana, making a decision in a flash of understanding. It suddenly became very clear. In front of her was her adopted daughter, raised by her and Brant since she was fourteen. Jana was looking back at her with a look of utter despair, a hopelessness so thick that you couldn't swim through it. There could only be one survivor. Thea took the stick and wrapped the thinnest portion behind her neck, grasping each end with her hands. Then she pulled with all her strength, using her neck as a fulcrum point. The stick bent, and bent, pain lancing through her spine as it put severe pressure on her neck. Then it snapped.

"What are you doing?" Jana asked in confusion.

"There can be only one survivor," the priest said again as the crowd watched on with silent anticipation.

Thea looked at the two broken ends, picking the thinnest and sharpest. Tears streamed down the side of her face as she looked at Jana. "I'm sorry," she said. "It is the only way. I love you. When Brant finds you, which he will, tell him I love him."

"Thea," Jana said in rising panic. "What are you doing? I don't understand."

Thea took a deep breath, then she rammed the sharp end of the stick in the side of her neck.

"No!" Jana screamed.

***

Brant was looking down at the landing when he heard Jana scream. Following the sound, he looked further below, his eyes trying to make sense of the scene. They were some ways away, but Thea was facing him. What he saw made him break inside. Blood was pouring from her throat. A hundred emotions slammed through his body in two eye blinks...despair, pain, anguish, loss, heartache, guilt, but in the end, anger found its home, exploding out from his center with more power than he had ever experienced.

Without a word, Brant leaped off the cliff side, aura energy flooding his legs, more vibrating through his limbs, its eagerness to be used nearly overwhelming. Landing hard on a flat place between rocks, his legs, supported by energy, took the impact, cracking the rock in the process.

Wasting no time, he jumped from boulder to rock, the energy coursing through him pushing him farther and higher than ever before. No one had seen him yet, their eyes and intent focused on the incredible scene before them. At the last minute he Fuzed, vaulting off a rock directly onto the stone benches carved into the rock. The Northmen near him didn't know what to do when he landed, his blue blade flashing left and right as he waded through them, cutting them down in massive sprays of blood. Then everything turned to chaos.

Cat was dumbfounded, looking at what Thea had just done with a sense of both dismay and pride. She had just sacrificed herself for Jana. Then there was commotion behind her and she looked up into the benches, not believing what she saw. It was Brant, and he was moving with a speed and precision she had never seen, cutting down Northmen, his blade arcs of devastating blue fire. Everyone near her turned to face the threat. The archers readied their bows and Orna and the priests stepped forward, Orna readied with her sword in hand.

Just then the rear door opened and men raced through with weapons drawn, one moving so fast that Cat knew he was a Merger. Then she saw Jarak. "Jarak!" she screamed. She saw him look her way, his eyes filled with hope seeing her alive.

The bowmen turned towards the door and the immediate threat. All bows thrummed, arrows ripping across the short distance. Cat screamed as an arrow struck Jarak in the chest, but relief replaced fear as she saw the arrow ricochet off his Kul-brite armor.

I am still alive, she thought. But Thea was in serious trouble. While the Northmen were occupied by the assault, Cat ran to Thea who was already slumped over, the tight leather strap holding her up, blood still pouring from the wound. Quickly she undid the strap at her ankles, then the one at her chest, lowering her the best she could to the ground. In the chaos of battle she heard Jana crying behind her, but her focus was on Thea. She was pale, the stick protruding from her neck as blood boiled from the wound. She ripped off part of her cotton smock and pressed it tightly around the wound. She had learned enough about battlefield injuries to know that removing the stick could cause more bleeding. So while the men fought for their lives, Cat fought to keep Thea from dying.

Baccus had launched forward so fast that he was nearly on the archers before they could fire. One arrow struck him in the thigh moments before he cut into them. Green fire flared brightly from his blade as Kul-brite steel cut through armor and flesh alike, equally with ease. He was a blur as he expertly maneuvered through them, the pain in his thigh forgotten as he focused on one thing, to kill.

Rizza and Jarak both followed the plan they had quickly set in motion, forming swirling air beneath them, lifting them high to land on several rocks rising above the pit. From there, Rizza pulled more energy from his tarnum and formed two swirling balls of fire, tossing them down amongst the throng of men below. The balls exploded in great force, incinerating the nearest men and catching others on fire as they were launched off the stone steps to the pit below. Other Northmen who had finally figured out what was happening, jumped off the steps onto the dais with weapons drawn, attacking Baccus and the three sentinels who were protecting the Dygon Guard's flank as best they could.

Jarak's focus was on the giant. The big beast had stood when Brant had attacked, its huge club held easily over its shoulder. But the space was limited and for the peak dweller to attack Brant he would have to wade through the Northmen. The great beast readied itself for an opening, but thus far stood back. It was a perfect opportunity. Pulling energy from his tarnum, he formed a great spear of magical energy in his right hand, the point as long as a short sword. He had used the spell once in combat when they had been attacked in the mountains by gullicks over ten years ago, huge white furred beasts who feared nothing. Since then, he had perfected the spell.

Jarak pushed a large amount of power into the weapon, the blue energy glowing brightly as he brought the weapon back to throw. His vantage point was perfect and the giant had not yet seen him. Snapping his arm forward, he released the spear, already pulling more energy from his tarnum as balls of flaming orange coalesced in the palms of his hands. The balls grew in size as he watched the spear cover the distance and strike the giant in its thick chest. There was an explosion of blue light and Jarak smiled grimly as he pushed more power into the flaming spheres. The giant stumbled and fell off the pit's edge, landing hard onto the stone floor, a hole in its chest the size of a man's head.

Then Jarak threw the balls of fire into a close-knit group of men who were converging on Brant. The explosion that followed was powerful, Jarak's power much greater than Rizza's. Bodies were ripped apart and pieces of flesh flew through the air. Even the men that weren't in the killing range were knocked off their feet.

Down on the steps, Brant saw Thea in his mind, the picture fueling each swing, each shift in movement, each snap of his wrist; all the while he was pulling energy from the earth around him. He had no idea how many men he had killed, but bodies were piling up around the benches as he ripped quickly through them. No sword or axe found his flesh, only kissing his Kul-brite steel before the blade snapped through their defenses, cutting into them with skilled proficiency.

Then suddenly a bullgon was before him, his huge bow at full draw not more than three paces away. The bow twanged and Brant didn't stop, his heightened senses seeing the arrow as he swayed forward, the huge sharp tip cutting across his cheek as he barely avoided it.

The bullgon was no Merger, but he was a bullgon, and Brant knew from experience, having fought one in the pits long ago, that they were naturally extremely strong and quick. As Brant's blade came up from a low angle, the bullgon snapped its large foot forward, catching Brant in the chest and knocking him two paces back to land on his back. The bullgon dropped his bow and pulled two hand axes from his belt, jumping towards Brant with both weapons raised.

Brant's chest hurt and he thought that perhaps the bullgon had broken a few ribs, despite the armor that he wore. But the pain he felt evaporated as he held onto the image of Thea's bloody neck. Roaring in fury he pushed energy into his blade and blue fire shot three paces, striking the bullgon in the chest and face. The creature howled and jumped back from the fire giving Brant time to regain his footing once again. He wasted no time in attacking.

The bullgon's thick skin was like a layer of stone and it did protect him some from the fire, but regardless the flesh around his chest and face were burnt badly and the pain from the wound was distracting. He was able to get his axes up to block Brant's attack, but they did little good as Brant's blade cut one in half, his powerful wrists knocking the other axe head to the side, his blue blade finding an opening, the point driving through the bullgon's stomach and erupting out its back. Extinguishing the fire, he quickly ripped the blade sideways, cutting halfway through the bullgon's torso. Blood and guts gushed from the wound as Brant leaped off the stone edge to the floor of the pit.

Quill was looking down at the carnage below, Bronas and a few others beside him. His focus was the closest Merger that was inflicting great damage to his men below. Growling, he lifted his right fist and blue icy frost swirled around it, forming a ball of freezing cold. A few moments later he threw the ball of frost and it landed behind the three sentinels as they fought to keep the Northmen from flanking them. The ball of ice exploded and shards of ice as long as knifes blew out in a circular pattern.

Tovar had stayed behind, knowing that he would get in the way of the skilled sentinels. He was good with a blade, but nowhere near the skill of a Dygon Guard and three sentinels. The ball of ice landed in front of him and he dove to the side, pulling a dead Northman over him. Shards of ice exploded around him and he heard men scream. Unharmed, he scrambled away from the body and

looked up. There were three men and a woman on
a veranda looking down on them. Frantically he
looked about to see the damage. One sentinel was
down, the backs of his legs embedded with shards
of ice. The other was fighting, but Tovar could see
that one leg was bleeding, the glinting piece of ice
visible as he fought to keep the enemy blades
away. The right flank was faltering. Holding his
sword before him, he jumped forward to fill the
space.

Rizza saw the ice ball explode and looked
over to the veranda. He only had enough energy in
his tarnum to fly down. He looked across the
clearing to Jarak who had just incinerated
handfuls of men with his powerful fire balls.
"Jarak!" he yelled. "The Veranda!"

Jarak looked up at Rizza's voice and saw the
men at the Veranda. It was a long shot, but he
thought he could pull it off. Again, he drew from
his nearly depleted tarnum, forming a bow of
orange fire in left hand. Reaching for the string, he
pulled it back and formed a long flaming arrow, the
head shaped like a knife. Pushing more energy
into the tip of the arrow, he raised the bow at what
he thought was the right arc, aiming down the
shaft of flickering flames. Then he released and
watched the shaft arc over the clearing toward the
veranda.

Quill saw it coming. "Look out!" he yelled as
he jumped off the veranda. The arrow struck the
woman and exploded in a powerful ball of fire.
Blood and flesh coated the wall behind them and
the force of the blow knocked Bronas and the other
man into the interior room. Quill landed hard and
felt his right leg break, groaning in pain as he

looked at the bloody bone jutting out from his ankle.

Cat was frantic. She felt Thea's chest slowly rise and fall, but knew she had very little time. "No, no, Thea, don't die on me," she cried as she looked at the battle around her to get a feel as to what was happening. It was chaos everywhere as the fighting continued. Northmen bodies were sprawled all around her as Baccus and the remaining sentinels somehow still kept them at bay.

"Brant," Thea moaned, bringing Cat's eyes back to her.

"No, it's me, Cat."

"Is Brant here?" Thea's voice was barely a whisper, her eyes fluttering open but seemingly not able to focus.

"Yes, he is here. He came for you."

She smiled and her eyes closed once again. "Tell him I did what he would've done. I saved our girl."

Tears streamed down Cat's face. "Tell him yourself. You're not going to die."

Thea smiled again, her eyes fluttering open. "It's okay," she said. By this time the blood at her neck was reduced to a slow trickle. Thea's face was as white as the snow around them. She looked at Cat. "Will you...kill...Bronas...for me?" Then she let out a long slow breath, her eyes glazing over.

Cat sobbed and reached out to close her eyes. "Yes," she moaned, "I will kill him." Then she stood and looked for a sword.

Jarak used the last of his energy to fly down to the melee below, his Kul-brite blade held in his hand. Rizza followed suit on the other side and landed with both short swords drawn. Together, they entered the fight, attacking the Northmen from the sides as Baccus, Tovar, and Lamwin, the only sentinel left, somehow managed to fend off the remaining enemy.

Orna stepped before Cat just as she gripped the blade and lifted it to defend herself. "So," the Northwoman said, "your king has come to save you."

"You ready to meet your god?" Cat snarled.

"Always." Then she attacked, her great sword coming down hard and fast for Cat's skull. Cat was tired and malnourished, but there was something else guiding her blade this day. She didn't know what it was, but she felt it, giving her strength she didn't know she had. Looking back at it later, she thought it was anger. But she realized that wasn't it at all. It was hope. She had witnessed the ultimate sacrifice; a selfless act to save another, and that gave her hope. In all the blood and carnage, the death and selfishness, she had just witnessed something grand, something great. It was a beacon of light to hold onto. It gave her something to fight for, something to defend.

Their blades clashed and immediately Cat knew she was in trouble. Under the best of circumstances, if Cat had armor and her own blade, and was strong and full of energy, the bout would be close. But Cat had none of those things, and Orna was extremely strong and fast. Using all the speed and skill that earned her the nickname Cat, she deflected and avoided, dancing, pivoting, and parrying, avoiding the powerful sword strikes of the Northwoman. But she was tiring quickly, the strenuous ordeal having already sapped most of her strength. Growling in defiance, she slipped inside a powerful swing and sliced her blade across the forearm of the woman. Orna snarled and kicked out with her foot, striking Cat in the chest and launching her onto her back. Orna lunged forward, her blade coming down hard.

Cat scrambled, pain lancing through her chest as she raised her blade. At least one rib was broken, the pain lancing through her as she took two strikes, the second knocking the blade from her numbed arm.

Orna stood above her as Cat scrambled back until she was butting up to Thea's body. The woman was smiling, her sword held low in her hand. "You are good," she added. She put the tip of her sword on Cat's chest and reached down with her meaty hand, gripping the old cotton smock at her neck.

Cat reached back and gripped the wood shaft sticking from Thea's neck. "Yes, I am," she responded, as Orna lifted her up with her strong arm, bringing her face close to hers.

The Northwoman was so strong that she was literally holding Cat on her tippy toes with one arm. "You would've made a great bed mate," she grumbled. "It's a shame you have to die."

"I don't think so," Cat whispered, snapping her arm up and ramming the sharp stick into her thick muscled neck. Twice, in quick succession, she stabbed the sharp point into her flesh, aiming for the artery that roped up her neck.

Orna's eyes widened as she tossed Cat aside, her hand coming up to her throat as blood gushed from the horrible wound. She dropped her blade and stumbled about, trying in vain to keep her blood from spraying forth.

Cat picked up her sword and stepped towards her just as she stumbled to her knees, her eyes wide in shock, horrible gurgling noises coming from her throat as she tried to speak. Without a word Cat yelled in fury and swung her blade in a powerful arc, cutting off her head in a shower of blood.

Brant saw Jarak land nearby and attack the remaining Northmen. Glancing to his left he saw the crazed Taresk, having no idea what kind of creature it was. The ripped and torn body of the woman beside the creature was unrecognizable. The beast was howling and lunging forward, trying to break the chains to get at all the flesh around it. But he wasn't focused on the others. He cut down two men as he moved towards Thea, his path suddenly blocked by two ghastly looking men. They were Northmen all right, but they wore different furs and armor, and their faces resembled white skin pulled tight over skulls, their dark hollowed eyes adding to their frightful appearance. They each held two long knives, the blades suddenly sparkling in blue glowing ice.

Were they Mergers Brant thought, *or something else?* It mattered little. They were standing between him and Thea. Brant engaged them both, their blades ringing loudly as energy erupted from each contact. Normally, a standard blade would not stand a chance against a Fuzed Kul-brite sword, but obviously these were no standard blades. Somehow, whatever power was in them, they were able to withstand the power of Brant's sword. But he doubted their flesh could.

Brant's forearms were nearly as big as his biceps, which were colossal in themselves. Years and years of practicing the Kilting Way, the secret sword forms taught only to the Dygon Guard, had added immense strength and power to his wrists and hands. Using them now in a two-handed style, he knocked their blades away with subtle snaps of his wrist, the same power used to avoid the attacks, was used to deliver precise hits, his steel cutting into exposed flesh before they realized what they had gotten into. Crouching low on powerful legs, Brant weaved right by them, their swords knocked aside as Brant cut one across his femoral artery, dropping him to the ground in a spray of blood. Spinning past the other, Brant hooked an arm around his neck and flung the priest hard and to the side, right into the waiting claws of the Taresk. The beast roared as it ripped the screaming man to pieces, blood splattering the already crimson stained stone around it.

Brant saw Cat standing near Thea, a dead enemy beside her. The fighting was roaring around them but he heard none of it. Cat was crying when she saw him, stepping aside as he neared, Thea's body laying behind her.

"I'm so sorry, Brant. I tried to save her," she sobbed.

All he heard was muffled tones as he knelt next to Thea, her eyes closed peacefully, blood drenching her dirty cotton smock.

He picked up her head and held it close to his chest, heaving in great sobs as he tried to wrestle with her death. Despite her disheveled appearance, her hair still smelt familiar to him. Looking up into the sky, tears streaking his blood splattered face, he roared with all his might, releasing the pain that was erupting from him. He held her longer, sobbing into her chest, the crescendo of fighting dying down as the last of the Northmen were killed.

***

Two men were found alive. Both were dragged into the arena, their comrade's dead and bloody all around them. Jarak's fire arrow had burnt them badly, but both still breathed. They had gathered up the bows and killed the blood covered Taresk, taking eight arrows to finally slay the thing.

One of the survivors was found upstairs near the veranda and dragged below. It was Bronas and his arm was broken, the side of his face also black and burnt. Bronas groaned in pain, his entire torso and lower neck burnt badly. They were pretty sure the Northmen was suffering some internal damage caused by the explosion.

The other man was Quill, his leg badly broken, caught trying to drag himself away from the fight.

Brant had not left Thea's side until the two men were dragged in and propped up against the stone wall. Rising without a word he walked to Quill, the Northmen smiling at his approach.

"Ann..." he began, but only got out one syllable before Brant slid his blade slowly through his neck. Gurgling on his own blood, his eyes snapping wide, his body suffered several spasms before he died. Brant casually withdrew his blade and stepped to Bronas.

"Wait!" Cat said, leaving Jarak's embrace as she ran to the swordsman's side. She placed a restraining arm on his shoulder. "Before Thea died, she asked me to kill Bronas. Please, let me."

Brant's eyes were pooled with tears and it looked like he was ready to crumble to the ground, the sheer weight of his despair sitting heavy on his shoulders. He thought for a moment before stepping aside.

Cat picked up a discarded blade nearby and stepped before Bronas. The big Northmen looked at her through one good eye, the other burnt along with his ear. "You deserve worse than death," she said, "but it will have to do." Then she placed the tip of the blade on his stomach and slowly pushed it in, the warrior's good eye going wide with shock as he sucked in the last of his air. Then she yanked the blade sideways across his belly, completely disemboweling him. It was a horrible wound, one that would not kill him immediately. His hands went instinctively to his gut as blood gushed from the wound. Moaning in pain he slumped forward as Cat's sword clanked on the stone floor. She walked back to Jarak without another word.

The fight was over. All three sentinels had died trying to defend Baccus who had unleashed a devastating amount of destruction. Bodies of Northmen were piled about him in a display of splashed blood and sliced flesh. The great Dygon Guard was nearly killed in the fight as well. An arrow had struck his leg, and he had been hit twice with blades, cutting him deeply on his forearm as well as his shoulder. They had stopped the bleeding, but he needed his wounds cleaned and plenty of rest. Tovar suffered bruised ribs as a sword thrust was stopped by his armor, as well as minor bruises and scrapes. Rizza had taken a bad cut on the leg, the Northmen's sword barely missing his femoral artery. They were a sorry looking lot, but the enemy looked far worse.

Brant stood on numb legs and looked up at the benches around him. He must have killed fifteen Northmen himself, their bodies sprawled awkwardly in death all across the perimeter seats.

Jarak and Cat stepped next to him. "What do you want to do?" the King asked. He didn't say he was sorry, for that was obvious and seemed to belittle Thea's death. There were no words that would make him feel better.

"I'm going to finish this," he said, his crackling green eyes turning to his friend. "I'm going to find out who did this, and kill them."

Chapter Twelve

ReeOnen had sent a message to TorGynin in their usual manner, asking to meet. They used a store front as their carrier, the owner of the mercantile paid to give sealed messages to the assassin when he came in, which he was required to do after every mission.

The Saricon moved briskly down the ally, the murky and foul-smelling path doing little to give her pause. It was evening, just before dark, when the assassin appeared from the shadows before her.

"Kulgarrion," he said, bowing his masked head only slightly as he whispered her title in the Saricon tongue.

"We are summoned," she said, "to appear before the Tongra. He wants to thank you personally for all your success."

"When?"

"Tomorrow at dusk."

The assassin paused, tilting his head sideways the way he did, as if analyzing whether or not he should kill you. His confidence was eerie to say the least. "I will be there as requested."

"Have you heard?" She asked.

"That the king is back?"

"So you know," she snapped, obviously perturbed.

"That the queen survived the ordeal, yes, I know, something that I will have to rectify."

"I knew we should've just killed her outright."

"Perhaps, but the original plan, if it would have been successful, would've been much more rewarding. Death is one thing, but wondering what has happened to your loved ones is even worse. Trust me, I know."

"No more games," she said. "I want her dead. He needs to pay for what he did to my family."

TorGynin paused again. "It will be done. Is there anything else?"

ReeOnen shook her head. "You may go."

The assassin backed away and was swallowed up by the night.

The next evening, just as the sun was setting, the assassin appeared next to ReeOnen, emerging from a side alley to join her near the gate of the inner palace. There were people about, and besides a few furtive glances, they gave the hooded man little notice. ReeOnen nodded and together they stepped to the huge guards standing before the gate. They were aware of her identity and meeting, and let them through after a few words. Several guards inside escorted them to a large interior training room, the tall ceiling and columned walls giving the space a grand appearance. At one point, before the Saricons' had conquered Eltus, the room had been a private worship center for the King of Kael. Now it was ripped of all things Argonian, emptied of statues, pews, and tapestries that had any resemblance to the gods Argon and Felina. Torches and braziers lined the room's long walls and weapon racks could be seen on both sides, filled with weapons of all design. The far end of the huge room was lined with chairs and tables. The Tongra was sitting in a huge wood chair flanked by his advisors known in the Saricon tongue as Talgrins. The room was lined with thirty Saricon warriors, their deadly javelins held in their hands.

Something was wrong. TorGynin felt it immediately and paused just inside the room as more Saricon warriors entered from behind, javelins blocking their retreat.

"Do you know why you are here?" the Tongra said from across the room as he stood from his chair and walked before them. He stared down at them both, his expression unreadable.

ReeOnen looked around the room, her concerned expression visible in the orange light shed by the hundreds of torches. "You said you wished to meet TorGynin, and so I have brought him."

Tongra Orgul stepped back to a table and picked up a black book, holding it up for them to see. "What is this?"

ReeOnen was taken aback. It was the Torgot, their religious text, everyone knew what it was. "It is the Torgot of course. Our sacred book."

"Then why have you defaced it!" he roared, stepping closer to her.

His sudden change in demeanor alarmed her and she stepped back. TorGynin remained unmoving.

"I...I don't know what you mean," she stammered.

"The Gratatuit is sacred...the rules are Heln's words," he growled, stepping closer to her. "You have pissed on his words by taking things

into your own hands. You have dishonored us all."
He stopped several paces away and looked at
TorGynin. "What is verse twenty nine of the
Nuracon?"

For six years DarPool trainers had
hammered into his memory, through pain and
torture, every verse of the Torgot. "The Gratatuit,
through pain of death," he said softly, "will be
honored for twenty years to the day of the blood
oath. No signer, or signer's family, shall be
harmed until the day of reckoning arrives, under
penalty of death."

Tongra Orgul stepped back to the table and
lifted a long piece of parchment, walking again
before ReeOnen. He held the paper up before her.
"Do you know what this is?"

She looked at it. "Yes, it's the Gratatuit."

The Tongra pointed to a signature on the
bottom, the choppy strokes written in blood. "Do
you know whose mark this is?"

ReeOnen gulped. "My father's."

The Tongra nodded and moved back to the
table, setting the parchment down. He turned
again to face them. "We know what you have
done," he said to ReeOnen. "You have broken the
agreement, and in doing so have sullied Heln's
word. And for that, you must die. Bring them
out!"

ReeOnen was sweating and she looked
around for an escape, but there was nowhere to go.
They were surrounded by over fifty Saricon
warriors, each holding a javelin. She would be
killed immediately. Trying her best to hide her
fear, she stood up straight, but nearly faltered

when she saw who emerged from the shadows behind the Tongra.

King Jarak walked next to the Tongra, with Cat by his side. Beside her was Brant Anwar, their expressions stern and uncompromising. Jarak wore his Kul-brite plate and the silver sparkled in the orange light. Cat was armored as well, her silver armor lined in gold filigree, a cape of a blue fluttering behind her. Brant narrowed his eyes when he saw the masked man, his fingers gripping unconsciously at his sides.

"What is the meaning of this!?" ReeOnen stormed, trying to find a way out of her predicament. "You bring our enemy here and claim it is I who have defaced the Torgot! You have no proof."

The Tongra ignored her and looked at Jarak and Brant. "Is this the man that accosted you?"

"It is," Jarak said.

"Yes," Brant replied, his voice low and ready to explode.

"There is your proof!" the Tongra yelled, his anger erupting again. He paused, taking a deep breath before looking at TorGynin. "Besides, we have had another assassin follow you. Your clandestine meetings are known to us. TorGynin, please step aside," he said as he hefted his massive axe off the table.

The assassin looked at ReeOnen, his masked face unreadable. Then he moved out of the way, leaving ReeOnen alone. "You cannot do this," ReeOnen said, looking to the Talgrins.

The Tongra stepped closer to her, his anger boiling and ready to spring forth, flashes of orange light flaring from his eyes as his Fury begged to be released. "Do not look to them. Their council supports your sentence." Then his eyes burst with light and he roared like a beast as his Fury took over. "Draw your blade and prepare to answer to Heln!" Then he charged.

ReeOnen's sword flew from her scabbard and met the Tongra's attack, the power of his initial attacks diverted as she expertly angled the attacks away, trying to lessen the Tongra's powerful strikes. But she could not keep up with his speed or match his strength. Moments later he batted her sword away and brought his axe down like a logger splitting wood, the blade of his axe striking her shoulder and completely cutting her arm off. The wound was devastating and her sword clanked to the floor as she dropped to her knees, her eyes unfocused as blood spurted from the wound.

The Tongra stood above her. "When you meet your father, beg for his forgiveness for dishonoring him." Then he swung his axe with one arm, the huge weapon cutting her head off, her body toppling to the floor. Tongra Orgul stood for a moment, his huge chest heaving up and down as he tried to reign in his Fury. Finally, he turned around and moved back to the table, leaning his bloody axe against it, ReeOnen's blood dripping to the stones. Then he looked to the assassin. "Step before me."

TorGynin paused for a moment as he was considering several things besides that. He had little choice. Even he would find himself riddled with javelins if he tried to fight or flee. Finally he obeyed, stepping in front of ReeOnen as several soldiers grabbed her arms and removed her, along with her head. "I am at your service," he said softly.

"You were following orders when you broke the Gratatuit, and for that you will be given a chance at life, just as ReeOnen had. You will fight Brant Anwar to the death." Brant stepped forward, his sword still sheathed on his back. "If you win," the Tongra continued, "then Heln still favors you and you will remain in his service. Do you understand?"

"Yes."

"Before we began, remove your mask," the Tongra ordered.

TorGynin hesitated. Then he pulled his hood back and removed his mask, looking up to them all, the torchlight dancing across his features.

Brant stepped closer as recognition flashed across his face. The face before him, although older and scarred, was known to him. The young man's eyes however, were different, deep pools of black with lightning gray scratched through them. But despite the unique eyes and the scars on his cheeks and forehead, he recognized the curve of his chin, the angle of his nose and mouth. His steadfast will and iron resolved faltered. "Ari," he stammered, "is that you?"

Ari's face was unreadable. "Yes, Brant, it is I."

Jarak and Cat were equally shocked, and they joined Brant. Brant couldn't believe his eyes. Brant had met Ari ten years ago when he was just a boy in the service of Kulvar Rand. He had liked him tremendously. As it turned out, he had been a Saricon spy, forced to do their bidding by capturing his parents and threatening their death if he did not obey. His true identity had been discovered, and he was tried for treason, a crime punishable by death. Despite the fact that he had been found guilty by the tribunal, in leniency, Jarak had banished him from the kingdom forever.

"You killed Endler and Serix," Jarak stammered, "because they found you guilty of treason?"

"Yes," Ari replied, again void of emotion. "They sought my death, while you decided to banish me. I could not kill you directly or it would destroy the Gratatuit. But it wasn't just that. My parents were killed when it was known that I was banished. You see, they were no longer useful to them."

"So you wanted to punish me by taking my wife?" Jarak asked incredulously.

"Yes. We thought her capture would not be tied back to us."

"You still broke the Gratatuit," the Tongra said, his voice calmer but still heavy with anger.

"We did," TorGynin agreed, "a small forgiveness, something we thought Heln would overlook after he saw what we had accomplished."

Brant stepped closer, his old anger returning. "Why me?" he asked. "I stood up for you?"

Ari gulped. "You did, which is why I did not kill you. I remembered what you did for me, but still, you had to pay for killing the Tongra. It was not my debt you were paying, but hers," he said, indicating the wet blood behind him.

"What happened to you?" Cat asked. "How did you become...*this*?" She spit the last word out in disgust.

Ari hesitated, not wanting to bring up the memories. "I wandered...I starved...I was beaten...violated in ways you can't imagine. I wandered more, living as a vagrant. I made my way here, and found out that my parents had been killed a year before, no longer useful as a tool against you. I was taken as a slave...beaten daily. Then they used my anger, turning me into a killer. The irony is that the pain I suffered gave me the strength to become what I am now, to enact my revenge on you for not standing up for me when you should've. I was just a boy," he said softly, the innocent Ari resurfacing for a moment.

"Even now, you don't see your folly," Jarak replied. "You had a choice then, as you have had every step you've taken since. I regretted having to send you away, but I did it in opposition of having to see you executed for treason. I gave you leniency, and you repay me with this! You have proven to me that my compassion was a mistake. I should have killed you then."

"Perhaps you are right," Ari said.

"Your actions killed my wife," Brant snarled.

"Yes, and now we are even in Heln's eyes."

"Even!" Brant stormed. "There is no such thing. Even as I draw my blade through your flesh, we will never be even! Nothing I do now can make up for her death!" Then he drew his blade from his back. "Ready yourself," he said, his thundering voice dropping to a controlled anger. "Death awaits you."

Brant's body was vibrating with energy as he shot forward in a blur, his sword erupting in blue energy. Ari's Kul-brite blade appeared in his hand and their steel clashed, again and again, the ringing of steel moving from a fast crescendo to a faster hammering, the speed of their attacks blending together to nearly one noise.

The two Mergers flew across the stone floor as the people watching tried to discern what was happening. The fighting continued for minutes as they danced over the stone pavers. Brant had no idea how Ari had become a Merger, but he shoved that thought away, focusing on the task at hand. Ari was fast, very fast, but he could not Fuze and he was having a hard time matching Brant's sheer power. Not to mention he was being forced to deflect the power of his blows, worried that his Fuzed blade would damage his own, despite the fact that it was forged from Kul-brite steel. Ari's aura energy was slowly diminishing, while Brant's energy was unwavering, pulled from the ground beneath him.

Switching tactics, the assassin moved in closer as he allowed Brant to use his power to bat his sword aside. Ari snapped his foot forward trying to connect to the back of Brant's knee, hoping to cause him to stumble. Brant pivoted the last moment, turning his leg and lowering into the *swaying oak*. Ari's foot struck his hard shin and Brant countered with an attack of his own. His right fist shot forward and it just grazed Ari's cheek as he swayed around it, like moving water pouring around a piling. He continued to spin a full circle with his sword leading, trying to cut into Brant's back. It was a beautiful move, one that would've found any swordsman in trouble, but not Brant. Brant dropped low into a powerful squat, flooding his legs with aura energy he shot back into the assassin, his back facing Ari's silver blade. The sword whistled over his head while Brant blindly angled his sword back and low, extinguishing the fire with a thought. Then, in an explosion of power, he spun by him as he ripped his blade outward and across Ari's inner thigh.

Brant stepped back as Ari slowly stood up from his fighting crouch, his mind not fully registering the massive amount of wetness pouring down his legs. Blood squirted from the wound several times, splashing crimson across the pavers. He reached down to touch his thigh, his hand coming back drenched in blood. Then he dropped to his knees as dizziness took him.

"I'm sorry," he mumbled, his eyes blinking rapidly.

Brant stepped closer and Ari tried to raise his blade. Brant swatted it away where it clattered across the floor. "So am I," he whispered as he slowly pushed the tip of his blade into his heart.

The assassin's breath caught in his throat as his eyes bolted wide. Then Brant slowly drew the weapon free as Ari let out his last breath, his eyes rolling back in his head as he thudded to the floor.

Epilogue

Jana stood before the fire staring into the mesmerizing flames, her mind adrift elsewhere. A dirty table was before her, various dishes and mugs scattered across it, her tray sitting empty amongst the mess. It was late at night and the five patrons staying at the Inn had left for bed, leaving Jana alone with her own thoughts.

"You okay?"

Jana blinked as she returned to the present, her troubled thoughts burning away with the flickering flames. Gorrin moved next to her and placed a hand on her shoulder. "Let me help you," he said softly.

It had been six months since their ordeal and still she could not get the images out of her head. Thea had died trying to save her. She would never forget that, nor did she want to. Despite the horrible image of her ramming a sharp stick in her own throat, she wanted to burn it into her memory, so she would never forget her sacrifice. Remembering it would bring her courage in the times to come. Gorrin had moved in from his cottage and together he and Jana, along with the help of a new young man named Jessup, had reopened the Inn. It had probably been the best thing for Jana. The first few weeks after she returned, she woke screaming to nightly nightmares, her thin cotton nightshirt soaked with sweat. The more she worked, however, the more she tired herself and the less restless her nights were. But still she often thought of what had happened, the images fresh in her mind. She doubted she would ever be the same.

"I cannot get the image of her out of my mind," Jana said softly.

Gorrin knew she was talking about Thea. "I imagine not."

"What am I going to do?" Jana asked pleadingly. "Will Brant ever forgive me?"

So that was it, Gorrin thought. She blames herself for Thea's death, hence thinking that Brant would also. Gorrin stopped loading the dishes and put his hand on hers. "Jana, it is not your fault. Brant does not blame you, this I know. Can I give you some advice?"

"Of course."

"Try to hold onto what Thea did for you, not the image of it. It is rare to find such noble acts in our world. It is something to live up to, to try and emulate. Be the woman that Thea would be proud of, for that is why she gave her life for yours. She died so you can live, and you cannot live if you dwell on her death." Gorrin paused. "I shall try to do the same with my son."

She looked at Gorrin as he went back to putting the dirty dishes on the tray. "I will do my best."

"It is all we can do," he added. "Let's promise to remind each other of this when our thoughts darken like a stormy night."

"Okay," she murmured, adding a few dishes onto the tray. "I miss him," she continued, "and I worry for Brant."

Her husband, and Gorrin's son, had been killed the night she was taken, and there wasn't a day that went by that she didn't think of him. And Brant, she was frightened for him. He had left soon after his return from Kael and no one had heard from him since.

Gorrin held her hand again as she reached for a dirty knife. "I miss him too," he said. "We will get through this, you and I. We will do it together," he added with a squeeze of her hand.

She smiled weakly. "Do you think Brant is okay?"

Gorrin sighed. "He is in a lot of pain. He just needs time."

"You're not worried for him?"

"I'm not worried about him. I'm worried about whoever gets in his way."

***

The cup was cold in Brant's hand as he pushed his chair closer to the fire, the sounds of drunken laughter muffled in his troubled mind. After he had killed Ari, and seeing to Jana's return, he had left, moving farther north than he ever had. Month after month he jumped from town to town, from Rygar west to Palatone, then north to a city called Gythona along the northeastern coast of Corvell. He was running, running from his memories, hoping that the pain in his heart would go away. But no matter how far he went, the pain followed, his mind flashing through images of Thea's dead body.

He took a long pull of the cold ale, the bitterness a fine companion to his troubled spirit. Snow had fallen weeks before and the northern regions were far colder than what he was used too. In fact, he saw very few Dy'ainians, the people this far north fairer skinned. The lands here seemed to be less homogenized. Brant even saw a few Gyths walking casually down the main road. He didn't know the local tongue, but luckily for him most people at least understood Dy'ainian.

"Do you mind?"

The voice pulled Brant from his plagued thoughts, his hand automatically dropping to the hilt of his sword that he now had buckled to his belt. Months ago in Ol'myr, a beautiful city in Rygar, he had a swordsmith expertly wrap the handle in black leather, as well as changing out the unique crosspiece that separated the hilt from the blade. Now, when sheathed, it looked like an ordinary sword.

The man was alone and wore a fur lined leather coat over a dust covered wool tunic, a long cotton undershirt beneath. The top of his head was bald, with long frizzy gray hair that ran the perimeter of his skull and went to the collar of his shirt. His skin was white and his eyes gray blue. He seemed innocent enough. Brant nodded towards the seat opposite him and the man sat down.

"It's cold out there," he said in Dy'ainian, his northern accent subtle. There was another fire in the tavern but it was surrounded by a boisterous lot. Other than those patrons, Brant was alone, the fire the only companion he needed, or wanted.

"You're welcome to it," Brant said as he indicated the fire.

"Thank you," he said as he scooted his chair closer, cupping his mug. "Me names Taggard."

"Brant."

"You from Dy'ain?"

Brant looked up from the fire, a little annoyed at the small talk. "Yes."

"I meant no offense," he said. "I came into town a week ago and don't know anyone. It's nice to have a conversation with a person instead of a stone wall." Brant looked at him strangely, not understanding his words. Taggard tugged on his dusty shirt. "I'm a mason, come into the city to help with repairs on the northern wall. My wife died six months ago." He shrugged. "Figure it would be better to move around than looking at shadows in my home, wondering if she was still there."

"You speak Dy'ainian well," Brant said, warming up to the man.

"My wife and I lived there for a few years after the Saricon Wars. King Dormath needed a lot of masons to rebuild. It was good work." Brant nodded and looked back into the fire; the mention of the wars bringing back more anxious images. "What brings you this far north?"

"Same as you I guess," he said softly. "Needing to get away."

"Running from something?" Brant's eyes narrowed, his rising anger fizzling out when he saw the mason's harmless expression. "I know the look." But he said nothing more.

The door to the tavern suddenly flew open and cold wind and snow flurries blew in, the chill shut off quickly as the trio shut the door behind them. They wore leather armor beneath thick furs, a mismatch of weapons evident as they looked around the room, eying the duo and the warm fire they sat before.

Brant saw one man, a bow held in his right hand, nod towards them before he walked their way. Two of the men had long dirty blonde beards caked in snow and ice. The other wore a fur hat, a sharp, nearly white growth of hair protruding from his chin. They stepped to the table and one of the bearded men glanced at Taggard.

"Get lost," he said brusquely. "We be needin the fire."

Taggard turned and looked at them, sliding his chair back. "It was nice talken to ya stranger," he said to Brant as he moved to stand.

"Stay," Brant replied. His tone was like a sword sliding slowly over ice. Then he looked back at the three men, his green eyes sparkling in the shadows. "This fire's taken. Find somewhere else to warm yourselves."

The bearded man smiled and looked at his two friends. Brant wasn't sure, but he thought they might be hunters, or maybe mercenaries. They had that look.

"Oh, don't worry about me," Taggard said, sensing the volatile emotions raging through Brant.

The man wearing the hat took it off his bald head and smacked Taggard in the face with it, startling the mason so much that he dropped his mug. "Shut up old man."

Brant stood up from his chair and stepped around the table to face the three men. "I said, this fire is taken," he murmured, his voice low and dripping with violence. "Leave us alone and you will walk away."

The other bearded man laughed at Brant's arrogance. "Who is this foreigner? Go back home and *you* might walk away."

"Leave you alone?" the bald man mocked. "You mean like this?" he sneered as he slapped Taggard again with his hat.

There was no warning, no shuffling of feet, no more bravado laced words, Brant simply attacked with a violence the men had never seen.

Dropping his hips, he shot forward with his right fist, launching low to high and striking the first bearded man in the chin with the palm of his hand. The man's head jerked back and he flew three paces into the air to land hard on the stone floor. The other bearded man reached for his blade, which was a stupid move in such tight confines. Brant lashed out and gripped the man's wrist in his iron grip, turning it out and jerking it hard towards him, all the while ducking and spinning, using the man's wrist and his vice-like grip to spin his arm around and throw the man to his back. The bald man was still holding his bow and swung it like a staff, aiming for Brant's back. But Brant expected it, and still holding the other man's wrist as he lay on the ground moaning, he snapped out with his left leg. There was crunch as the bowman's knee caved in, his swing halted as he fell to the floor.

Brant was still holding the man's hand when he turned it, putting enormous strain on his wrist. The man cried out, his anguish adding to the bald man's whines as he held his shattered knee. "I told you," he said calmly. "This fire is taken."

He let go of the man's hand and moved back to his chair, dropping nonchalantly into it, casually grabbing his mug off the table. "Leave now," he said, not looking back. The bearded man that was thrown got up quickly, nursing his wrist. Reaching down, he frantically helped the bald man up.

Together they limped away, the man Brant had punched groggily joining them, stumbling behind with his hand to his broken jaw.

The small crowd was silent for a moment, weary eyes looking his way. Then the talking started up again, leaving Brant to his thoughts.

"You didn't have to do that," Taggard said, his eyes newly appraising him. "But thank you."

Brant took a sip of his ale, glancing towards Taggard. "Do you believe we all have something dark inside us?"

Taggard thought for a moment. "If you mean, do I believe we are all capable of dark things, then yes. There is a beast in all of us, but sometimes it's necessary to unchain it."

"You really believe that?"

The old mason pursed his lips. "I do. What else is going to protect the weak from the oppressors? What else is going to stand up to those who care little for life?" The mason shrugged and drank from his mug, leaning forward to get closer to the fire. "It's like this fire," he continued. "It burns bright, hot...it destroys, but also gives life." As if sensing the difficulty that Brant was wrestling with, Taggard added, "The beast inside us, if controlled, can be a good thing."

Brant was staring deeply into the hot embers. "I am that fire," he muttered.

"I know. I just witnessed that." The old mason drank again from his ale, thinking as he savored its malty flavor. "Be careful Brant, do not let the fire consume you."

"That too is my concern."

And together, they shared the silence of their own deep thoughts, the warmth of the fire doing little to warm Brant's cold heart.

The End

About the Author

Jason McWhirter has been a history teacher for twenty two years. He lives in Washington with his wife, Jodi, and their dogs, Meadow and Tucker. He is a certifiable fantasy freak who, when he wasn't playing sports, spent his childhood days immersed in books and games of fantasy. He'd tumble into bed at night with visions of heroes, dragons, and creatures of other worlds (he still does actually), fueling his imagination and spurring his desire to create fantasies of his own. When he isn't fly fishing the lakes and streams of the Northwest, or wine tasting and entertaining with his wife and friends, he spends his spare time sitting in front of the computer writing his next novel.

Join Jonas in the Cavalier Trilogy! Look for it on Amazon and Barnes and Noble!

Praise for the Cavalier...

"This intensely written novel of fantasy and magic, good and evil, draws you into a tapestry; the world that the author Jason L. McWhirter has created."
Fantasy Book Review

"The writing is crisp and polished, and the narrative has a good level of description for a fantasy novel. Jonas is a sympathetic character who the reader immediately cares about..."
Sift Book Review

Check out McWhirter's Steel Lord Series....

In this extraordinary fantasy epic, Jason L McWhirter, author of the Cavalier Trilogy, leads readers into a world where the fate of a land, of a people, rests in the hands of two young men, one an untried prince, the other a scarred fighter forged from a life of violence. Can they save the lands from its new threat, a violent race far from the west, whose goal is to subjugate the people under the shadow of a new god, Heln?

Look for them on Amazon and Barnes and Noble!

Looking for something fantastic to read?

The Life of Ely is Jason L. McWhirter's first non-fantasy book. Twenty two years in the classroom as a teacher and coach has given him a unique perspective on the trials and tribulations that some students experience as they attempt to survive their adolescence. This story, although fiction, is inspired by these experiences.

Look for it on Amazon and Barnes and Noble!

www.ingramcontent.com/pod-product-compliance
Lightning Source LLC
Chambersburg PA
CBHW070831250626
47159CB00003B/732